491

D0677164

 M

Mathis, Edward.

September song.

$18.95

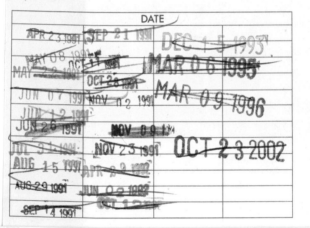

DATE		
APR 2 3 1991 SEP 2 1 1991	DEC 1 5 1993	
MAY 08 1991 OCT 1 1 1991	MAR 0 6 1995	
MAY 2 3 1991 OCT 2 8 1991	MAR 0 9 1996	
JUN 0 7 1991 NOV 0 2 1991		
JUN 1 2 1991		
JUN 2 6 1991 NOV 0 9 1991		
JUL 3 1 1991 NOV 2 3 1991	OCT 2 3 2002	
AUG 1 5 1991 APR 2 9 1992		
AUG 2 9 1991 JUN 0 2 1992		
SEP 1 4 1991 OCT 1 3 1992		

© THE BAKER & TAYLOR CO.

September
Song

September Song

— / ◆ / —

EDWARD MATHIS

CHARLES SCRIBNER'S SONS
New York

Collier Macmillan Canada
Toronto

Maxwell Macmillan International
New York   Oxford   Singapore   Sydney

M

3-91 BT 18.95

Charles Scribner's Sons
Macmillan Publishing Company
866 Third Avenue
New York, NY 10022

Collier Macmillan Canada, Inc.
1200 Eglinton Avenue East, Suite 200
Don Mills, Ontario M3C 3N1

This is a work of fiction. Names, characters, places, and incidents either are the product of the author's imagination or are used fictitiously. Any resemblance to events or persons, living or dead, is entirely coincidental.

Library of Congress Cataloging-in-Publication Data
Mathis, Edward.
    September song / Edward Mathis.
        p.   cm.
    ISBN 0-684-19262-4
    I. Title.
    PS3563.A8364S47   1991   90-42237
    813'.54—dc20

10 9 8 7 6 5 4 3 2 1

Printed in the United States of America

This book is for
Bettye and Hank Stone, Jimmie and Ray Porter,
Helen and Elson Fortune, and their families

September
Song

/1/

When I finally ran him to ground, Henry "Big Boy" Doheny lay sprawled behind a clapboard honky-tonk near Breckenridge, Texas, lodged there like a bad penny in a crack, sleeping off the granddaddy of all hangovers, whining moans and stentorian snores blasting the peace right out of a peaceful Sunday afternoon, fouling the air with the effluvium of self-indulgence and sloth.

I felt no excitement, no sense of a job well done, only a quiet kind of weariness and apathy; sniffing the wind, and wrinkling my nose at the noxious odors of booze and grass and vomit that clung to him like a pall of nascent fear, wondering if I had ever looked that bad, stunk that bad, knowing full well that I had, knowing I probably would again.

This latest biannual binge of Doheny's was one day over two weeks old and, like all the other times, would have gone on for another week if I hadn't found him. But judging from the condition of his giant coffee-colored frame, it was a toss-up whether he would have made it much farther or not.

I had seen him this way before, gaunt almost to the point of emaciation, his skin a curious shade of mottled brown tinged with saffron, straining mightily to contain the massive bony rib cage as he sucked for oxygen in the dry September air. Spittle bubbled at one corner of his mouth and crawled sluggishly across the hollow of his cheek, then wound its meandering way through the stubble on his jaw to dribble in long glutinous strings into the West Texas soil.

I had seen him this way before, all right, too damn many times, but somehow it never seemed to get any easier. Only sadder.

His white Dodge pickup with the orange Day-Glo camper rested patiently a few yards away, and after I snapped the Polaroids I walked around it, kicking the tires, checking the molded plastic hull for fresh bullet wounds, tracks of incipient madness, midnight delirium. And they were there all right, two of them, mute evidence of another try at the demons, the green scaly creatures that crawled the walls and infested the drunken mind of Big Boy Doheny, inveterate warrior, uppity nigger, and just maybe the best offensive linebacker the Dallas Cowboys had ever sacrificed to computer age statistics.

I had never met him face-to-face or shook his hand, but I had followed him too many times and too far not to know something about him beyond the one-dimensional photos his wife had sent me the first time, beyond the enormity of strength and stoutness of heart that had cut a mighty swath through opposing lineups on Monday night football. And sometimes, filled with melancholic introspection, working my way to oblivion in one of his recently vacated bars, I wondered if maybe we weren't chasing the same dream, fleeing the apparitions that beset all old soldiers—the haunted past, the dreaded future—searching for impossible perfection in an unregenerate world, our own Epiphany, or maybe our own small niche somewhere in Valhalla.

I walked past him again on my way back to my car, averting my eyes from this latest proof of man's inherent foolishness. I was saddened by the dreary fruitless game we played twice yearly, this fool's game of hide-and-seek with no real beginning and no end and little meaning that I could see.

I found a roll of quarters in the glove compartment of the car. I locked up the Polaroid camera and opened a fresh pack of cigarettes, then crossed the short distance to the phone booth at the corner of the silent honky-tonk.

I pushed quarters into the tinkling bandit and punched out Big Boy Doheny's home phone number. I had never met his wife, but I knew what she looked like from seeing her on TV a time or two. The first time was when she married Big Boy, a wedding that would have done the Kennedys proud for pomp

2

and circumstance, an event that rattled the bones and curdled the blood of wealthy bigots all over Texas. The second time was an interview by Susie, something to do with an upcoming charity telethon. Susie used to be one of Texas's most popular TV reporters. She also used to be my wife.

Mrs. Doheny had not been a handsome woman as I remembered, too much curve and length to her jaw and not enough distance between her eyes. But she had cornered the market in beautiful smiles and had the sweetest voice I had ever heard. She had one other thing going for her: she was easily the richest woman in Dallas, if not in Texas, and after the initial bigoted knee-jerk reaction to a union between one of Texas's leading socialites and this brash, good-looking refugee from South Dallas, her power and position reasserted itself and brought about in high society a universal color blindness that astounded ophthalmologists from the Panhandle to the nose of the bear.

While I waited I watched Doheny through the fly-specked window of the booth. He hadn't moved that I could see, his head and one hairy thigh still lying free of the crushed green blanket, his hands knotted into fists and pressed against his stomach. He wore orange-colored walking shorts, cowboy boots, and a pearl-gray Stetson lay crumpled a couple of feet from his head. A half-empty fifth of whiskey sat waiting within easy reach of his arm.

A cruising redneck deputy's dream, I thought, and instinctively craned my neck to look up and down the highway.

"Hello." The voice was still as sweet as in my memory.

"This is Dan Roman, Mrs. Doheny."

"You've found him, then. Of course you have or you wouldn't be calling."

"Yes, ma'am, I've found him." I gave her our approximate location and the name of the bar.

"Very well, Mr. Roman, you may go home now."

"He's not in real great shape. I haven't forgotten the rules, but don't you want me to . . . to do something?"

"You've done your part, Mr. Roman. Please go home now."

She paused, then asked the question she always asked before she let me go. "Is he alone?"

"Yes, he's alone," I said, lifting my hand to light a cigarette and pausing as the rear door of the camper swung suddenly open. A woman stepped down, a slender dark-skinned blonde in a skimpy bikini and high heels. She picked her way daintily through the weeds to where Doheny lay and began kicking him on the soles of his boots.

"Very well, Mr. Roman, thank you. You are finished"—she paused again—"for this time."

"There won't be a next time," I said flatly, watching the blonde pour the bottle of whiskey over Doheny's hairy chest, her knees flexed, poised for flight.

"As you wish," she said, ignoring the fact that I had said the exact same words six months before . . . and six months before that.

"Goddammit!" I was suddenly raging, choking with anger I only partially understood. "I can't do this anymore. I can't handle this sorry childish shit. I've chased this man up and down this state six times in three years, and caught him every time. And yet . . . and yet I've never looked him in the eye, never shaken his hand, never seen him up close when he wasn't unconscious, sleeping off a drunk. I'm damn tired of chasing a ghost. This is a crazy game you've got me playing, a fool's errand, and I'm not doing it anymore. I don't need you rich folks to mess up my head; I can do that all by myself."

She listened quietly until I finished, then made a sound that could have been a compassionate cluck or a gentle snort of derision. "I'm sorry, Mr. Roman. You're right, of course, it is a game of sorts, perhaps a foolish one. But it's the only game that he has left and I'm afraid I'm compelled to play."

"Well, I'm not, and I'm turning in my jersey." I tensed a little as Big Boy came roaring off the blanket, catching the squealing blonde before she had gone five paces, sweeping her into his arms and nuzzling her jaunty breasts. Then I heard him bellow the rutting call I had heard about from more than

4

one giggling barmaid, and had heard once before myself, faintly, on the beach at Boca Chica.

"Go home, Mr. Roman," Clarice Doheny said gently. "Now that he knows you've found him, he'll be coming home himself."

"He doesn't know it yet," I said. "I have the Polaroids here in my shirt pocket. Unless you tell me what this is all about, give me a reason for all the hours and all the miles, make me understand this idiotic game we're playing . . . well, maybe I'll just keep them as souvenirs and drive away."

"It's your decision, of course," she said, then followed with a low dry chuckle. "It's his game and his rules. Why don't you ask him?"

"Maybe I will," I said, watching the black giant toss the blonde through the door of the camper, clamber through behind her, and slam the door. "Enough is enough. Pretty soon I'll be as crazy as he is."

Her low sweet voice came again. "He isn't crazy, Mr. Roman. He's just trying to survive."

"Aren't we all," I said, then slowly hung up the receiver as I realized I was talking to an empty line. I cursed softly, then lit another cigarette and stepped out of the booth.

Doheny's pickup was fifty feet away but I could see it rocking and faintly hear the lusty bellows and high girlish laughter, and I suddenly felt put-upon, disgruntled, my vague sense of dissatisfaction crystallizing into cold hard purpose. Not this time, dammit. I had always walked away before, left my calling card like a thief in the darkness, slunk away like a Peeping Tom after the lights were out. But not this time; I had caught him fair and square, and like a ragged old hound with his last coon I needed to bay a little and worry the carcass.

I crossed the empty lot again, passing the dirty crumpled blanket under the live oak, the folding table with the metal Igloo water cooler and the crusty, flyblown remnants of somebody's meal. Whatever else she was, Doheny's blonde wasn't any great shakes at housekeeping.

I drew up at the back of the camper, stiff-legged and wary, listening to the sounds, the growls and squeals, the metallic clatter of worn shocks bottoming, the unholy cacophony that had no continuity and no rhythm and sounded like it might go on forever.

I thought about waiting, but rumor had it that he could go on like this for hours, and often did. And since listening to two strangers making love is only a little less desperate than watching, I stepped forward and pounded on the door.

"Go away, dammit, whoever you are. Can't you see we're busy?" His voice was a deep baritone rumble and, as far as I could tell, more amused than annoyed.

"Can't do that, man," I said, making my voice light and friendly. "You've been treed fair and square. It's high time I got a look at what I've been chasing."

"Roman? Is that Dan Roman?" The pickup stopped rocking and I heard a protesting feminine wail.

"Hey, man, this ain't the way . . . come on, man, what's got into you?"

"Too many bars and too many miles, Doheny. You're making me old before my time."

"Hey, man, don't ruin it. Next time, huh? Next time when you catch me, me and you'll get together—"

"No next time for me, Doheny."

"Why, man?"

"Hell, I don't know why. Maybe I'm finally growing up."

"Aw, man, that ain't no good reason. Listen—"

But I had stopped listening. There was too much pleading in his voice. A drunkard's whine I had heard too often in my father's voice and in my own. So I stuck the Polaroids in the crack of the door, turned my back on his plaintive plea, and walked away, rocking on my heels, a keening whistle in my ears that only I could hear and only I could understand.

But it wasn't enough.

I felt empty, cheated; something was ending and there had been no grand finale. Only the clowns doing pratfalls and belly whoppers. I walked around in a tight little circle, kicking empty cans and cursing. I spotted Doheny's Stetson and sent it flying, smashed the whiskey bottle against the honky-tonk's foundation.

It still wasn't enough; I was coiled too tight, all my strings on stretch and thrumming.

I kicked Doheny's hat again on the way to my car. I took the .38 out of the glove compartment and stalked back to the center of the lot. I was squaring off when Doheny yelled: "Hey, Dan—"

The rest was lost in the slapping roar of the gun and the continuous roll of thunder as I emptied it into the Igloo cooler, watched it quiver and jerk and spout arcing streams that would have made a Boy Scout troop proud around a dying campfire.

I felt better almost at once. Easy, loose and easy.

I grinned at Doheny's startled face in the camper window, bowed, and swept my baseball cap across the toes of my boots. I was still grinning when I got into my car and drove away, leaving him to muddle through whatever was left of his charade. I had other things to do. Important things. I knew a half-dozen good bars on my way home. I just might curl up in one, maybe find a blonde of my own and play my own damn games for a change.

/2/

There's no accounting for the physiological changes wrought by time, no way to estimate the damage done by man himself in his constant search for gratification or painless oblivion. Sharp perceptions dim and fade into confusion; the senses dull, blunted by ennui, induced euphoria, or just plain boredom. Emotions atrophy or shut down, and the organism, in a valiant effort to survive, will oftentimes compensate for the impact of five lagging senses by augmenting the sixth.

The sixth sense; an empirical will-o'-the-wisp that some men label instinct and others deny altogether.

But it exists; it must. There was no other way I could have known that Susie would be waiting for me, sitting quietly in my den, her dark eyes wide with uncertainty. But I did know. Standing in the entry hall, unsnapping the gun from my belt, hanging it in its accustomed place in the closet, I knew. There had been no sound, no telltale aroma of perfume, but I knew with an undeniable certainty that she was there, and I stepped through the doorway without surprise, with only thudding shock to contend with. But shock was fine; it was better than pain—the pain would come later.

I lifted a hand without looking at her, her image an indistinct blur in the far corner of my right eye as I crossed the room to the bar without stumbling once.

"Jesus Christ," she said incredulously.

"In person," I said, a programmed response to an old barroom joke that was never very funny in the first place.

"How did you know I was here?"

I grinned at her. "Secrets of the profession." My grin felt

funny, too tight, and my cheeks were beginning to ache. I began building a simple drink of Canadian Club and ice cubes; my hands needed something to do, and I had a hunch I was going to need it.

"You're no slouch yourself, kid. How'd you know I was coming home today?"

There was a touch of the old impudence in her hesitant smile, a hint of defiance in her graceful shrug. "No big deal, Danny. You had a call from Clarice Doheny on your phone recorder. I just called her back, is all. Clarice told me she thought you'd be home this afternoon."

"Clarice, huh? Sounds like you know her pretty well."

She nodded without answering, wetting her lips nervously, one tanned hand straying to a tangle of thick black hair curled loosely at her shoulder. The late-afternoon sunlight streaming through the patio door gleamed dully on the plain gold wedding ring on her third finger.

I took a drink of bourbon and wondered if the movement could have been deliberate. But her warm brown eyes were guileless, her lovely face arranged along compassionate lines. I moved my eyes away from her finger and tried not to think about it, tried not to remember how it was to be married, the things that people did.

Finally she broke the uneasy silence. "How've you been, Danny?"

"Fine, fine. I'm doing just great. How about you?"

She nodded again without speaking, then cocked her head like an inquisitive puppy and smiled crookedly. "You don't look so great."

I raked a hand across my face. "I could do with a bath and a shave and about twenty hours of sleep." I leaned forward on the bar and cupped the glass in both hands. "What is it, Susan? I can't make myself believe this is a social call, and since I'm not a very likely candidate for one of your high society interviews—"

"I don't do that anymore, Danny. I quit when I got . . .

when I got married. It was too much for me. But maybe I'll go back." She crinkled her nose. "Haven't you missed me on the six o'clock news?"

"I had to choose between you and a game show. Sorry." I finished the drink and began building another, a rising swell of resentment keeping my gaze away from her, away from dark liquid eyes that worked in devastating harmony with flawless skin that had the bloom of an early-summer tan, pale pink lips glowing with their own natural color, bringing the small oval face into bright and shining focus, softly turned and utterly feminine.

"Do we have to be enemies, Danny?" Her voice reached me faintly, low and throbbing, her hands coming together in her lap, clenching, then slowly opening, palms upward, fingers slightly curled in an unconscious gesture of supplication. "I can't believe that you . . . that you hate me."

I rubbed my eyes with a hand that smelled of gasoline and gunpowder. "I don't hate you, Susan, you know better than that."

"Then why did you let me go?" she asked quietly. "Was what I did with Jack so . . . so terrible? It wasn't important, Danny. It meant nothing."

"I didn't send you away; you took yourself away." I raised my head and looked at her finally. "And it meant something to me."

Her gaze met mine squarely, blazing out of a face that had grown strained and pale. "I'm sorry. I asked you to forgive me and you said you would. You said it was a human thing; you said that flesh was weak, that no man, be he self-righteous prophet or a sapless wino, was above the call of irresistible nature, that no man could stand firm before the winds of desire. You said—"

"All right. That sounds like some of my bullshit. The kind I spout when I'm drunk. But you'll notice I didn't say a damn thing about women."

"See," she said, smiling wanly, "you asked more of me than you did yourself."

"No," I said evenly. "I never asked anything of you. It's just that where I came from we expected our womenfolks to be faithful the way we expected our coon dogs to have good noses and a lot of heart. Maybe it's different over here in North Texas." I dumped the rest of the drink down my throat, the tight dryness giving way before its stinging bite. "What's the point in all this, Susie?"

Her right hand curled into a small brown fist, beating against her thigh. "Dammit . . . it was your fault as much as mine." She tried to build a smile around quivering lips and failed. "You were the one who brought Jack here to live with us—"

"Not to live," I said, "only to stay until he found a job and got on his feet. His father was a friend of mine, Susie. I owed him."

"You didn't have to spend a week deer hunting, go chasing Mr. Doheny all over Texas . . ." Her voice faltered, steadied, then gained volume. "Three weeks we were here alone together. I was honest with you. I didn't have to tell you, but I did. Just that one time . . . too much wine, too much music, too much loneliness . . . and just a little bit . . ." Her voice faded again, her head lowered in uncharacteristic humility, lips compressed and trembling.

My laugh was as biting as I could make it. "A little bit of what, Susan? Making out, love, sex . . . what? Does that mean you didn't come? Or maybe you kept your clothes on? Come on, honey, tell me, explain it to me. Maybe I'm not with it anymore, but how does one go about fucking a little bit?"

"All right, Danny." She stood up, her hands automatically smoothing the tailored slacks along slender hiplines, snugging the magenta blouse across moderate-sized breasts, slopes and contours and valleys I could close my eyes and see with painful clarity. Her smile was soft, but her eyes were brimming. She swept the shining cascade of black hair back across her shoulders and thumbed angrily at her eyes in the same fluid motion.

"All right, Danny," she said again, "I'm not sorry I came. I wanted to see you . . . it's been good to see you again. I was hoping . . ."

"Hoping what, Susan? That we could be friends? That we could sit and chat and maybe have a beer and giggle over old times? I could tell you all about my fascinating life these last two years, a fool chasing other fools. You could tell me about your new marriage, the raptures of young love, the joys of a home and hearth and a loving husband. I could tell—" I broke off, the blip of anger gone, wondering if my words sounded as self-pitying to her as they did to me.

"I waited a year, Danny. And you never called. Not once. You never tried to see me."

"Roads and telephone lines. They have one thing in common: they work both ways."

She shook her head, crossing the short distance to the bar, standing two feet away, her features soft again, blurred and working with emotion I could only speculate about. "No. It had to come from you. All my life it seems I've been chasing you, ambushing you in ways you never even knew about. Fighting. Always fighting. I waited. I waited and plotted and planned. But none of it did any good because you were hung up over the difference in our ages. It was a nightmare I couldn't wake up from. I hated that, Danny. I hated having to scheme—"

"Susan . . ."

"No," she said fiercely, "let me finish." Her hand came out and clamped around my wrist. "I need to say these things, get them out of my system, maybe . . . maybe get you out along with them. We were left unfinished, Danny. Dangling. All those years together when I thought you loved me—"

"I did," I said hoarsely.

"—the way I loved you," she went on relentlessly, squeezing harder, her other hand flashing out to join in the throttle hold on mine. "But you didn't. You couldn't have and still have thrown me away because of one silly little mistake."

"I didn't," I said coldly. "You're exaggerating again." I scanned her flawless features, searching for imperfection: a blemish, or a mole—anything. Something I could focus on to break the power of her spell. The magnetic force of her sensuality flowed through our joined hands, weakening me, shattering what little was left of my resolve.

"Are you saying you made a mistake?" I cleared my throat huskily. "Are you trying to say you're still in love with me?"

Her eyes searched my face with fulgent clarity, punishing in their intensity. Finally she shook her head, laying my hand on the bar and stroking it once with warm lingering fingers. "No, I'm not saying that at all. That wasn't why I came." She smiled briefly, then she turned and walked across the den to the kitchen door.

"I'll need to use your phone. Jack thought it best to drop me off instead of staying with me."

"Sure," I said. "I always said Jack was a smart boy."

She disappeared into the kitchen. I stood rubbing my tingling wrist, wondering if I had missed some vital part of our conversation, a word, some nuance that would give me a clue to the reason for her visit beyond the turning of the screw.

The murmur of her voice rose and then died and a few seconds later she appeared in the entryway hall.

"I'll wait for Jack out front. It's nice and shady under the oaks."

"Fine," I said. "Take care."

"Good-bye, Danny." Her face was composed, her eyes cool and remote.

I heard the muted click of the front door latch. I sat for a while without moving, watching the ice cubes melt in my glass, feeling the pain awaken, stretch, stand up and take a few practice swings at my insides.

I glanced at my watch: at the rate of one drink every five minutes, in a half hour or so I could be beyond feeling. I reached for the bottle of Canadian Club.

Along about the fifth or sixth drink, approaching stupor, I decided the gentlemanly thing to do would be to forgive her.

/3/

The sun woke me, glaring balefully through the east window in my bedroom. I had forgotten to adjust the air conditioner and I was bathed in a slick slime of perspiration, the raw rank odor peculiar to whiskey-sweat rising in waves around me.

Surprisingly enough, I had no hangover, only a slight dizziness that vanished with the first spray of cold water in the shower. I braced my hands against the wall and let the water pound full force, blasting through the film of road grime and washing my pores free of accumulated poisons. Then I turned off the shower, soaped everything, and did it again.

I came out pink and tingling, cleaner than I had been in two weeks. Motel room showers gave me the horrors—visions of scabrous bleeding feet and worse—and I tried to avoid them whenever possible. I toweled briskly and dug out a fresh set of clothing. Somewhere along the line my stomach had wakened and was making noises, the piteous whining sounds of a good hound on a bad trail. I scraped a hand across the stubble on my face and decided a shave could wait until after breakfast; I turned down the air conditioner and padded barefoot down the hall to the kitchen.

Breakfast was a simple affair: four scrambled eggs, a half pound of bacon, toast, a small glass of orange juice and a larger one of milk. A drinking man's breakfast: protein, vitamin C, and more than enough good animal fat to coat my stomach against whatever harmful substances might chance to come its way. For some reason, most heavy drinkers never learn the secret of prolonging the joys of drinking, the basic fact that the more you eat, the more you can drink—the deleterious side effects of obesity notwithstanding.

But since we exist in an imperfect world, each remedy has its malady, each simple truth its countervail in complicated falsehood. My malady was that I drank; my simple truth was that I had no clear idea why.

I had lost Susie. True. Driven her away with neglect and pompous indignation, shamed her with self-righteous absurdity and thrust her into the arms of a man far younger than I, handsomer, and probably a hell of a lot smarter to boot. Was that not reason enough to despair? to beat my chest and howl with anguish? to drown my sorrow the way men have done since the first man squashed a fermenting grape between his toes and stooped to taste the nectar?

But even I wasn't foolish enough to believe that: I drank long before Susie, drank long before the years with the Law even, the years of being a cop in a cop-hating society, the times of triumph and travail, of happiness and pain. The times of loss: of another woman I loved and a fine handsome son.

I could blame it on the war, on the desperate need of a frightened young warrior to still the demons and blot out the stark reality of his own mortality.

Or I could blame my father, a gentle man who drifted aimlessly to the bottle after my mother's death and, like Willie Nelson's song, found a whiskey river of his own, bobbed helplessly a couple of times, slipped silently beneath the current halfway to the other shore.

Or I could stand flat-footed and face up to it the way I had done a time or two before. It had never amounted to much; I still didn't know why I drank, but I had garnered some dark suspicions. I had hunches, vague notions, flashes of insight that made me uneasy and filled me with a restless desire to have done with this fruitless self-analysis and go have a drink.

And that's the way it always ended, ice cubes and amber liquid, a clinking glass and a solemn promise to stick with it the next time, to probe my psyche, invade my id, adjudicate my findings, and set to right this miserable flaw in an otherwise sterling character.

I finished eating and cleared away the mess; the paper plate and plastic knife and fork went into the trash, the juice and milk glass into the dishwasher. A quick swipe at the table with a dish towel and I was finished. I stood in the doorway to the den and lit my first cigarette of the day, feeling smug for a change, obeying the American Cancer Society's fifth commandment: DO NOT smoke before breakfast. I was reaching for the stack of mail on the coffee table when the front door chimes began chiming, a hard-knuckled fist rapping shave-and-a-haircut by way of accompaniment.

I sighed and walked toward the door. Only one man did it exactly that way.

"Okay, Homer, I hear you," I yelled.

The cacophony continued.

"Dammit!" I threw off the chain, clicked the lock, and yanked open the door.

Captain Homer Sellers of the Midway City Police Department glared at me with mock ferocity, his fisted left hand still upraised, his right against the bell. Behind me the chimes still pealed.

"You can stop with the bell now, Homer," I said. "You've got my attention."

"Good," he grunted, the scowl melting into a grin. "Figured you might be laying up in there all drunked out, or something." He poked at my belly with a thumb as big around as a hoe handle. "Or maybe shacked up with some poor widder woman with no taste and less brains." The grin widened. He had large white teeth in a big shaggy head that went well with the rest of his oversize body.

"What were you going to do, Homer? Bust me on a morals charge?" I stepped back out of his lumbering way and closed the door. Four inches taller than my six feet and fifty pounds heavier, he sometimes seemed overwhelming.

"Hell no," he boomed, stepping into the den and heading

16

straight for my new rocker-recliner. "I figured I'd join you. I ain't had me an orgy in some time."

"I don't think me and you with one woman would constitute an orgy, Homer. That'd be more like black comedy."

He laughed, a rough grating sound that always made me want to clear my throat.

"This is nice," he said, pushing the recliner into the first position and crossing his thick ankles on the footrest. "New, ain't it?"

"Yeah." I lit a cigarette and sat down on the end of the couch. I glanced at the clock above the TV. "What're you doing running around in old work clothes, Homer? Goofing off at taxpayers' expense?"

His head rolled back and forth against the headrest. "First day of vacation. I gotta lot of stuff to do around the house, scraping, caulking, painting, crap like that."

"Sounds like fun. Hell of a way to spend a vacation, though."

"Thought I might run down to the coast for a couple of days, snapper fishing, scuba diving, things like that."

I nodded and wondered if he was working around to asking me to go with him in his usual convoluted fashion. "That sounds great."

"Yeah, don't it." He yawned and stretched his hairy arms. He smiled sheepishly, then cocked his head, squinting red-rimmed eyes at me. "You look like hell."

"It's been a rough two weeks," I said, resisting an impulse to yawn myself.

"Two weeks? You been chasing that big black mother again? You better watch out that big sucker don't turn on you sometime, make a lot of little ones out of your big one."

"He's nothing like that. He's harmless. He just likes to play games, is all. We play hide-and-seek until I catch up with him, then he just goes on home until the next time."

"Dumbest thing I ever heard. How much does he pay you for that kind of shit?"

I grinned and shook my head. "None of your business. You working for the IRS now?"

His short pug nose twitched. "Come on, dammit. I'm not being nosy, I just want to know."

"There's a contradiction there somewhere."

"Don't try to throw me off with big words. How much?"

I shrugged. "Four thousand."

His lips curled in disgust. "You never used to lie to me, Dan."

"I'm not. Four thousand plus expenses."

"Jesus Christ! No wonder you don't want to come back on the force. Two thousand dollars a week for following some guy around bars all over the state, drinking and carousing and I don't know what all."

"I have to work for it. He doesn't always make it easy."

"That's the damnedest thing I've ever heard of. Why's he do it, you reckon?"

"I don't know exactly. I've thought about it a lot. I suppose he has to break out every so often. He's a black man living in a white man's world. Maybe it just backs up on him. He sure as hell crams a lot of living into two weeks or so."

"Sounds like you got yourself an annuity."

"I gave it up."

"Gave it up? Why, for pete's sake?" His eyebrows leaped upward, creating a ladder of inverted V's down the center of his broad forehead.

"It's not fun anymore." I got up, crossed to the patio door, and opened the shade; sunlight flooded the room. One of my three resident squirrels leaped out of the large stone pot I kept supplied with hickory nuts, walnuts, and pecans. He scampered leisurely across the patio, down the bank, and up the trunk of the large oak in the center of the yard. Out of this year's litter, he was all tail and fluffy hair, his body no larger than one of Homer's sausage fingers.

"I guess you saw Susie," Homer said. He was unwrapping a fat cigar with a plastic tip, always a prelude to something, a sure sign that we were getting around to the reason for his visit.

"Yeah, I saw her," I said, determined not to show my surprise. "How did you know she was here?" I went back and sat down on the couch.

He shoved the raw end of the cigar inside his mouth, wallowed it around, then withdrew it and lit it with a kitchen match. He shook his head, then brushed a hand through mud-colored hair, his face suddenly sober. "She called me, said she was coming by here to see you. She wanted to know if I knew how you felt."

"About what?"

He gave me a sidelong glance. "About her, dammit. What else?"

"Why would she call you? Why wouldn't she call me? Come on, Homer, you're shucking me, man. What's going on?"

He sucked on the cigar, his round face gloomy. "I guess she didn't ask you, huh?"

"Ask me what?"

"She said if you hadn't forgiven her, she wasn't going to ask."

"Ask me what, dammit?"

He shoved the recliner into a normal sitting position and laid the cigar in the ashtray stand beside the chair. "You remember the Wagermans? Dalton Wagerman and his son Tony? Six or seven years ago. Susie and that other girl, that girlfriend of hers—"

"I remember," I said, "Susie and Betty Asterman testified against them. . . . What about it?"

"I don't know," he said. "I only know what Susie told me. I did run a check and she's right about them being out."

"Out? Out of prison? What the hell does that have to do with Susie?"

He spread his hands eloquently. "I only know what she told me . . . but Susie thinks they're going to try to kill her." Normally as stolid as those of a hibernating bear, his blunt features were beginning to show signs of agitation.

"Kill her?" A ripple of shock reaction brought a surge of adrenaline, a rapid acceleration of my heartbeat.

"That's what she thinks. She came here to ask for your

help." His wide mouth curled sardonically. "But I guess too much of your dumbass stubbornness has rubbed off on her over the years."

"She didn't say a word. I wondered why she came. Why didn't she say something if she's really worried? Why didn't she—?"

"Don't ask me questions I can't answer, boy. Thing is, I didn't put much stock in it myself when she came to me a month or so ago." He paused and puffed on the cigar, his expression noncommittal. "That was before that friend of hers turned up dead."

"Jesus Christ! Betty Asterman?"

"Not Asterman anymore. She was married. Name was Rawlings now." He paused, his face suddenly tight and hard; a cop's face. "She was killed, Dan, killed in the worst way there is: beaten and raped and tossed into a ditch like a bag of trash."

"Jesus Christ," I repeated inanely, my mind numbly sifting through his words, suddenly realizing their significance. "And you think the Wagermans—"

"I don't think anything," he said roughly. "It's not my case. She was dumped out on Dellerman Road. That's County. Deputy named Wally Prentice working it. I talked to him a few days ago, but so far he's got zip."

"How about the Wagermans? Did you tell—"

"Susie did. They got alibis tight as a gnat's ass. Or so Prentice says, and I got no reason not to believe him. I've heard of him. He's an old hand, a good man, thorough."

"Alibis can be set up."

He shrugged, puffing smoke. "Anything's possible."

"Dammit. Why didn't she tell me about it?"

"She's got pride too, Dan," he said, pushing out of the recliner and crossing to the door. He stood looking at me, his eyes behind the new contacts glassy with reflected light. "She says they've been hounding her, that everywhere she goes they turn up, that she's seen them following her when she's alone in her car." He blotted his eyes again with a corner of the handkerchief. "The question is, what are you going to do about it?"

I shook my head. "I can't help her if she doesn't ask me."

His lip curled again and became a sneer. "Sure. Good chance to make her crawl a little, huh?"

I smiled thinly. "She'd let them kill her first."

He opened the door. "Yeah, that's what I'm afraid of." He stood there limned by sunlight for a moment, then went out and quietly closed the door.

/4/

People never seem to profit much from the mistakes of others. For years Texans have been watching Californians on the evening news, watching homes worth millions of dollars slipping and sliding all over the sides of hills and mountains, being inexorably engulfed in a tidal wave of goo or mindlessly crushed like matchstick dollhouses in the hands of a demented child.

And yet, hardheaded realists that we are as a group, we learn little; we still go for the high ground every time—when there's high ground to go for. Maybe it's instinctive, this need to live among the eagles, to overlook the valleys, to smell a cleaner wind untainted by the prosaic lives below, to feel Godlike, perhaps, to feel immune to the mundane affairs that stultify and fret the luckless lowlanders. Maybe it feels that way; I don't know.

There are prerequisites for modern mountainside living: a certain amount of courage and a lot of money. Courage to battle the icy grades in winter, washouts and erosion after the spring rains, plumbing and sewage that can become a nightmare overnight.

It takes money to cope with these problems, and while I was sure Susie had the fortitude necessary for living on the lip of a mountain, I was wondering about the money for this outlandish creation of brick, glass, and aluminum as I gunned the Dodge up the steep incline to a four-car detached garage almost as large as my eighteen-hundred-square-foot home. I braked and parked on the apron in front of the fourth stall, pinning the car to the slope with the hand brake and a fervent prayer.

I sat for a moment, a little stunned by the enormity of the one-story structure that seemed to go on forever, following the concave contour of the hill and sprawling in unrestrained majesty amid stunted post oak and threadbare elm. Glossy wood trim sparkled pristine white beneath a cedar shake roof that was no longer allowed in the city below, and three giant plate glass windows facing the southwest splashed my eyes with late-afternoon sunlight. I counted five fireplace chimneys and four dormers set into the moderately sloped roof at regular intervals.

A million dollars in today's market, I thought, a sum equal to five times the amount Susie had been given by her mother a short time after she left me. Invested in money market funds, the two hundred thousand would have yielded something more than thirty thousand a year, hardly enough to pay the energy costs on this home.

As for handsome Jack Farley, he had been practically penniless when I came home and threw him out of my house in the grip of cold righteous rage. A tall, well-built man possessed of an ingratiating manner, he had a predilection for beautiful women which I had recognized instantly but ignored to my sorrow.

His father had been my crew chief in Vietnam, had volunteered for one too many missions and lost his life. I owed him for that, the way I owed all the ones who died. So maybe it was just guilt that made me take in his son Jack when he came to Dallas from Iowa to look for work. But jobs were scarce for economists that year, or so it seemed, and he was still unemployed when I came back from two weeks of loping around the state after Doheny.

I saw nothing amiss in his cerulean eyes and bland smile, but one look at Susie and I knew. I waited until she told me, knowing she would, knowing it would gnaw at her until she did. She could never lie to me, and not telling me would have been a lie of omission. Shaken by her honesty, bleeding from her truth, I had turned my back on her.

Then I had thrown him out. Bag and baggage, as they say. I

had brushed her aside, my face as cold as stone, my heart sick and unforgiving. For two days I was on a rampage, slaking my whiskey lust and taking my empty revenge amidst the uncaring bones of some forgotten whore.

When I finally came home she was gone. A year later she divorced me and married Jack Farley, an event I wouldn't have known about if not for Homer Sellers's raging at me for being a dumbass stubborn fool.

And now, seeing the house they lived in, talked and laughed and slept in, made love in, brought a sweeping rush of desolation.

Despite the heat building inside the car I shivered. I lit a cigarette and got out of the car, shutting down my thoughts by sheer force of will.

Filled with ambivalence, I walked toward the front door, suddenly conscious of my scruffy appearance, faded Levi's and a wrinkled shirt, regretting vaguely my decision not to wear the blue sport coat and contrasting pants that Susie had made me buy before she left.

But it was only Susie after all, I reminded myself, and she had seen my worst and my best before, seen me tall and proud and almost handsome when we married; seen me white-faced and moaning, groveling in my own filth; listened to my sorry rationalizations, the lying litany of all drunks everywhere: "Never again, Lord, never again." There was not a lot I could do to fool her; she knew me.

But it wasn't Susie who finally answered the door. Jack Farley stood there, wet and dripping in vermilion swim trunks and clogs, his auburn hair pasted to his face like streaks of dark blood above a small uncertain smile. My faint hope that he had somehow grown ugly during the past two years died a pauper's death.

"Oh, hi, Dan," he said, his smile gaining breadth and strength, his pale eyes watching me warily.

I nodded without speaking, turned and flipped the cigarette butt down the driveway. I turned back. "I'd like to speak to Susie, Jack." I could hear faint sounds of laughter from behind him, a noise that sounded like the rebound clatter of a diving board.

He grimaced and snapped his fingers. "Damn, Dan, I'm sorry. She just this minute left—" He broke off and looked past my shoulder as if she might still be in the driveway. "A wedding shower," he went on, the cheery grin returning, "one of our friends. She's marrying the governor's nephew, by the way. You know—"

"What can you tell me about the Wagermans?"

His face sobered instantly. "I thought Susie didn't tell you anything. How did you find out about—?"

"Never mind that. What do you know about it?"

"Not a hell of a lot. Susan told me about the trial, the way that old bastard threatened her and—"

"I was there," I interrupted again. "What I want to know is what's happened recently. Why does Susie think they're trying to kill her?"

His eyebrows shot upward. "Kill her? I think that's a little strong, Dan. Scare her, would be more like it. Sure, we've seen them a lot lately, but they haven't done anything to make me think they were trying to hurt her, let alone kill her. I'm sorry, but to be honest, I think Susan is getting a little paranoid about all this." He leaned down and scratched the calf of his left leg, the long flat muscles rippling across his chest, the deeply tanned skin almost golden in the sunlight. A golden god, I thought, and pictured raven tresses spilling across bronzed flesh, cascading around their faces in iridescent splendor as she hovered over him, magnificently uninhibited, with those nibbling lips and warm butterfly kisses I remembered so well . . .

I turned away and fumbled for a cigarette. "I'll be the judge of that," I said harshly. When I looked back, he was standing erect, eyebrows raised again above knowing eyes, a glint of something in their pale blue depths that could have been pity. The smile was back, austere, but friendly enough.

"I'm sorry," he said quietly, "but Susan is my responsibility now."

"No," I said, just as quietly, mimicking his tone. "She's only your wife. As long as I'm alive, she's my responsibility." I sucked in a deep breath. "I promised her mother."

Our eyes met and held steady while I lit the cigarette. I was thrumming gently inside, a slow tensing, cloaking my mind like warm dark liquid. Signals, harbingers of violence that a tiny part of me recognized in startled wonder and was appalled. A small worm stirred in my brain, coiled, waited eagerly for the wrong look, the wrong word.

But he nodded finally, his face solemn, yet somehow mocking. "Okay, I can buy that. We both love her. But you had your time with her. She's mine now. I don't want you trying to take her back."

"You'll be the first to know," I said coldly. "Now tell me about the Wagermans and what you've done—if anything."

"All right." He stepped to one side. "Come on in—"

"This is fine right here. I don't want to interrupt your party."

"No party. Just some guys from my office building." He gestured vaguely. "We have an indoor pool."

"Good for you. Now, about the Wagermans. You said you'd seen them a lot lately. Where have you seen them?"

"Well . . . let's see, at the Ranger ball game in Arlington two weeks ago and at a flea market in Fort Worth. We saw them twice at the Belmond Dinner Theater in Dallas and at Casa Mañana—that was about three . . . no, four weeks ago." He stopped and frowned, stroking his square chin, his eyes squinting. "There was one other time . . . yeah, just before July fourth, at that meat market out on Highway 157. They were running a special on eight-ounce fillets. Six for—"

"Did they approach Susie, say anything, stare at her—what?"

"Nothing like that, that I saw. They were just there. Always close by somehow. At the Ranger game they were seated two rows behind us, at Casa they were directly in front. They were a couple of tables away at the Belmond Dinner Theater—like that."

"You said 'they.' Was it the man and his son?"

26

"The old man and two sons. The younger son is named Karl."

"And that's all there is?"

"Yes . . . except Susan said she was sure they were following her on at least two other occasions." He paused and frowned. "But I'm not sure about that, Dan. She said they were in cars both times and both of the boys own pickups. The old man drives a Ford panel truck with the name of the machine shop on the door."

"How do you know so much about them?"

He grimaced wryly, his face slowly turning pink. "Okay. I wasn't going to say anything because nothing came of it, but when Susan began to get upset, I hired a private detective—"

"Who?"

"A man named Mort Grossman. His office is in Fort Worth. I hired him to follow the Wagermans, check them out, you know."

"And what did he find out?"

He shrugged. "Nothing much we didn't already know. They never came anywhere near Susan during the three weeks Grossman worked for me. All I got for my money was a list of stakeout reports as long as my arm. Nothing at all out of the ordinary. He did find out that the girl—woman now, I guess—is back living with her daddy and brothers. Evidently what the old man said at the trial was true." He shifted impatiently as another outburst of noise came from behind him.

"That doesn't alter the fact that it was incest with a minor, consenting or not."

He nodded. "I understand that, but Grossman thinks all three of them are still banging the hell out of her."

"It would still be incest and still against the law. So your money wasn't wasted if we need to apply a little pressure. If they're just trying to harass Susie, they'll back off quick enough. The old man got out almost four years early, so he'll be on parole. I'm not sure about the son. I think he got only five years."

Farley nodded. "That's right. And he served every day of it.

27

He couldn't stay out of trouble in prison. He spent over a year in solitary, according to Grossman. A real mean mother." He moved restlessly and raked long-fingered hands through thinning auburn hair.

"How long has this been going on?"

He screwed up his face. "About ... two months, I guess. The first time was the meat market. We just thought it was a coincidence. After all, their machine shop is not far from there and they only live about two miles away. Of course, we didn't know that at the time. It upset Susan a little, seeing them like that, but nothing like the other times since."

"You have their addresses, home and the shop?"

"I can dig them up for you, but they're both in the big phone book under the old man's name ... Dalton A. Wagerman. He calls his shop DAW Machine and Tool Company."

"And both the sons live with the old man."

He nodded. "The younger one is supposed to be married, but I guess he must have split from his old lady. At least he was living there during Grossman's investigation." He shifted his weight and leaned a shoulder against the doorjamb. "Sure you don't want to come in, have a beer or something?"

I shook my head and turned slightly to avoid a splinter of reflected sunlight from one of the large windows. "No thanks." I lit another cigarette. "I'll need to talk to Susie. You can tell her I'll be home most of tomorrow, but she might call first."

His eyes flickered. "All right," he said evenly, "I'll tell her you came by. I have to be honest with you, I don't think she'll call." His face was solemn, but there was a trace of arrogance in his voice, a tightening around his lips that could have been annoyance.

I felt the grin coming and did nothing to stop it. "You just tell her, sonny."

His face reddened, the thin white line spreading around his lips. "I'll tell her, Dan, but you remember what I said. You had your time with her and now she's mine." His posture had become unconsciously defensive, his left hand coming up to press against the opposite doorjamb, barring my way.

"You make her sound like a parking meter," I said lightly. "Susie made the decision to leave. I didn't try to get her back then. What makes you think I would now?" I let the grin twist and become what I hoped was mocking. "Are you that unsure of her, Jack?"

"Not at all," he said, his eyes suddenly hard and bright. "You're just a father figure to her. She worries about you, your binges. And the way she left you bothers her. Susan's emotional. I don't have to tell you that. She likes things tidy, neat, and your relationship had a lot of loose ends." He straightened and unconsciously squared his wide shoulders. "Anyhow, she's my wife and I'll protect her." He wet his lips, his face suddenly contorted. "We don't need you."

"I'm crushed," I said, the taut band inside me snapping, splashing anger like an acid rain. I reached out and poked his bare chest with a stiffened forefinger. "You tell her, sonny. You tell her I was here and why and let her make her own decision." I turned and walked toward my car, my head throbbing. I flipped the cigarette butt in a high arc toward the bluff that bordered the street.

I was climbing into my car when he began yelling: "Hey, goddammit! Listen to me! You stay the hell away—!"

I muted his words by closing the door, then drowned them out by racing the car motor. For one small burning second I debated getting out, settling a debt that was two years old and long overdue. But reason prevailed and I drove away. Reason, and a snide little voice in the back of my mind postulating the possibility that I might just get my ass whipped.

/5/

The DAW Machine and Tool Company was located in northeast Tarrant County, a half mile beyond the city limits of Midway City. Housed in a ramshackle wooden building, it sat twenty yards off the road and seemed to tilt precariously with the prevailing winds. Sometime in the ancient past the dilapidated structure had been a buggy manufacturer's dream; the faded silhouette of a fringed surrey complete with prancing horse still haunted the cracked, scabrous walls. A truncated rock chimney poked ragged edges through the roof, and a battered weather vane with proudly crowing cock had been preserved when the new metal roof had been installed.

Despite immense double doors that gaped open in the center of the building, the interior was dim. In one corner a stout-looking young man in a black tank top and jeans stolidly watched a chugging machine wrest tortured screams from raw smoking metal. Three other machines sat silent and brooding, patiently waiting their turn at the hapless stock of bar, plate, and ingots stored in racks along the far wall. A small pallet heaped with oily, gleaming discs sat just inside the doors, and a bundle of shining coreless rods that looked as if they might some day become gun barrels lay neatly banded together on a table. The unpleasant odor of burning oil lay heavy in the air.

I stood in the doorway for a moment, rocking on my heels, trying to decide if the muscular young man resembled the barrel-chested, brutish lout Susie had pointed her finger at in court. I was deciding that he did when he looked up. I had a fleeting impression of pale shaggy hair atop long square features before the moving light behind him thrust his face into partial shadow. I could still see his eyes, dark and deep-sunken, watching me critically, as if I were a broken-down old machine he could possibly cannibalize for spare parts.

I nodded and smiled genially. "Dalton Wagerman," I said loudly.

He stared back at me placidly, silently, his square chin rotating rhythmically as he chewed the cud bulging his right cheek. I was cupping my hands around my mouth to yell again when he lifted one heavy arm and pointed to my right, jabbing it once toward a small rectangular enclosure in the corner.

I nodded and smiled again, but he had already turned back to his machine, his head canted as if listening to magical strains in the tortured sounds that only he could hear.

I walked around the pallet of discs, across a concrete floor dark and dank with an oily accumulation of grime. I made a mental note to scrub my boot soles before venturing onto my new den carpet and found myself thinking idly about the young square-jawed man at the machine, wondering if he had followed his father and brother down the unwholesome trail to incest, the lust-sickness that according to the experts invades one home out of four in one way or another. A sad commentary on modern man, I thought.

There was a plain unpainted door set into the plywood partition, but I didn't bother to knock. Only salesmen knock at office doors and what I had for Wagerman wasn't for sale, I was giving it away free.

It was a mean, depressing little cubbyhole, raw plywood walls with one door and no windows, a filing cabinet, a water cooler, and a scarred antique desk that looked older than the man behind it.

He was hunched over the cluttered desk writing when I opened the door, and if he looked up I missed it when I glanced quickly around the room. I sidestepped, closed the door, then sidestepped again to bring me in front of the desk. I stood there a full sixty seconds, staring at the top of his bald head, watching his thick square hand move steadily across the paper, feeling foolish over my melodramatic entrance, feeling more foolish over being ignored.

I coughed and shifted my feet and said his name out loud just in case he thought I was the kid from the machine: "Wagerman."

Nothing about him moved except the hand scribbling large looping words across the paper.

"Susan Farley," I said. "Used to be Susan Morgan. She testified against you in court, sent your fat ass to the pen for banging your own daughter."

He frowned suddenly; I could see the wrinkles spreading across the front of his head. He laid down the ballpoint and picked up the pad. He hunched forward, adjusted the gooseneck light, and began to read what he had written.

I stared down at him, flabbergasted.

"Susan Farley," I said. "Don't play dumb with me, asshole."

He grunted, laid down the pad, picked up the ballpoint, and began writing again.

"Jesus H. Christ!" Enough was enough. I took out the .38 and held it down in the light where he could see it. He went on writing.

"Goddammit!" I shoved the barrel under his nose, hooked the recurved sight in his left nostril, and began lifting. His head followed.

I saw his eyes first, bright and glistening, hot crazy eyes, smears of darkness against a field of marbled white. The eyes of a man who has done it all or had it done to him and thinks that makes him special and inviolable.

I thumbed back the hammer and grinned, pushing the barrel farther up his nose. "This sear is filed to a monkey's whisker, friend; a baby's fart could set it off. I wouldn't move if I were you."

He opened his mouth to breathe and stared up at me, unblinkingly. His skin was seamed, checkered like old leather, and someone in prison had put a mark on him, a long thin scar from his ear to the point of his chin.

"Susan Farley," I said again. "She's bored as hell with you.

Overexposure. If she ever sees you again it better be your ass, 'cause you better be running like hell in the other direction.''

His glaring eyes never left my face and he made no attempt to back away from the gun. He was either the coolest son of a bitch who ever lived or he was stone crazy; I couldn't decide which and wasn't sure I wanted to know.

I pulled the gun out of his nose and wiped it on a fold in his shirtsleeve, a cool tickling on the back of my head. I couldn't shake the feeling of unreality, of objective detachment, as if I were watching poorly written summer stock acted out by demented players. He had not blinked once that I could recall, but suddenly his eyes were veiled, opaque, dark and murky with malevolence.

I sneered to hide a shiver, opened my mouth to add to my threat, then closed it again with a snap. He either understood or he didn't; he would heed my warning or he would not. More empty words would do nothing except add to my own eerie feeling of uncertainty, add scope and dimension to confusion already alive and working.

I put up the gun and stepped backward to the door; I turned the knob and watched in utter disbelief as his head dropped, his hairy hand picking up the pad, adjusting it, thick fingers curling around the pen, pushing it across the yellow paper . . . a mindless automation in blind pursuit of esoteric imperatives only he could understand.

I walked back the way I had come, past the captive metal whose screams had died to a low grinding groan, past young Wagerman snapping his fingers and swaying to some inner beat.

I stepped out into the last gasp of a dying day and lit a cigarette with trembling fingers. One thing about it, I thought dryly as I wheeled the Dodge into the rutted, potholed street, the crazy son of a bitch knows that intrepid Dan Roman, fearless champion of old ladies and orphaned children, relentless foe of all that is evil, was standing squarely between him and Susie now. That oughta give him pause, scare the living shit right out of him.

*   *   *

I saw him as I turned the corner, my headlights sweeping along the gleaming sides of the silver Rolls-Royce. He was backing out of my driveway and paused to let me pass. When I didn't, when he saw my turn signal, he pulled forward again, gave me room to make the turn and pull in beside him. I parked and set the brake, then turned off the motor with a faint tickle of apprehension fluttering somewhere in my chest.

Dammit, I'd had enough craziness for one day.

He was out and standing when I climbed out of my seat, grinning broadly at me over the top of the Rolls, big hands held shoulder high, palms outward, fingers wriggling in a curiously feminine gesture.

"Peace, brother," he said. Tall as a tree, he looked considerably more substantial than he had the day before beneath the live oak. Despite the heat, he wore a lightweight tan jacket, and he had either straightened out his old hat or bought a new pearl Stetson.

"Hello, Big Boy."

"Hey, man, I thought I'd better get my black ass on over here and cheer you up. You looked like you was swinging pretty low yesterday."

"Sorry about your water cooler."

"Hey, no sweat. Hardly ever touch the stuff, anyway." He slapped his palms on the roof of the car and laughed. "Makes a damn fine target, don't it? I might just start carrying a couple extra. Come to think of it, makes more sense than blowing holes in my camper walls."

I walked around to the front of his car, eyed the sleek massive grill and the pretentious hood ornament. "Nice car."

He grunted and shrugged. "Yeah, it's okay for street driving. Ain't worth a shit for back roads and climbing hills and like that." He took off the hat and raked a hand through his tightly curled hair, obviously ill at ease. He replaced the hat, hesitated, then took two quick steps forward and shoved out his hand. "Reckon me and you oughta shake hands or something."

I mustered up a smile and took his hand. "It's good to meet you at last, Big Boy." His hand was smooth and warm, surprisingly limp.

"Hell, don't call me that," he said gruffly, smiling to take the sting out of it. "That's the fans' name, the fans' and the sportswriters' and the groupies'. That Big Boy's a holdover from when I was a kid. I was always a head higher and thirty pounds bigger than everybody my age. Call me Henry . . . or Hank. Mostly I go by Hank."

"Okay, Hank," I said.

"Getting back to yesterday. Man, you made my bowels loose when you came stomping across that field with that gun. I thought maybe Clary had finally got pissed and put out a contract on me. What happened, man? Everything just back up on you, or what?" The light from the street lamp streaked across the bottom half of his face, illuminating his wide grin.

"Something like that."

"Maybe you ought to go off on a binge, let me chase you for a while."

I laughed and lit a cigarette. "I'm about binged out. That's one of the problems."

"Aw, man, don't say that," he said, a groan in his voice. He opened the rear door of the Rolls and reached inside. I heard the clink of bottles as he brought a small cardboard box into view. "Scotch, bourbon, vodka, and brandy. I happen to know you're partial to all four."

"I could live without brandy," I said. "But how did you know?"

He cocked his head and brought back his smile. "You don't think I'm dumb enough to let some guy with a gun chase me all over Texas and not know a little bit about him?"

"I never for a minute thought you were dumb—only crazy."

His laughter boomed in the balmy evening air. "Goddamn, I think I'm gonna like you even if you ain't black." He rattled the bottles suggestively. "These sure ain't doing anybody any good in here."

"Why don't you come in and have a drink, Hank?"

"Shee-it. I thought you'd never ask."

/6/

"That first time, man, I wanted your ass bad." Big Boy grinned across the kitchen table at me, his bloodshot eyes watering from the double shot of bourbon he had just gunned. "I'd only been out five days and here come Clary and Mamma and two of my sisters busting into that motel room screaming sweet Jesuses at me, scaring the shit out of that pore little gal I'd been kind enough to take in out of the cold. I was too hung over to wonder much how they found me so fast. They never had before. Clary told me later, but she wouldn't tell me your name, not until I came up with the plan." He filled the two shot glasses again, shaking his head ruefully, his face shifting between melancholy and amusement. "I was right proud of the plan," he added a little wistfully.

"It wasn't bad," I conceded, sampling my Bloody Mary, feeling a pang or two of nostalgia of my own. Even now, neck-deep in post-chase exhaustion, I could feel the seductive tug of the wide-open spaces, hear the lilting susurrus of tires and motor, the siren song of moving on.

"You had some fun too, huh? It wasn't all work chasing me?"

I laughed. "How hard can it be chasing a seven-foot black millionaire in cowboy togs who just happens to have been a Texas football hero for eleven years? You tend to stick out a little. I'd compare it with tracking a gut-shot bear across an open field covered with snow."

"Aw, it wasn't that easy, was it? I covered my tracks real good sometimes, doubled back and everything."

I grinned and finished my drink, then I lit a cigarette. "If that's so," he continued, his voice pained, "how come you never caught up with me for at least two weeks—except that first time?"

I shrugged. "I've run away a time or two myself. It takes about that long to work out the kinks, to convince yourself that it's not the way, that it's time to put up the toys and go home, take up being a man again."

He nodded thoughtfully, his deep-set eyes on the wall behind my head, dark and gloomy. "You got that about right, I reckon." He tossed an ounce of bourbon into his mouth, then delicately stroked his lips with thumb and forefinger. "I always wondered why you didn't show up with Clary and Mamma that first time, to help get me back home."

I shook my head. "My job is finding people, not dragging them back home, or anywhere else for that matter. Sometimes it's a shitty job and I feel shitty doing it. Sometimes I don't succeed. Other times I do and say I don't. It depends on who's looking and why and who I'm looking for. A lot of times it's somebody looking for some kind of revenge and I stay away from that. But I don't always get a clear picture when I start and they fool me. One thing's sure. I'm not stupid enough to tackle a seven-foot, two-hundred-seventy-five-pound linebacker without a posse to back me up."

He patted his stomach and grinned. "Only two-fifty. I've been off my feed lately. Anyhow, I'm really a pussycat when you get to know me. I want to be remembered as a lover, not a fighter."

"One thing I've been wondering," I said. "Buzzy's Place outside of San Antonio. Was that you?"

He leaned back and grinned, showing a glint of gold in the back of his mouth. "Naw, that was Buzz Williams. He fought with me in 'Nam. Sucker's bigger'n me even." He leaned forward on the table, his face gleeful. "How'd that happen anyway?"

"I'm not sure. I drifted in quietly and had a couple of drinks. Everything was cool. And then I asked a couple of questions about you. First thing I knew four or five brothers had me pinned to a table muttering something about checking my jiveass liver for spots, and they had the hardware to do it, too. Next thing I remember I saw this mountain Dean blowing through them like a high wind. Somebody got in a lick, though, and put out my lights. I woke up in my car a couple of miles away, my head hurting like hell, my pants down, and a cute little yellow ribbon tied around my dick. I got the message."

His booming laugh rattled the glasses on the table. "Goddamn. You was lucky. That's a mean place, man. You wasn't supposed to know anything about Buzzy's. I slipped off over there to see Buzz and didn't tell a soul. How'd you find out, anyhow?"

I shrugged. "A barfly at the Jackrabbit Club overheard you on the phone, picked up on the name. It cost me two bar whiskeys."

He nodded sagely, still smiling. "Could've cost you a lot more than that. Lot of mean mothers hang around there. I don't feel none too easy myself and I'm mostly black."

I glanced instinctively at his peanut-colored arms on the table, then looked away, but not quickly enough to forestall his rumbling bellow. He pounded the table, almost toppling the empty bourbon bottle.

"You think I got this color washing with Purex? Man, you ought to see my granddaddy. He's black as a tar pit. Rumor has it that there's a honky somewhere in my grandmamma's pile."

He threw down the other ounce of whiskey, then drank half a can of beer as a chaser. He wiped his mouth with his hand and grinned at me owlishly. I suddenly realized that he was drunk, that we both were. I glanced at my watch, surprised to find it was after midnight, even more surprised to find that I had been enjoying myself for the first time in too long a time. Whatever his failings, Big Boy Doheny was an entertaining man, a prince among clowns, a free spirit skipping blithely like a butterfly along a mountain stream. The mental image tickled my funny bone and I laughed.

"What's so funny? You think it's funny some horny white bastard pronged my grandmamma in a woodpile?"

"It was probably spring," I said.

He nodded solemnly, swaying a little, his lips pursed thoughtfully. "It's our minds, son," he said heavily, "that always screw us up. A hard-on ain't got no conscience, can't see worth a shit, and damn sure ain't prejudiced. I married a white woman, a good woman, and we get along great most of the time . . ." His voice faded, his lower lip drooping. "But it's just that damn money . . . all that damn money."

"It's a handicap," I said dryly.

He fixed me with a glaring eye. "Hey, man, I'm serious. I didn't marry Clary for her money. I was a millionaire in my own right." He paused, squinting his eyes reflectively. "Well, maybe partly because of the money. Hell, I don't know, maybe I wanted to see how it felt to be the big he-coon for a change. But it's worrisome, man, real worrisome. Bullshit up to here. Sometimes I think if you pricked me I'd bleed brown blood. That's why I have to break out every so often, feel the wind in my face, burn out my system with a dab of the dew."

His words had a practiced ring to them, and he stared soulfully out the bay window into the darkness, wagging his head, his broad face incongruously boyish, sad-eyed, and appealing.

"Hey, man, you don't have to sell me. I'm on your side."

He heaved a huge gusty sigh. "I have to go on like that for days sometimes before she gives in. In her own sweet way Clary's a damn strong woman."

He took another shot of bourbon and we were silent for a while, pondering the endearing whimsy of womankind, the gentle sex who made things like haircuts and wearing clean clothes important, who understood the worth of innocence and vulnerability, the power of wantonness and lust.

At least I pondered; when I looked over at Big Boy he was sound asleep.

I cleaned off the table, stacked the glasses in the sink, and carried the rest of the booze to the bar in the den. I came back and lit a cigarette and fuzzily considered my alternatives. I could try to wake him, bellow in his ear, shake his shoulder and take my chances on dodging any wild swings. Or I could leave him to topple like a giant redwood sometime in the night. Or I could open the window and fire off a round close to his ear. That ought to do it.

I chuckled as the idea took hold, even reached for the gun in its accustomed place. Then I remembered taking it off and dropping it on the entry hall table as we came in. No problem, sport, I told myself and, the chuckle degenerating into an insane giggle, I threaded my way unsteadily across the den toward the front door. I stumbled on the step up into the entry hall, wavering, a tiny portion of my consciousness indignantly demanding to know if I were really going to do such a stupid thing. I giggled helplessly, seeing the gun on the table between a small potted plant and a stack of mail, making up my mind in that instant.

"Hell yes," I said aloud, and stepped toward the table—stepped head-on into a sizzling rocket that exploded somewhere near my right eye.

I had a sensation of flying, a sweet euphoric moment of graceful gliding in a silent world of soothing darkness spiced with psychedelic lights and surrealistic shapes. I floated effortlessly, marveling at my consummate skill. . . .

And then something popped inside my head, and there were sounds in my beautiful world; sounds and feeling—low guttural words and incredible stabbing pain.

". . . careful, dammit! Don't kill him like you did that other one."

". . . an eye on that big mother in the kitchen. That honky is . . ."

". . . out of it, man. Stay the hell away from the jiveass bitch."

Low voices, dim shapes. I tried to suck in breath to scream and discovered I was suffocating. I clawed at the hand over my mouth, jerked and rolled with the thud of blows. I wrenched at the thumb blocking my nose and heaved air into my tortured lungs, but the hand hung on, hard and horny, stinking of oil.

". . . Farley woman, man. Stay out of it . . . stay away . . ."

The voice broke into fragments, reverberated inside my head, became a ululating chant, merged with the noise of crashing waves rushing to engulf me in a cold swooping black hole that smothered all sound and all pain and finally me.

There were holes in my velvet canopy of darkness, shimmering circles of light in the outer reaches of my interior vision, pyrotechnic patterns that glittered with naked brilliance, comet tails of blue and green and arterial reds. And there was pain. Squirts of pain racing gleefully along tattered pathways, loading the junctions, bursting in my head like the rocket that had started it all in the first place.

I groaned and opened my eyes, then rolled frantically on my side as my stomach lurched and Big Boy's expensive booze gushed across the terrazzo tile. I dry-heaved for minutes after there was nothing left, breathing through my mouth whenever possible. When the spasms finally stopped, I scooted painfully backward, away from the unpleasant mess that was threatening to start it all over again.

I bumped against the table, felt it teeter on spindly legs, then cringed in paranoid terror as something spilled across my head and something else thumped into my side. Logic told me it was the stack of mail and the gun, but I cringed anyway, and gave it a full minute before I opened my eyes.

The mail lay scattered in the vomit; the gun lay two feet away.

I inched forward again, my side hurling white-hot barbs at my brain with each tiny movement, my brain sending back expanding waves of darkness studded with pulsating pinpricks of light. Finally I decided I could reach the gun without rolling on my face, and I put out a hand and touched the worn leather lovingly, patted it, and worked the gun free using my thumb and two undamaged fingers.

I held the rough butt in my hand and lay quietly a moment thinking about it, wondering what had happened to Doheny. I tried an experimental yell, but heard only a dry rasping croak. No damn good. I needed noise. A lot of noise. I cocked the gun and looked around for a likely spot, noticing for the first time that the front door gaped open, that by craning my neck I could see a narrow strip of brilliant Texas sky.

I pivoted painfully, using my left elbow as a fulcrum, and levered my agonized body around until my head lay swimming on the doorsill, dark clouds suddenly swooping, blotting out the pristine stars and the glow of Dallas burning on the horizon.

The first one was easy since I already had the gun cocked, but the concussion buffeted me, threatening my fragile hold on consciousness. I had to work at the second and the third, calling on reserves of strength and determination I didn't know I had. But three was the signal and I did it three times, then lay smugly listening to the echoes, the faraway sound of muted voices, the lonely wail of the roaring locomotive that somebody had just let loose in my head. . . .

/7/

Somebody was standing on my chest; somebody in big high-heeled boots and Mexican rowels; somebody who kept telling me to try to relax, try to relax and breathe deeply, please. And every time I tried, the son of a bitch raked me from stem to stern with one of the spurs.

"He may have hairline cracks, but none of his ribs are broken. He should have X rays, nevertheless. Everything else looks superficial except for some deep bruises around his kidneys and spleen. I'd advise you to take him to the hospital, Captain."

"Too damn late for that," Homer Sellers rumbled. "Hardheaded sucker's waking up. You'll never get him to go anywhere now."

"Hardheaded sucker's already awake," I said. I opened my eyes and looked up into a young serious face hovering a foot above my own myopic eyes and watching me intently through oversize glasses. A short upper lip and protruding front teeth gave him the look of an eager young rabbit. Behind him another young man stood watching silently.

"How are you feeling, sir?" He wore the pin-striped shirt of a Midway City Hospital paramedic, and a yellow polyester baseball cap advertising Bell Helicopter perched precariously atop a mass of tightly curled red hair. He looked about fifteen.

"Give me a little time, I just now woke up."

"You took a pretty good lick on the side of the head, sir. There's a possibility of concussion. Do you feel light-headed, dizzy, sleepy, have double vision—"

"Does pain count?" I heard a snorting sound, the clink of a bottle against glass, and a few moments later Homer Seller's placid face came into view. He handed me a glass half filled with amber liquid.

"What's that?" the young medic asked.

"Chicken soup," Homer said blandly.

"If that's alcohol, sir, I don't know—" He broke off as I handed Homer back the empty glass. He looked at his waiting companion, shrugged, and picked up his medical kit. "I can only advise you, sir." Behind his back his partner grinned at me and lifted his eyebrows.

Homer draped a heavy arm across the paramedic's frail shoulders and steered him gently toward the door. "You can't reason with hardheads, son. They have to learn the hard way." He patted the boy's shoulder. "Don't worry, I'll see he gets his ass in to get checked out."

I closed my eyes and homed in on the warmth spreading slowly throughout my body, dulling the aches and pains as it went. By the time it reached my feet I was feeling pretty good except for the dull heavy ache behind my right eye. I had a hunch it would take more than a double shot of bourbon to help that.

I heard the front door close and Homer's heavy tread in the hall. I opened my eyes again as he dropped into the recliner across from the couch.

"He's right, you know," he growled. "That's a sick-looking lump you've got on your head. Looks like he used a sap to me."

"Felt like a mortar round."

He popped the cellophane skin from a plastic-tipped cigar. "What the hell started this hooraw, anyhow?"

"Well, Homer, I don't know. I was just an innocent bystander."

He rolled the cigar around in his mouth. "You'd think that asshole is big enough he wouldn't have to use a damn blackjack." He eyed the cigar reflectively. "Hell, maybe he didn't."

I raised my head and looked at him. "What?"

"Maybe he didn't. Maybe he used his fist." He jabbed the cigar at me. "You're losing your touch, boy. I know he's a big mother and all, but you didn't lay a hand on him."

I struggled up on one elbow. "Homer? What the hell are you talking about?"

He grinned wolfishly. "That big black mother. I warned you he'd turn on you—"

"Jesus H. Christ! Doheny! Homer, goddammit, are you talking about Doheny?" Memory and realization struck at once, bringing a spurt of adrenaline, an explosion of dizziness.

"Damn right. We got his black ass in a cell. Funny thing, though, he was loop-legged drunk and come along as meek as a—"

"Aw shit, Homer! Call them up, dammit; turn him loose."

He wagged his shaggy head. "Now, look, son, I know you ain't one to hold no grudges, but a crime has been committed—"

"Dammit, Homer, turn Doheny loose. He didn't do it; he didn't even know it was happening."

He stared at me, the cigar halfway to his lips, his eyes, red-rimmed and watery from the new contacts, a burning blue. "You doing a number on me, Dan?"

"Hell, no, dammit. Doheny was passed out in the kitchen. They ambushed me when I came into the entry hall. Three of them, maybe more."

"I'll be damned. How'd they get in?"

"Probably walked through the door. I don't remember locking it." I swung my legs to the floor and lurched to a sitting position, closing my eyes as another wave of dizziness struck, the effort undoing the palliative effects of the whiskey, bringing sharp splinters of pain from all areas of my body. I leaned back and breathed slowly and carefully.

"I'll be damned," Homer said again. "Looks like all the ruckus would've woke him up."

I rolled my head wearily back and forth. "They kept it down, kept me choked down. And anyhow, nothing short of a howitzer will wake him when he passes out drunk."

"They said he was passed out in the kitchen, all right. We just thought he had—"

"Well, go call, will you? Get him out of there."

"Ain't no hurry about that. He's damn sure too drunk to

46

drive. He's probably asleep again by now." He hesitated. "Unless you want me to call his wife."

"No, don't do that. If he's asleep, just let him sleep it off."

"Well, who the hell you reckon it was, then?"

"The Wagermans," I said.

"Wagermans? You mean them bastards that've been giving Susie a hard time?"

I shrugged, regretting it instantly as a dibble of pain lanced across my chest. "They're the only Wagermans I know about."

"How do you know that? Did you recognize them?" His voice was sharp and crisp, all cop.

"No. I didn't recognize anybody. I never really saw anyone. But they told me to stay away from Susie, to stay out of it—whatever 'it' is."

He took a clean handkerchief out of his jacket pocket and carefully blotted his eyes. "I'm never gonna get used to these damn things." He blinked slowly, the contacts and dampness giving him a soft blurred look. "Then it looks like Susie was right."

I lit a cigarette and took an experimental drag. I nodded. "It could be. Or it could be I hurt his feelings."

"Who?"

"Dalton Wagerman." I sighed and pointed toward the bar. "If you'll get me a jot of that Wild Turkey there, I'll tell you about it."

He brought the drink. I took a small sample and told him what had happened at the machine shop, watching his bushy eyebrows climb upward. He raked a hand through his mud-colored hair, then smoothed it back with both palms pressed tightly against his head. A sure sign of agitation. While I talked his face worked its way from interest to cynicism to disgust.

"Dammit, Dan, you can't go into a man's place of business and stick a gun in his damn face."

"Maybe I can't, but I damn sure did. Don't worry about it, Homer, he's outside the city limits." I finished the miserly portion of Wild Turkey, closed my eyes, and waited patiently for the healing warmth.

"And he didn't turn a hair, huh?"

"If he did it was on his ass. He had damn good control of his face."

"What do you plan on doing now?"

"Recuperating."

"No, I mean about the Wagermans."

I opened one eye and squinted at his flushed face. "I don't plan on doing anything. What do you want me to do, Homer?"

"Well, dammit, now we know for sure they're planning on doing something to Susie—"

"Bullshit, Homer. Wagerman may be a lump of suet, an emotional cipher, but I don't figure he's completely stupid. They may as well have advertised in the *Star Telegram*, coming here and stomping on me, then warning me to stay away from Susie."

"But why would they tell you to stay away from her if they weren't planning—"

"I don't know why. Anyhow, you're not asking the right questions. Ask me why they would come in here knowing Doheny was with me. They had to know. All the blinds were open. They could see us from the front of the house and through the kitchen window. That big-assed Rolls of his was in the driveway. Hell, they could have heard us if they'd listened. Why not wait until I was alone?"

"All right, why?"

"I don't know why, dammit. All I know is I'm hurting and I want to go to bed."

His lips pursed thoughtfully. "Maybe they were carrying and didn't give a damn about Doheny. Figured they could handle him with a gun. Maybe they just didn't give a shit. Maybe the old man was hot and wanted your ass bad enough not to care. Who knows? Bastard has to be nuts banging his own daughter like that." He stubbed out the cigar and fastened bleary eyes on me. "Who's gonna take care of you?"

I made a sound meant to be a laugh. "Who always takes care of me, Homer?"

He shook his head. "You can't stay by yourself. If you do have a concussion and go to sleep you may never wake up again."

"That should throw the world into chaos."

He tightened the slack in his heavy features. "Quit talking like a dumbass. And quit feeling sorry for yourself. It's your own damn fault you ain't got Susie here to take care of you when you get yourself all banged up like this."

"Right on, good buddy," I said, deciding there was no sense in pointing out the irony in his statement.

He heaved to his feet and thrust a hand into his jacket pocket for the handkerchief. "Why don't I just wheel you on over to Midway Emergency, get you checked out right?" He gingerly blotted his eyes.

"Forget it. That medic knew what he was doing. I've had beatings before. Nothing's broken or busted. It just hurts like hell."

"How the hell do you know that?"

I raised my head and looked at him. "Pain, buddy. I can feel it."

He waved a thick hand impatiently. "I don't mean that. How do you know nothing's broken?"

"I've been sitting here taking tally, one bone at a time. Everything works."

He snarled in frustration, wheeled around in a tight little circle. "Dammit, sometimes it's a strain being your friend."

"Anything worthwhile is worth straining for," I said, giving him a grin, "just like taking a good shit." Making him mad was the quickest way I knew to get rid of him. I needed rest more than I needed conversation; an evening of solitude and Wild Turkey would be even more comforting than the well-meaning concern of a friend.

He stomped toward the door. "Okay, Dan, I know you're running a number on me, but I got feelings too. You can go to hell." He went out quietly and closed the door without slamming it, under the circumstances an admirable display of restraint.

I closed my eyes and leaned my head against the couch, wishing I had asked him to hand me the bottle before he left, wishing suddenly that he was back, but wishing most of all that there was somebody to take care of me.

/8/

All drunks have fearsome dreams. Countless hordes of wyverns and goblins prowl their sleep the way fear haunts their waking hours, mindless creatures fashioned in the tortured crucibles of convoluted minds, acting out in endless drama the small tedious fears of life, of failure or success, of loneliness or love, the fear of dying alone, of having to live with others. Fright stalks them like a running sore, molds their thoughts and actions along cunning lines. One dread overshadows all others in both their uneasy slumber and their amorphous reality: the fear of waking to a bone-dry bottle.

My father had that fear, so he spent hours searching out unlikely nooks and crannies, secreting flasks and flagons against that inevitable day of reckoning. But his hiding places were secret only in his imagination, and since I was old enough to hate him for his weakness, yet young enough to love him for himself, I forgave him.

It was then, when I was still young enough to see the humor as well as the sadness, that I came home from school and saw him drunk for the first time, found him retching in the bathroom, on his knees before the toilet, the whiskey bottle still in his hand, his knuckles gleaming like smooth white stones against the amber glass.

I watched silently, feeling my own sickness, trying not to despise this one last person I had left on earth to love.

While I watched he rinsed his mouth with whiskey, spat and drank again. It came back up, a gushing spewing stream. He tried again . . . and again, and finally it stayed down. He tilted the bottle on its end, drained it, then climbed wearily to his feet, turning startled bloodshot eyes to see me standing in the door.

His smile was sickly, somehow endearing, almost shy. "Never mind, son," he said, "never again." He held up the bottle, tossed it firmly in the wastebasket. "See, son, the last one. I'll quit tomorrow . . . tomorrow."

Tight-lipped, my face dry and burning, I brushed past him, raising the cover on the porcelain tank. I lifted the dripping bottle, dried it carefully on a towel, and pushed it at him. He took it.

As I went out the door, I tried again not to hate him, tried to see the humor in his crestfallen face, his guilty shifting eyes, unshaven chin, and dripping nose. But there was none and I could not.

And now, a few years younger than my father had been that day, I spewed whiskey-vomit into my own toilet, watched my own mucus string from my nose into the brown-clabbered water, made my own lying promise to a son I had lost a long time ago: "Never mind, son, I'll quit tomorrow."

When I finished retching, I crawled out of the bathroom on my hands and knees, humble but not repentant, crept into my warm cocoon again, lay huddled, waiting for oblivion, and the demons that would surely come.

She came first in the murky depths of my dream, fresh and bright and lovely in the sweet innocence of youth. We lay crushed together, cried hot forgiving tears, talked of love and loving. Her voice throbbed in the soft air as she begged my forgiveness, humble and penitent, beseeching. Bursting with a profusion of emotions I didn't understand, I held her, told her that in my memory what she had done seemed not sorry after all, only human.

But dreams are only dreams and have no substance, and she faded, left me crying in confused delirium, my arms aching and empty . . .

And when I awoke from sleep, climbing painfully out of comforting darkness into the day, she was there. Sitting there beside my bed, hauntingly beautiful, head bowed slightly under the heavy mass of glossy raven hair. Her eyes were closed, the corners of her mouth lifted in a secret knowing smile, remembering, perhaps, some special moment in our time, before the specters of age and the vicissitudes of youth swept us apart.

I watched enthralled, afraid to move, afraid to blink, the clinging residue of my dream still too fresh, too vivid in my mind. One sound and she might smile that sweet forgiving smile and disappear, dissolve before my eyes, leaving me with nothing but my raging thirst and my pain.

But I finally had to close my mouth and swallow, a dry gulping sound that brought her instantly alert, her dark intense gaze sweeping my face, finding my eyes and locking.

"How do you feel?"

"Better," I croaked. I opened my mouth and made drinking motions. "I need a drink."

She nodded and stood up. I lay back and closed my eyes, marveling at my sudden feeling of serenity, the sense of security one glance from warm brown eyes could bring.

She was back moments later, leaning over me. "Here, drink this."

I raised on one elbow and stared at the glass of water in horror. "I said I needed a drink."

"Drink," she commanded firmly, those brown eyes suddenly stern and unrelenting.

I curled my lip and sipped at the water, then found myself swilling it as the cool liquid fought the thick gummy coating inside my mouth.

"See," she said, smiling. "Want some more?"

I shook my head and handed her the glass. "How did you know?"

"Uncle Homer called—"

"Damn nosy old woman," I grumbled.

"Hush. He was worried about you." She carried the glass into the bathroom.

"How long have you been here?"

She smiled at me from the doorway. "For a while. Why?"

"I had a dream."

Her smile widened, became an infectious grin. She came back and sat down.

"Stop grinning or tell me what's so funny."

"You. Your dream. I was in it. You were telling me what you were going to do to me." She leaned an elbow on the arm of the chair and cupped her chin in her palm.

I grimaced and shrank farther under the covers. "Good things or bad things?"

Her face had turned pink without me being aware of it. "Mostly good things—I think. Some I'm not too sure about." Her head tilted on her palm, her eyes suddenly blurred and soft. "It's been a long time since you threatened to spank me, Danny."

"I never threatened to spank you."

"Yes, you did. One time, remember? When we were first married. I told you to go ahead, that I thought I might like it." She braced both elbows on the chair arms and laced her fingers.

"You always were a smart-ass kid."

"You liked me that way. You told me so." The grin had downgraded to an indulgent smile, a hint of white even teeth between finely shaped lips. A smile so much like Barbara's in my memory that I thought of love long lost and the endless chill of death and shivered.

"Are you all right, Danny?"

"No," I said, dragging myself back from old sorrows and old pains, finding her eyes under the wide smooth brow, searching for love in their fulgent depths, and if not love, kindness. "No, Susan, I'm not. I'm freezing to death."

She sat perfectly still; her face completely blank.

"Freezing, honey," I said softly, my voice not far from a whining plea. "I can't stop shaking."

Her lips quivered, an eyebrow twitching as her face moved swiftly out of the dead zone, came alive with understanding, cynicism, something I couldn't identify and was afraid to try.

Her breath expelled in a long sibilant sigh. "Yes, I can see," she said, her tone normal, matter-of-fact. "Do you want me to help you, Danny?" Only her dark burning eyes betrayed her.

"Yes, please," I said, speaking hoarsely through dryness and fear.

"All right." Her voice was oddly small and filled with compliance, as if she had abandoned all will to resist, all thoughts of womanly restraint or virtue.

"Only if you want to," I said faintly, my own voice stilted and waspish. I wanted her, needed her with a fierce compelling desire that transcended all spurious honor and stiff-necked manly pride. I wanted her, but I wanted her coming at me, wild and eager and unrestrained, not nobly acquiescent, a placebo for times gone by. I hungered for her desperately, but need demands need the way darkness demands the sun and I wanted no part of empty mockery.

"Susan," I began, but she silenced me with a look. Her fingers worked deftly, swiftly at her simple summer clothing. "Remember, Danny? That first time? I stood here just like this taking off my clothes. But maybe you don't. You were really cold and shaking then; delirious. You had the flu. You thought I was Barbara and you begged me to hurry."

"Please hurry," I begged.

"Hush," she said softly, smiling, stepping free of her clothing, natural and uninhibited in splendid nakedness, fingers splayed on gently tapered waist, hipshot in teasing provocation. "Do you still think I'm beautiful, Danny?" Her eyes glowed liquidly, as if melting from her own inner heat.

I nodded mutely, reached for her with hungry arms, crept into her radiant warmth whimpering like an old thin-blooded hound on a bitter winter day.

We bumped noses in fleeting awkwardness, searching for old rhythms, the old cadence of a love too long abandoned but not forgotten. "I wanted you to say my name that first time, but you never did," she said sadly against my neck.

"Susie," I said, "Susan, Susan—" and she squeezed me mightily, crushed me against pliant softness until pain rico-

cheted off my ribs to my brain and back again in bright
squirting flashes.

"Easy," I groaned. "Easy, honey . . ."

"I'm sorry, darling," she whispered. "I'll be gentle."

There was something inordinately splendid about making
love with my body on the verge of collapse; my senses reeled,
dissolved, flowed gently; pain retreated amid imprecations
and gnashing of teeth and sore muscles stretched and flexed
again. Kissing became an end in itself and caresses on con-
tused and lacerated flesh seemed to flow all the way to the
bone.

And when I was finally inside her, embedded and helpless
in the secret electric flesh, she pulled her lips away from mine
and caught my eyes in a glance filled with infinite wisdom, a
look that said as clearly as words: It was always you, Danny.
Only you from the beginning. Why couldn't you understand
that, accept it without guilt?

But I closed my eyes to her silent message, listened only to
the call of our demanding flesh, fierce poundings and gentle
rhythms, broken words that sounded like a sob.

The end at hand, the inevitable glorious end, she searched
frantically for my mouth again, her breath hot and strangely
exotic as she spasmed, shuddered, clutched blindly at my own
failing flesh.

I followed her, shut down my mind, leaped headlong into
the tumultuous wake of her convulsive frenzy, intoxicated by
her power, infinitely grateful for my own.

Later she stirred in my arms, her hair tickling my chin, her
body warm and lax against my side, her soft breath jetting
across my chest.

"Do you remember the first time? You made me a woman
that night and the sad part was you seemed as frightened as
me." Her head shifted in the pit of my shoulder and she made
a small contented sound. "But that was all right. The das-
tardly deed was finally done. I knew what it was I had been
having fantasies about all those years. But you didn't just

make me a woman. You made me *your* woman. You spoiled me, you old bastard, for anyone else. The hell of it is, I'm only fully alive when I'm in your arms like this."

She lapsed into silence when I didn't answer. I felt her body relax, her breathing deepen, become slow and even.

And minutes after I was certain she was asleep, she whispered: "But maybe you did know, you old fox, all the time."

/9/

"You promised you wouldn't hurt me," I said, pressing gingerly on a red-and-blue patch on my chest where her elbow had rested during a tense moment. I could see her through the bathroom door, toweling her slender body, blotting more than wiping, working downward from rounded shoulders and jutting breasts that had yet to succumb to the inexorable pull of gravity.

She looked up and threw me a kiss. "Was I too rough on the poor little thing?"

"It's not a poor little thing, and, anyhow, I was talking about me." I propped a pillow against the headboard and lit a cigarette.

"How do you feel?"

"Let's take five before we go through that again."

She laughed as she came through the door. "The funny part is, you were really shaking after all."

I nodded. "Suppressed emotion, pent-up need. Take your choice."

She paused beside the bed, wholly unself-conscious in her golden nudity, her dark eyes soft and tranquil, a small smile playing around bruised lips. She stood hipshot again, hands curled on her hips, unconsciously provocative.

"Pent up? How long pent up?"

I huffed a ball of smoke at her. "None of your business, missy." I took another pull at the cigarette. "Too long."

"How long—about?"

I shook my head in weary disbelief. "You're as bad as Homer." I looked at her through the smoke. "Two years—about."

She stared at me incredulously, her mouth opening. "You? I don't believe you, Dan Roman."

I shrugged. "It isn't important enough to take an oath on, Susie." I mashed out the cigarette and gingerly scooted toward her side of the bed and the bathroom beyond. She sat down abruptly on the edge, blocking my way. Her hands fluttered, the right one coming to rest above my knee. She squeezed; I winced.

"Tell me the truth," she said, her voice small and quivering. "You mean you haven't . . . had anyone since . . . me?" Her oval face was solemn, working its way through disbelief, her eyes already collecting moisture, bright and glistening.

I put a hand against the side of her face. "It's not an earth-shattering thing, Susie. I never cared much for groping in motel rooms or cars, and the kind of bars I go to . . . well, the women who come there come to drink. They don't come for sex." I ran a thumb beneath a brimming eye. "I'm an old man, kid. Come on, gimme a break already."

"Don't shit me," she whispered fiercely, "you're as virile as you've always been." Her fingers dug into my thigh again; I winced again.

"Once," I said.

"What?"

"Once I'm as good as I've always been. Twice, who knows? Tomorrow or the next day . . . ?" I let it trail away and shrugged.

"Oh?" Her hand finally relinquished its stranglehold on my thigh, slid suddenly upward, gaining a firm yet somehow gentler handhold. "Oh?" she said again, "we'll have to see about that, won't we?"

"You're going to hurt me again," I complained, feeling an incredible surge of power, an astonishing tumescence. "I thought you were going to nurse me, not—"

"I might do that too if you don't shut up," she murmured, hooking an arm beneath my knees and tugging me flat on the bed. She climbed astride, joined us with a swift fluid movement, then lay flat against my chest, her gleaming eyes only inches away from my own.

"You don't feel like you're done, old man," she said softly. She kissed me long and passionately, her lips firm, then soft, then melting into mine. She pulled back again, her eyes shining, her body moving slowly, sensuously. "Well, what do you have to say now, old-timer?"

I grinned up at her. "Only one thing . . . my mamma didn't raise no stupid kids."

"I can't believe I let you work me like that."

She lay spread-eagled beside me, her hands pressed against her rib cage beneath her breasts, a small catch in her voice as her breathing returned to normal. At some point during this second, even more exquisite frenzy, she had pressed the palms of her hands against my head and now the lump behind my eye throbbed spitefully. Another hurt among many. It had become painfully obvious that the narcotic effect of sex lasted only as long as the sex, and my pain center was once again being bombarded with distress signals from the nether regions of my body.

"Only because you wanted to be worked."

She sighed. "I guess so." Her head moved on the pillow. "Were you lying about the two years?"

"No, but I don't want to talk about it." I could almost feel the weight of her eyes against the side of my face. She rolled on her side facing me and began tracing the black-and-blue marks that were turning a nasty-looking yellow-green around the edges.

"That makes me sad," she said.

"What?"

"That," she said, her voice small and warm. "Not having any . . . not being with a woman for two years because of . . . of me."

For once I had sense enough to keep my mouth shut. I sighed deeply.

"I'm sorry about this, Danny." She leaned forward and brushed her lips across a purplish patch above my right pectoral muscle. "I know these must hurt terribly."

"Only when I'm awake or breathing." I lit my second after-sex cigarette of the day. I took a deep drag and closed my eyes, concentrating on the pain, listening to the ragged nerve impulses colliding at the intersections. "I've had worse. I'll survive."

Her hand drifted down my chest to my stomach, gathering a fold of flesh. "Maybe now someone will believe me," she said.

"About the Wagermans?"

"Yes."

"I'm not sure about that, Susie. I think it was personal. I think I plucked the wrong string and Dalton Wagerman was coming back at me."

"What for?" Her head lifted, her face startled.

I finished the cigarette and told her about my futile trip to Wagerman's machine shop, endured a few excruciating moments as she hugged and kissed and tugged at me in a frenzy of maternal concern. But beneath the stern censure her voice was warm, her eyes darkly shining.

"But, Danny, I thought . . . Uncle Homer told me this had something to do with the Wagermans . . . with me, but he didn't tell me you had been there."

"He wouldn't. No point in getting you stirred up any more than you already are." I stopped and grinned. "He was probably testing you in some weird way. He's always testing people in one way or another. Particularly me."

"That was a brave thing you did," she said solemnly, stroking my battered chest with the light-fingered reverence women usually reserve only for mink.

I snorted a laugh and lit another Carlton. "It's easy to be brave with a gun poked up a man's nose." I shook my head. "That old man. He's either a stone psycho or somebody stomped his nervous system dead up there in the pen."

"His eyes . . . my God, did you get a look at his eyes?"

I nodded and gently disengaged my biceps from her clutching fingers. I swung my legs to the floor, then after a moment, creaked cautiously to my feet. Nothing fell off or came apart, but I stood swaying in darkness for a time, watching bright sparkling dots dance and shimmer behind my eyelids. Vertigo, I thought, and patiently waited it out.

"Do you feel better, or a whole lot worse?"

I hobbled toward the bathroom. "If you're talking about old hammerhead here, he feels just great. The rest of me feels about the way it looks." I propped a hand against the wall above the commode, seeing her drift through the door out of the corner of my eye, coming to rest with one slim hip slung against the sink cabinet. We listened in silence to the splash and splatter. I examined myself critically, gave it one last flip.

"He says you can get dressed, we're through with you for the day."

Her throaty laugh rang loudly in the small room, subsided quickly. She moved a minute distance so I could reach the sink to wash my hands, then: "What happens now, Danny?" Her voice was low and flat.

I dropped my hands on her shoulders, rubbed my thumbs in the small depressions above her collarbones, then pulled her against me, marvelling at the lush softness, the coolness of flesh that had been so intensely taut and burning such a short time before.

"We eat," I said. "That's what happens now. I take a manly shower and you fix a womanly breakfast and then we eat and maybe talk. It probably won't settle anything because I'll probably get mad and you'll probably cry . . . but what the hell, let's take a run at it, anyway."

"All right, Danny," she said meekly, moving against me, pressing lightly, giving me a cool passionless kiss before tugging herself gently away. "Bacon and eggs, I suppose."

"Right," I said, slapping her bottom as she turned away. "And don't forget to clean out the eggs."

/10/

"I've been wanting to ask you," I said, glancing at her face, then back to the yolk-smeared plate I was using as an ashtray. "How can you afford that warehouse you live in? The payments alone must be—"

She shook her head, her face slowly turning pink. "There aren't any payments, Danny. I—I bought it outright." She brought a hand up to cup her chin in her palm.

I stared at her for a moment, then turned my eyes to the backyard beyond the bay window, trying to gather my scattered senses. I looked back at her.

"You own it?"

She nodded, her lips quirking in amusement, the color mounting in her cheeks. "It was a good buy, Danny. It's only a year old. The builder couldn't sell it because of the recession. He got into a bind and had to drop the price way down. It was valued at a million and a half, but I—we got it for only nine hundred thousand."

"Oh, well, hell," I said, "if that's all you paid for it—"

She laughed, her hand swiveling to cover her mouth, her eyes twinkling.

"A million dollars, Susie? A goddamned million dollars?"

She nodded, the color deepening, flowing into her neck, into the upper slopes of her breasts. "I know it's a lot, Danny. If—if you won't think I'm bragging or something, I'll—I'll tell you about it."

I bobbed my head wordlessly. I lit another cigarette from the butt of my old one with shaking fingers.

She sat up straighter and dropped a hand to fiddle with her

knife, her voice almost prim. "Well, you know about the money Mother left me—"

"I didn't know she had a million dollars."

"Not exactly," she said stiffly, the color suddenly flooding her face again. "Her small real estate investments paid off well during the boom here. It was more like two million." She watched my face, her eyes anxious, lips slightly parted, poised to go either way, to laugh or to cry.

I puffed on the cigarette, stunned, watching a rift between us grow into a small rocky canyon, watching faint hope become a jeering dream.

"Jesus Christ," I said, feeling my breakfast congeal into a hot sticky ball and plummet to the pit of my stomach, feeling the earth tremble as the canyon became a yawning chasm. I stabbed at the plate with the cigarette, keeping my face lowered, knowing I wasn't fit to look at just then, doubting if I ever would be again. Two million dollars! It was a formidable sum; a high mountain.

"Danny!" The anxiety in her eyes had bled into her voice.

I looked up and smiled. "I'm proud for you, babe."

She watched me long and earnestly, her hand knocking over the salt on its way to grapple with mine. Her nails bit into my flesh, tightened painfully, but my smile didn't waver. Only my eyes. I could see myself in the clear sparkling depths of hers, and I finally had to look away, away from the reflection of a man who has seen his worth and his destiny, and is appalled.

"That's something, babe," I said. "That's really something."

"Oh, Danny," she said miserably, her hand leaving mine, meeting with its mate en route to cover her quivering lips and chin.

I rubbed the angry new-moon indentations in my hand and smiled ruefully. "You've got a grip like a stevedore, kid."

"It's only money, Danny; it doesn't have to matter."

I gazed at her curiously; my goddamned face was cracking, but the smile was still in place and working, whatever it looked like. "Matter? Of course it doesn't matter. Of course not. You're still the same sweet lady—just rich, is all. You look the same, taste the same, make love the same—"

"Why are you angry with me, Danny?" Her eyes ambushed me over her hands, deep-set and haunting, her face crumpling as she struggled for comprehension.

I rubbed my face briskly with both hands, eradicating the smile, bringing life to frozen flesh, surprised to find the pain had retreated again.

"Oh, hell, Susie," I said. "I'm not mad at you. You're right, it's only money. It's only money and you're only married and I'm only a damn fool for thinking it could ever be any other way again."

I took her cold hand in mine and studied her downcast face, the sweep of long fine lashes against her skin, the curve of pouting lips that were meant for laughing or loving.

"You must love Jack, Susie, or I don't think you'd have married him. You couldn't have changed that much in two years."

"I thought I did," she said faintly, then lifted her face. "I—I do, Danny, I guess . . . but not like I love you . . ."

"I know, honey," I said soothingly, hating my syrupy voice, the mealymouthed words I was saying, would have to say. "But think about it this way, Susie. You were gone for two years. You didn't come to see me. You didn't call. That must tell you something. Right now you're scared. Right or wrong, you think you're in danger. You feel safe with me. I've always protected you before, kept you from harm. Jack's an unknown quantity. You don't know about him yet, his strengths, his weaknesses. He looks like a man, Susie, walks and talks like a man. Let him be the man I'm sure he wants to be for you. Go back to him. Give him a chance." I patted her hand and laid it on the table, busied my own hands with a Carlton. "You can afford around-the-clock protection if you think you need it. If it makes you feel better, do it." I dug out my smile, dusted it off, and pasted it back on. "But I really don't think you'll need it, honey. Now go home—go home to your husband."

She nodded and stood up wordlessly. She looked around, her expression wild and oddly strained, perplexed, as if she were trying to orient herself to new and frightening surroundings. She looked at me once with a strange inarticulate compassion in her eyes, and I felt my heart lurch as she marched firmly from the room, ramrod straight, black hair tossing, never more lovely in my memory than at that moment.

I listened for her at the front door and moments later heard the throaty rumble of her car. She laid down tracks all the way to the corner, and then the car screamed shrilly into second halfway up the long low hill that led to the highway. I lost her in the dim rumble of freeway traffic a mile away.

I got up and went into the den to the bar; if I hurried maybe I could beat the return of the pain. I had driven her away from me again, but this time I knew I was right.

/11/

An hour before dark, Henry "Big Boy" Doheny showed up on my doorstep bearing gifts that clinked enticingly under his huge arm, his shining eyes telling me that he was already half drunk. But I was mellow enough myself not to care a damn, forlorn enough to welcome him with gleeful sounds and open arms, friendly punches and affectionate obscenities. And as the day wore on to dying we sat at the bay window in the kitchen telling lies and toasting life, watching dark crimson streak the horizon over Fort Worth, as if some giant hand had opened her collective veins and splashed her blood across an unwitting sky.

We drank my beer to chase his booze and while away the hours in the way of drinking men everywhere, comrades all beneath the skin, a vociferous profane army seeking solace more than excitement, peace instead of war, sweet oblivion rather than painful love.

"Love without penalty, boy," Big Boy said once, banging his hand on the table, glaring at me with his walnut-colored eyes shot with blood. "Love without penalty. It's only as far away as your wallet. Remember that."

"That's only sex," I said, and watched him watching me as if I were the last pork chop on the plate and he was trying to decide if he was still hungry or not. But his big face screwed up in painful deliberation, his eyes closed, his lips moving as if committing my eloquent words to memory, then breaking suddenly into a beaming admiring smile.

"That's deep, son," he said, pounding the table again, lifting his glass and booming voice to toast the lonely ladies of the night, those truly humble servants of man, used and abused and enduring, but always coming back for more, taking without complaint the slings and arrows of grave misfortune, the misbegotten lusts and passions of man for willing breasts and pliant thighs. When he paused to gather his breath, I jumped in. "That's sad, Big Boy," I said, "and poetical." He stood up and bowed solemnly, and we drank a toast to sadness and poets, both living and dead.

I told him he was the whitest black mother I had ever met and, his eyes glistening wetly, he said I had a lot of soul for a goddamned honky. It was along about then when the front doorbell began ringing.

Big Boy lunged to his feet. "Let me get that mother! Might be them mealymouthed krauts coming back for some more of your ass." He lurched across the kitchen, one big hand clenched in a wave, the knuckles as big as black walnuts. "Man! Goddamn, I hope so! Sheee-it, I hope it's them mothers . . ." His voice trailed off, garbled with incoherence. I sank back in my seat and thought about praying.

I heard the front door rip open, a fearful moment of silence, then a startled exclamation.

"Hey! Hey, man! What're you doing here? You see my car parked out there, or what?"

A voice I couldn't understand, that seemed familiar, mumbled something.

"No shit! Imagine that. Goddamn, if it ain't a small world, after all. Come on in here, man. Old Dan's in the kitchen drunker'n a coot." His laughter rumbled closer.

The mumbler mumbled again. I caught one word: Susan.

"No, man, not since—" Big Boy broke off as they came through the door, his big arm draped across the shoulders of Jack Farley. A Jack Farley I had never seen before, his handsome face pinched to the point of ugly, his clothing in wild disarray, hair disheveled, a pinpointed, glassy look in his cerulean eyes I had seen too many times not to recognize.

Big Boy grinned happily, foolishly. "Lookee here, Dan'l. Look who I rounded up standing at your door like a lost calf.

Goddamn, I didn't know you knew old Jack Farley. Best goddamn investment man in the—"

"Hello, Jack," I said quietly, feeling a tightness across my
chest and a coolness behind my ears. He was wearing a lightweight worsted suit, the right-hand jacket pocket bulging
under the weight of his hand, a hand that was holding a gun
unless I'd drunk so much whiskey my eyes were playing
tricks on me again.

Farley shrugged deftly out of Doheny's heavy embrace, took
two paces forward, and brought his hand out of his pocket. I
silently congratulated my eyes with fond wishes for a long
and healthy life.

The hand held a gun, a small gun, to be sure, but at a
distance of four feet that doesn't matter as long as there's
determination and staying power.

"Where is she, goddammit?"

"She's not here, Jack."

"I know that, you son of a bitch! But you know where she
is." Anger and whatever he was on had leached his bronze
skin to a sickly shade of ocher. "She was here today, goddamn
you, deny that!" The gun, a small nickel-plated .32 automatic, jabbed threateningly.

Big Boy watched Farley in amazement. "Hey! What the
hell—?"

"I won't deny it, Jack. She was here," I said evenly. I
carefully fished a cigarette out of the pack on the table and
reached slowly for my lighter lying in plain view.

"What's this shit?" Big Boy rumbled. He took a step forward.

Farley half turned. "Stay out of this, Mr. Doheny. This is
personal. Please."

Big Boy lifted his hands shoulder high, pink palms outward.
"Hey, man," he said, and shrugged.

"Why was she here?" Farley's voice rose again, shrill,
ragged, his eyes unfocused, the hand with the gun beginning
to shake.

"Hell with this shit," Big Boy said. He reached across

Farley's shoulder and closed a hand over the younger man's, gun and all, pointed it at the ceiling, then plucked the gun out of the nerveless hand like the last banana on a stalk.

He grinned at me over Farley's head, the gun a tiny toy in the palm of his hand. He rolled his eyes. "Man, where's you get this thang? Out of a Cracker Jack box, or did you send off box tops?"

Farley sagged against the cabinet, rubbing his right hand. "It isn't loaded," he said dully.

Big Boy clucked his tongue. "Man, man! You white folks sure do act strange sometimes." He worked the action, dropped the clip, then looked at me and shrugged. "It ain't," he said.

I lit the cigarette and stood up, leaning a little on the table as a wave of dizziness struck. "Are you saying Susie isn't home?"

Life came back into Farley's face. His lips tightened. "You know damned well she's not. You know goddamned well what's going on. She said in her note—"

"What note?"

"The note she left, dammit."

Big Boy glanced from me to Farley and back again, his black eyes puzzled. "You know Susan, man? His wife Susan?"

I nodded. "What about the note, Jack? What did she say?"

Farley sneered. "You know what she said, you son of a—"

I went into his chest with my shoulder, wrapped my hands in soft pliant cloth that felt like silk, and slammed him against the oven cabinet, did it again and again to keep him off balance, his head popping against the solid ash wood with each slam. Then I stopped and got right up in his face.

"Listen, asshole, you've got fifteen years on me, and I'm more'n half drunk, but you're stoned so maybe it'll even out. Don't matter either way. We're gonna fight if you don't tell me what was in that goddamned note." I slammed him one more time and turned him loose, stepped back a pace and stood waiting, breathing hard and feeling finer than I had in two years.

He looked at me dazedly, rubbing the back of his head. "Hell, Dan, I—I . . . shit, here!"

He dipped into his left jacket pocket, thrust a crumpled ball of paper at me. "Read it your own damn self." He glanced at Doheny, grimaced a shrug, then went back to rubbing his head.

I smoothed the note on the table, recognizing instantly Susie's small neat script:

Dear Jack:
    I'm frightened, honey. I'm scared and confused and I have to go away for a while—a place I know I'll be safe and alone and can sort things out. I want to be honest with you. I saw Dan today and I'm more confused now than ever. I have to find out if I'm what I thought I wanted to be or some other person entirely. This may not make much sense to you, but please remember

                        I love you
                        Susan

I read it once more, then folded it and handed it silently to Jack Farley. His face, taut and strained, had regained some of its color, the belligerence almost gone.

"You really don't know where she is? She didn't tell you where she was going?"

I shook my head and turned back to my seat at the table. "No, she didn't say a word."

"I hope I can believe that."

"You can goddamned believe whatever you like," I snarled, suddenly raging, remembering the three small words above her signature on the note, feeling a yawning emptiness inside, a sudden savage need for violence ripping through me like a small hot wind. I pushed back from the table and looked at him.

"Hey, man." Big Boy Doheny moved up beside me, between me and the young gunslinger who no longer had a gun, between a battle-scarred old rooster and a strutting young cock who could crow like hell but had no spurs.

"Hey, man," Big Boy said again, and turned away from me. He laid hands on Farley, none too gently, and deposited him at the other end of the table. "Come on, man, let's have a drink and forget all this irascible shit. Hell, I thought you two was friends or I wouldn't let your ass in here."

"We were friends once," Farley said sullenly.

"No, man," I said. "Your father was my friend. I just knew you. Not well enough, as it turned out." I poured scotch into a glass and dropped in ice cubes.

Farley tasted the raw whiskey Big Boy handed him, made a face. "I didn't set out to steal Susan away from you, Dan. She'd been gone over a year when I married her."

"You had nothing to do with her leaving, I suppose."

"That was your own damn fault. We didn't plan what happened, it just happened. I was sorry about it but you didn't give me a chance to explain. We just got carried away, is all." His eyes gleamed glassily in the bright fluorescent light.

"Anybody want some pretzels?" Big Boy ripped a plastic bag and dumped pretzels on the table, sorting them into three separate piles.

"Bigger than both of you, huh?" I said, wondering what the hell I was doing. We were acting like two spoiled kids in a marble game fighting over the same taw. I watched him take a healthy slug of bourbon, wondering sardonically if he knew the results of mixing alcohol and drugs.

"Better lay off the booze," I said, surprising myself, "if you're on anything stronger than grass."

"Don't tell me what to do." He gunned the rest of the whiskey, then wiped his lips with two fingers and fixed me with a bleary stare. "I suppose you're going to tell me you and Susan didn't . . . didn't get it on today?"

I looked at Doheny. He was stacking pretzels, his broad face bland and noncommittal.

"This is stupid, Jack."

Farley's face split into a sneer. "Yeah. Now the shoe's on the other foot. Come on, man, did you bang my wife today?"

I shrugged and lit a cigarette with fingers that were beginning to tremble again.

"You chickenshit bastard! Answer me! Did you screw her?" I scanned his angry snarling face and wondered if I would have to fight him after all. Maybe hurt him or be hurt, kill him or be killed. It was man's oldest and craziest game with woman both the curse and the prize in the battle, and as always came the burning question: Was she really worth it?

I leaned forward on the table and bared my teeth at him. "Yeah, I did. Twice."

I saw Doheny's left nostril flare from the corner of my eye, watched Farley's handsome face go from white to pink, then back again. I gathered my feet beneath my chair, my eyes on Farley's frozen features, and watched in utter disbelief as he suddenly collapsed, the life force draining out of him along with the sobbing air from his mouth. His head fell forward on his arms with the fluid laxity of a dead man.

But Jack Farley wasn't dead or even dying; he was only crying.

/12/

I finally got up and went to bed. Left them sitting there consoling each other in mawkish sentimentality, boisterous and tragic in turn, Farley's tear-streaked face driving me away with haunting memories of my own lonely tears. But male tears, like true love, are hard to come by and should be earned. Jack Farley, golden boy millionaire, had not earned the right to cry for the woman I loved: not with a drunkard's tears, shallow and vain and reeking of self-pity.

But I left only to dream: dark tortured dreams, heavy with menace, fraught with chilling panic and hopeless fear, breathless chases and long spiraling falls. A part of me that watched my blind staggering antics with cool detachment intervened only as I approached madness, interjected bright silvery interludes in sylvan glades filled with dark-eyed, raven-haired maidens who beamed sweet lovely smiles and threw themselves at me with wild and joyous abandon.

So I slept and I dreamed and when I awoke at mid-morning Farley and Doheny were gone, the field of battle deserted except for a few crushed pretzels.

I drove by police headquarters to see Homer. Partly to mend my fences, but mostly to trick him into confirming my notion of Susie's whereabouts.

He looked up as I walked into his office without knocking, glared at me briefly out of red swollen eyes, then said brusquely: "If you got business here, see the sergeant."

I grunted amiably and sat down in his visitor's chair. "Susie took off, Homer. Just up and left without telling anybody where she's going. Not even her husband."

He laid down the report he was reading and picked up another. "So? She's a growed-up woman. Reckon it's her own business."

"You're not worried about her anymore, huh?"

He stared hard at the report, moving his lips to show me he was reading. I let the silence grow and finally he looked up, scowling. "Dammit, Dan, I'm too busy to play games."

"Don't shit me, buddy," I said softly. "She calls you Uncle and you love her like you really were. So don't jack me around. You know where she is. You know and now I know because she doesn't have a key and she'd have to come to you to get it."

"Dammit, Dan!" He dropped the paper, his florid face suddenly earnest. "Leave her alone. Let her be for a while. She needs time to think. She told me. It's about you, man, and her husband and—"

"And money." I smiled thinly. "Money and power and precious magical youth. That's powerful artillery, Homer. And I'm sitting here with a peashooter. An old broken-down peashooter at that. No, buddy, she needs help making up her mind. My help."

"Be fair, Dan," he said gently.

"Fair? What the hell does fair have to do with it? Was it fair for that son of a bitch to eat my food, sleep under my roof, then get my woman drunk and—"

"That wasn't exactly the way it happened, Dan, and you know it."

"How do you know so damned much about it, Homer?"

He shrugged and looked down at his blunt fingertips, his face a shade darker.

"Does Susie tell you everything? Did she tell you about yesterday? How great it was with us? For that short time, just like it used to be. Maybe better. Did she tell you that in my goddamned perversity I ran her off again? Sent her back to that crybaby she's married to? And had the goddamned stupidity to feel noble about it? Noble, my ass. I was panic-stricken, man. I found out she was rich and I couldn't handle that. The same way I couldn't handle my wife's ghost, the difference in our ages, my damned drinking all those years. But something's changed, Homer. I've changed. I'm going to get her back."

He gazed at me over pyramided fingertips, his bloodshot eyes unimpressed. And why not? He had heard it all before. Different words but the same whining litany. It had taken years for him to lose faith in me, years of specious reasoning and lame excuses for all the sorry things about me he couldn't understand, years of covering my shortcuts and detours when I worked for him as a cop.

He should never have been a cop himself; he still believed a friend couldn't look you in the eye and lie.

He cleared his throat and leaned forward. "I hope so, Dan. Will you give her some time?"

"Sure," I said, rising to my feet and looking him in the eye. "Sure, Homer, if that's what she wants."

Except for a five-dollar bill and some loose change, my father died a penniless drunk. Drunk and alone a few feet from the door of a hunting cabin he and I had built on four hundred acres of substandard land left to me in irrevocable trust when I was born. The rest of the fifteen-hundred-acre ranch was gone, sacrificed to slake an insatiable thirst. My mother's death had set him off, loosed him like a redbone hound on some new and exotic game. For four years he never stopped running, his shoulders hunched before a Texas norther only he could feel, looking forward only to the next drink, the next drunk. He had drowned his pain and sorrow in a river of good whiskey, solved his whole life by lying down and freezing to death five yards from safety. For years afterward, off and on, I wondered how grief could so whip a man that he would just lie down and die. I try not to think about it anymore, but if I do, I know the answer.

* * *

She was wearing cutoffs and a T-shirt, standing in the open doorway of the cabin, one bare foot rubbing across the top of the other. Her arms were folded beneath her breasts, head high, her back stiffly erect, a position I had come to associate with annoyance. Driving the last few yards to the cabin door, I decided on the truth, discarded the carefully constructed lie I had worked on off and on all the way from Dallas, a hundred miles to the northwest. A plausible lie, something I did every year about this time. And she would know that, probably believe me. She almost always believed me. A sad state of affairs that had made it next to impossible to cheat on her over the years.

I looked through the windshield in her direction, pantomiming surprise, deliberately not focusing on her face to see if she was smiling; I would find out soon enough.

I killed almost a minute lighting a cigarette I didn't want, another thirty seconds rooting around in my cooler for a beer I didn't want, either. Then, as ready as I'd ever be, I climbed out of the car. I walked toward her wearing a lopsided grin that I knew looked foolish, feeling fragile, old and fragile and incredibly vulnerable.

"Hi," I said from six feet away, daring to look at her face for the first time, seeing a faint curve to her pale pink lips that brought a swelling rush of relief.

"What are you doing here, Danny?" Her voice was quiet and reproving, but not challenging.

I opened the can of beer and held it out to her. "Want some?"

She shook her head, eyebrows arched, waiting.

I took a quick drink, started to wipe my mouth with my hand, and took out my handkerchief instead. "Well, you know, honey, I always come up here in September. See about the deer stands, put out some feed blocks, stuff like that."

"Deer season isn't until November, Danny." She tilted her head, eyebrows climbing.

"Yeah, but if you'll remember, me and Homer and Lee

and Tom always come up in September to get things ready." She looked past me. "Oh, are they still in the car?"

I grinned. "Okay. That was going to be my story. I even stopped and bought a couple of deer blocks, but ..." I let it trail away and gave her a cunning grimace. "But you know damn well I never could lie to you."

"Then Uncle Homer told you I was here." There was something approaching sadness in her voice, as if she had just learned her best friend had betrayed her.

"No, he didn't, Susie. You know how he is. He can't hide anything from me. I tricked it out of him. But I knew you were here, anyway. Where else could you go to be safe and alone and still drive your car?"

"You must have read my note." It was a statement and not a question, her dark eyes insistently finding mine. "Did Jack call you?"

"He's upset," I said, seeing no point in going into lengthy explanations about male posturing and vacuous whiskey tears.

"Well, I'm sorry," she said, her lips tightening. She looked beyond my shoulder, her eyes cloudy, sweeping the horizon slowly, coming finally back to me, limpid again, as if somewhere in the monotonous vista of rolling hills she had found answers to vexing questions. "In his own way, Danny, he's as stubborn as you."

"Hey, gee, thanks, honey," I said warmly, stepping quickly forward and kissing her, stepping back, catching the crinkling around her eyes, the involuntary upward curl of lips that tasted of hickory nuts and sweet maple syrup.

"Aha," I said, "you had pancakes for breakfast and you've been into my cache of hickory nuts."

"For lunch," she said, smiling at last, a stingy smile by her usual standards, but warmly glowing. It was a good omen.

"And you smell of pinecones and pitch and moss-covered stones in twinkling streams," I said, "which means you've been wading in the spring branch again and probably lying wantonly under the pines." I wagged a finger at her. "Don't you know the cottonmouths and rattlers are losing their skins and are meaner'n snakes?"

She laughed, then crimped her lips firmly. "Don't try to divert me, Danny. Why did you come?"

I lit a cigarette and did some vista rambling of my own, a slow troubled scan of hardwoods and elm, cottonwood and pine, the small patch of original timber that surrounded my cabin, a hard-won concession from the creeping mechanical monsters that had plundered the land for lignite coal and laid waste to thousands of acres of age-old timber and lofty, if not majestic, hills. Beyond my three-acre oasis the land lay in undulating waves, monotonous and dull, as featureless as a dirty green carpet scuffed and wrinkled by uncaring feet, a sad tribute to man's unceasing effort to rape the earth.

Susie cleared her throat and I brought my eyes guiltily back to hers, meeting her cool punishing gaze and faltering inside, seeing vivid images of a young tanned god and a nubile goddess, intertwined, linked together in fierce embrace, thudding power and softly whispered words as golden thighs spread wide in sweet surrender . . .

"I could lie," I said hoarsely. "I could tell you I came to cut these sprouts around the cabin that have been needing it for two years. I could say I came to cut the brush out back that's getting too high . . . but I won't, dammit. I came because of you. I know what's on your mind, or think I do. You're trying to choose between me and . . . and all those other things like money and power and prestige . . . and a young husband who probably loves you. It's pretty one-sided, babe. I need all the help I can get. I need to see in your eyes, hold your hand, make love to you if you'll let me. I was my usual dumb-ass self yesterday, the same way I was two years ago. We should have talked it out then." I reached out and laid my hands on her shoulders, glanced fleetingly at slightly parted lips, wrenched my gaze upward to meet serene brown eyes. Something in their cool depths flickered, blazed brightly, then faded.

"That sounded like a speech. Did you practice it on the way down?"

"Some," I admitted.

She gripped my wrists and lifted my hands from her shoulders. "All right. This is your place and I couldn't ask you to leave even if I wanted you to. To be honest it's a little scary around here at night by myself. And I'll help you cut the brush and the sprouts. We'll do some fishing and some work and maybe talk like grown-up adult people."

"That's cool," I said.

Her eyes sparkled. She placed her hand flat against my chest and gave me a slight push. "But no touching, Danny, no holding hands and no making love. It wouldn't be fair."

"It would be to me."

"I know," she sighed, "and maybe even to me, but it wouldn't be fair to Jack."

"Jack who?" I said.

/13/

I worked leisurely the next two days, with no sense of urgency, grubbing the knee-high sprouts that had grown up around the cabin over the last two years. Susie helped, digging fiercely at the obstinate hardwoods, straining mightily to rip the tenacious roots from the soil, dragging them triumphantly to a neat pile behind the cabin near the spring. Then, more often than not, wandering over to stand in the ankle-deep spring branch, flushed and heated, but serene, her face as peaceful as I had ever seen it.

Once during the second afternoon, impelled by a cosmic loneliness that dried my throat and shuddered in my stomach, I walked over and held her, hugged her tightly and kissed her, my mind empty of everything but her, the feel of warm lips and smooth heated skin, the natural heady fragrance of her, of sunshine and moss-covered rocks and sweet-smelling wood.

"Hey," she murmured against my lips, "no touching, remember? No kissing . . . no loving."

I dropped my arms and stepped back. "Right. Try to control yourself next time."

I went back to my chopping and digging, sawing and sweating, feeling her eyes on me, wishing I could slip inside their clear depths, curl up and watch the world from her side, see myself as she saw me. . . .

On second thought, maybe not, I thought wryly.

That evening, an hour before dark, we walked down the hill to the small lake a hundred yards behind the cabin. Primarily spring-fed, it was slightly more than three acres in size, a teardrop bubble of shimmering blue water held at bay by an earthen dam bulldozed across the mouth of a narrow rocky canyon. Fifteen feet at its deepest point, with numerous rocky ledges along its sides and just beneath the top of the water, it made an excellent swimming hole and spawning ground for catfish and bream.

By dark we had caught nine good-sized channel catfish and twice as many bream. All but five of the largest catfish went back into the lake, and by the time I finished cleaning the hapless ones by Coleman lantern it was full dark, a three-quarter moon sliding over the low rim of the hill, burnishing the still water, painting a ghostly streak of old silver across the center of the lake.

Somewhere a turkey hen yelped at a nightbird invading her roost, and Susie touched my shoulder and pointed toward a half-dozen graceful gray shapes cautiously approaching the water at the shallow end. As silent as wraiths, the deer lingered only long enough to drink, then drifted away up the canyon as quietly as they had come.

Silently, her face unreadable in the shadows cast by the lantern, Susie handed me a towel, a washcloth, and a bar of soap.

"Would you like for me to wash your back?" I asked.

"I can manage, thanks." She had tied her hair into a ponytail that swung thick and heavy almost to the center of her shoulders, and her face, in bold relief, gleamed like pale gold in the moonlight.

"Okay," I said cheerfully. "Watch out for snakes." I turned and walked a decorous fifteen yards along the bank of the lake. "You can take the lantern," I called out as I slipped out of my Levi's, "I won't peek."

Standing knee-deep in the warm shallows I washed myself, scrubbing copious amounts of suds into my sweaty gummy hair. Then, taking in as much breath as my rusty lungs would allow, I hit the water in a low flat dive. I swam underwater until my body had absorbed all the oxygen, then surfaced, blowing and spouting, hooting as my legs drifted downward into cold water.

"How is it, Danny?" Susie called, her voice sounding as if she was standing ten feet away.

"Great," I said, looking at her for the first time, her tanned body astonishingly pale in the moonglow, limned with fire from the lantern on the shore.

"Stay right there," she said, and her hands rose to wind her hair into a rope, pinning it somehow to the back of her head. A moment later she was in the water, streaking toward me, a smooth effortless stroke she had tried to teach me for years.

She pulled up a few feet away, treading water, smiling broadly, her breathing light and even. "You're right, it's great."

"A little chillier here than near the shore."

"I can hardly feel it," she said.

"Women have an extra layer of subcutaneous fat."

"Oh, really?" She drifted nearer and I felt her fingers probing my chest and stomach. "I'm not so sure about that. I seem to feel a nice layer of fat right here."

"Let's compare," I said, making an effort to keep my face from revealing the metamorphosis occurring below.

She wiggled her eyebrows and smiled coyly. "You just want to get your big old hands on my fair body."

"You damn bet I do," I said, reaching for her under the water, finding her waist and yanking her against me, catching her lips with mine just as we sank beneath the surface. She lay passive in my arms, not struggling, but not responding either. I held the kiss as long as I could, then pushed her away and kicked for the surface.

She treaded water six feet away, watching me quietly while I gathered in breath. Moonlight glinted briefly in deep dark eyes and I could see a faint gleam of white between lips slightly parted in an uncertain smile.

Feeling foolish, I grinned at her, then turned and began my laborious crawl toward the shore.

"Danny! Danny, I'm sorry. I didn't mean to . . . to arouse you."

I stopped twenty feet away, my feet scraping bottom. I watched her move slowly toward me, the cool water somehow comforting around my diminishing erection, remembering what Big Boy Doheny had said.

"It's not your fault," I said. "It can't see or hear, and it damn sure don't have a conscience." I turned and started swimming again, her laughter filling the night around me.

It was hot and stuffy inside the two-room cabin, and after I put away the fish I turned on the small air conditioner while Susie went around closing windows. We carried beer to the redwood picnic table under a stand of hardwoods near the brow of the hill.

I smoked, and we sipped at the beer and talked desultorily for a while, listening to the night sounds, watching the twinkling lights of Butler Wells at the head of the valley, hearing above our heads the stealthy rustle of restless leaves, a tiny mournful dirge to the inevitability of winter and dry withering death.

I fetched another round of brew and, driven by compulsions beyond my comprehension, waxed loquacious, as they say, regaling her with tales of not-so-derring-do, of tarnished knights on stumbling horses, winning sometimes, but mostly losing in this unending battle that some sardonic wag had labeled life.

Nostalgia crept in swishing its shaggy enticing tail, and I talked on, told her things I had never told anyone before, not even myself; I told her about my mother's swift unexpected death, my father's deliberate lingering one, told her about my first wife Barbara, the good years and the bad, her courage in the face of painful death. I talked about my son Tommy, his drug-induced death, told her of my vengeance on the man who had started him on that one-way path.

I talked sadly of that useless Asian war, my part in it, the horror of endless nights made bright as day, the smell of phosphorescence, napalm, and death; the mindless fear that drove men to mutilate themselves, to fill their clothing with the sour odor of urine, the slick-slime stench of terror-sweat, the noisome slither of uncontrollable bowels.

We talked briefly of her mother Lucille, oddly and in muted

tones, not as her mother, but in curious detachment as if she had been some beloved stranger, some awesome entity adored and revered by all who knew her. Which, in some limited measure, she had been.

Susie talked about her early years, her childhood and the early teens that I had not known. I listened with grave attention, but watching her lovely mobile face sent my mind wandering back to other places, to good times and harder times, to times when she had braced my soul and found me wanting, to times when she had called out to me and found me deaf.

I had an overwhelming need to touch her; I reached across the picnic table and took up her hand.

She stopped talking and looked at me, her face barely discernible in the pale moon-shadow, her eyes gathering light from somewhere, darkly gleaming. "Are you okay, Danny?"

"I'm fine," I said, my smile feeling awkward, strained, not telling her that watching her made me feel used up, as old and wasted as the gutted land around us, as gnarled and hollow as the old den tree that teetered on the edge of the bluff. Not telling her, but wanting to, that youth is only a little less grim than middle age and has no clear-cut priorities on love and sorrow and heartbreak. Not telling her anything, just working on my smile until it was loose and free and easy, basking in the glow of her radiant face, tingling from the warmth of her hand in mine.

In tacit agreement, we rose and walked toward the cabin, my hopes high and climbing, her hand still clutched tightly in mine. But, inside she turned, sighed regretfully, and kissed my cheek. Silently we went to our separate beds.

An hour later I still lay wide awake, drained and empty, yet somehow curiously alert and thrumming from my emotional catharsis, my avalanche of verbal diarrhea that now had me worried, wondering if I had said too much, revealed too much about the Dan Roman that nobody knew, least of all me. I lit a cigarette and swung my feet to the floor. I padded across the small room to the water cooler, glancing once at Susie curled in the other single bed in the far corner. Her eyes were closed, her face placid in the reflected glow of moonlight splashing across the bed.

She's having no trouble sleeping, I thought glumly, washing down a couple of aspirin for the pain that clung as persistently as that of a phantom limb. I stubbed out my cigarette and tried it again, pounded the pillow and turned into the wall.

I must have slept, or dozed, or maybe it was just the dreamlike quality of her voice drifting into my awareness that brought me rolling onto my back like an old dog panting for a belly rub.

"Danny."

She stood straight and fine and naked beside the bed, hands limply at her sides, hair down again, billowing around her face and shoulders, her features full and bold with puffy lips and eyes gleaming down at me from under lowered lids. I felt a thudding shock in my solar plexus; it was a look I knew.

"Danny, I'm hot." Her voice was low and plaintive, a thread of husky harshness that made my heart pound.

"I can turn down the air conditioner," I said.

She swayed forward, settled on her knees looking as if she wanted to laugh and couldn't. "Not that kind of hot, you dummy. I've been turned on all evening . . . ever since I felt you beneath the water . . ." Her dreamy voice faded and she leaned down and kissed my chest, nuzzled, crept upward to bury her face beneath my chin. "God," she whispered, trailing her lips across my neck to my ear, her body unfurling, stretching flat on top of mine. "I need you. Can you get horny again, Danny?" A rhetorical question if ever there was one.

"Nope," I said, ignoring the undeniable fact of burgeoning tumescence. "You had your chance, lady. Anyhow, remember, no touching, no kissing, no . . ." I hesitated. "No charity, Susan."

She chuckled throatily, warm lips pouncing, soft and yielding, yet still voracious, searching for more than kissing could bring. "Charity, my ass," she said softly a few moments later, pressing her hands tightly against my face, then sliding them eagerly between our bodies, finding me, shifting to fit us together, her breath hot and sweet against my mouth.

"Not this time, love," I said, doing some shifting of my own, scooting sideways on the narrow bed, turning, flipping her onto her back with ease born of long practice.

"Good, good," she murmured, her body suddenly changing, becoming fluid, supple, melting, flowing upward to meet mine, clinging and submissive—yet not passive—but subtly demanding. Her eyes grew wide, darker, more beseeching, her mouth forming into a tremulous O of supplication.

It was a game we had played before and she knew well its devastating effects.

Somewhere nearby a coyote bayed its ululating message at the sky and I felt her belly tremble with suppressed laughter. It came again and died, and there were no other sounds but ours, uniquely ours, as would be the ecstasy that was sure to come.

/14/

"You big gorilla," she said, wiping my forehead and smoothing back my hair in the same caressing movement. "You don't think for a moment that we're finished."

"Not for a moment," I echoed valiantly. "I'm only girding my loins, as they say."

"You can sleep for ten minutes. I'll lie here and watch you . . . and hold you," she added suggestively, finding actions to fit her words.

"That's cool," I said, fighting an overwhelming need to sleep, wondering fretfully why women never seemed to understand the physiological necessity for sleep imposed by gentle nature on the human male as both penalty and reward for a job well done.

"I'm only teasing," she murmured, warm breath puffing against my shoulder. "It's just that I'm still coming down. Lordy, I was high tonight." She made a quiet sound and pressed into my side, crushed her breasts beneath my arm, thrust the curly tickling mound against my hip. Her hand, holding me, felt both comforting and warm, yet strangely disquieting, and in my imagination I could feel the silent disapproval of the gleaming golden band, could feel in my insides the desperate anxiety her husband must be feeling.

"I was sooooo excited tonight." She trudged on, her voice low and dry, almost a monotone. "I wanted you at the lake, but . . . and then later when you talked to me for hours . . . you've never talked to me like that before, Danny. Never. About important things, I mean, things that have deep meaning to you." She stopped with a sound that could have been a sob. "I never understood before how tragic your life has been, how . . ."

"Not tragic, babe," I said lightly, "only foolish." I twisted my neck to look at her face; all I could see was a tousled tangle of glossy hair, the clean lines of rounded hip and supple thigh.

"Losing your mother and father both the way you did, Tommy, then Barbara . . ." Her voice trailed off sadly. She rubbed her cheek against my shoulder and murmured consolingly, then raised pursed lips to be kissed.

"Out there tonight," she said after a moment, "when you were talking, you looked so sad. I ached to hold you, comfort you."

"I was aching a little myself, if you want the truth."

She lifted her head and stretched to bring her face even with mine, her hair spilling over our heads, creating a deeper pool of darkness from which her eyes gleamed like droplets of shiny wax.

"I love you, Danny; that's not news to either of us, but what I never knew before I married Jack is that nobody can do for me what you do . . . here in bed, I mean. Why is that? Can you tell me why that is, Danny?"

"Dedication and technique," I said, feeling a rush of pleasure at her words, half embarrassed by her naïveté, her unsophisticated flattery. "Smart old dogs learn new tricks."

"Come on, don't be flippant. I'm serious."

"It has to do with love, I guess. Giving and taking. And maybe giving is the most important of the two. And practicality. How does that song go? 'Nobody does it better than you.' There's sense in that. Hell, I don't know. I stopped sweating the mystical stuff a long time ago. I just go with my instincts, and right now my instincts tell me if I don't go to sleep, I'm gonna die."

She laughed a throaty resonant laugh. "All right, baby, you go ahead. I'll just lie here and hold you for a while, until you're good and asleep. Doesn't that sound nice?"

"Sounds great," I said, despite my thorny misgivings.

She cleared her throat and began humming, a low sweet crooning sound.

I closed my eyes and began sleeping.

89

* * *

The next afternoon I drove into Butler Wells. Susie declined my invitation, citing a desperate need for a couple of hours more sleep. "So I'll be bright-eyed and bushy-tailed tonight," she said, giving me a long sultry look, her eyebrows arching.

I bought supplies at the gleaming chrome-and-glass-and-tile supermarket that had replaced Elmer Jetson's old general store, then drove slowly along the potholed main drag twice without seeing a single face I knew. I bought two dollars' worth of quarters from the man at the Shell station, and while he poured amber gold into my gas tank I walked to the phone booth at the edge of the apron.

I lost a quarter and five minutes obtaining Jack Farley's office phone number from the Dallas operator, then spent another fruitless two minutes trying to talk myself out of calling him.

But guilt or conscience, or whatever it was that was bugging me, won out. I lit a cigarette and dialed the number.

"That will be one dollar and sixty-five cents for three minutes, sir."

I dropped in my remaining seven quarters. "Just keep the change, Operator."

I heard a snicker and a ringing phone and then an impatient male voice. "Hold on a minute . . ." He was gone before I could object, even if I had wanted to.

I smoked patiently and watched the sweep hand circle the face of my watch twice. Fine. It was my two dollars, but it was his anxiety I was trying to dispel. And maybe, thinking about it, it wasn't such a hot idea after all. Knowing where she was was one thing, but knowing she was with me was quite another.

"Hello."

"Uh . . . hello. Farley? This is Dan Roman."

"Where the hell are you, Roman?"

"Look, I just wanted to tell—"

"She's with you, isn't she? Goddammit, I want to know where you are!"

"Look, Jack. I only wanted to tell you she was okay . . ."

"I'll goddamned bet she is! You look, you son—"

"Your three minutes are up, sir."

"I don't have any more change, Operator. Okay, Jack, she's okay . . ."

"Don't you get off this phone! Operator! Operator! Charge this call to 555–6785."

"Is that your number, sir?"

"Of course it's my goddamned number! Now, look, Roman . . ."

"Is this your residence or business phone number, sir?"

"Goddammit, it's my office! Now, will you get the hell off this line?"

"I'd watch the profanity if I were you, sir."

"Aw, shit . . ."

"There's nothing more to talk about, Jack. Susie's fine. I wanted you to know that."

"I'll just bet you did, you back-stabbing asshole! Where've you got her, Roman?"

"I don't have her anywhere, Farley. She came here of her own free will and she's staying the same way. I'm sorry, man . . ."

"You're goddamned right you are! You're the sorriest son of a bitch I've ever—"

"Are you smiling, man?"

"What?"

"I said are you smiling? When you call me that, you'd damn well better be smiling."

"Aw, shit, Roman—"

I cut him off, expelling my breath in a long whistling sigh. I'd had worse ideas in my time, but for the life of me I couldn't remember when.

We stayed three more idyllic days, working the brush with whatever was left of the mornings after late risings and leisurely breakfasts, lazing away the afternoons beneath the hardwoods and pine, smelling the clean westerly wind, the fragrances of nature and each other, listening to the tinkling stutter of the tiny creek, the sounds of nature, each other . . .

We made love beneath the giant oak beside the spring, and once more in the cool waters of the lake the way we had both wanted to that second night. Appetizers for the nights, the long languorous nights rife with self-indulgence and total satiation, replete with sighs and moans and savage exultation.

Completely absorbed in each other, we talked of nothing or no one not concerned with the here and now, not concerned with us as we were at that moment. We might well have been two young lovers, castaways in our own Blue Lagoon—and maybe we were: after all, she was only twenty-nine and I was very young at heart.

"I guess this is the only thing left," Susie said, propping the cased .243 Remington against the inside molding on the door. She held out her left hand. "And we have a banana left. Want half of it?"

I shook my head and watched her peel the yellow fruit. She dropped the skin into a small bag of trash just outside the door, then leaned against the doorjamb and put the end of the banana in her mouth. She looked up to find me watching and, her face slowly gaining color, bit off a chunk. She looked away while she chewed, then glanced back and caught my eye and broke into a laugh. "You've got a dirty mind, Dan Roman."

"I didn't say a word."

"Yes, but you were thinking plenty. Sure you don't want some? Banana, I mean?"

"I believe I will," I said, moving into the doorway with her. I leaned against the opposite doorjamb. "We'll each take an end and work toward the middle."

"That's a sneaky way to get a kiss."

"Messy, too, but I saw it once in an Italian movie. It led to all sorts of interesting things."

"I'll bet. Okay, the rules are, you have to chew steady and slow and not gulp. I'm already at a disadvantage. Your mouth is bigger than mine."

"You've already had a bite, so it'll even out. All right. Ready—"

"Go," she said, shoving the banana into my mouth, standing on tiptoe and closing her lips around the other end, her hands pulling mine around her hips, grinding her groin into mine, forcing me back against the edge of the doorjamb, her eyes over the banana bubbling with merriment.

"Mmmmmmph," she said, still chewing on the first bite. I hated bananas.

That she was going to win was evident from the beginning, devouring her half of the banana with astonishing gluttony, cheating outrageously by grinding her lower half into mine, creating a tactical diversion while her strong white teeth went about their work with systematic expertise.

And I couldn't have cared less, absorbed as I was in what was happening down below, wouldn't have cared even when the damn thing blew up in our faces if it hadn't been for the slapping crack of the rifle.

For some fraction of time—a second, maybe two—I stood frozen, my lips tingling, staring into Susie's half-dollar eyes, correlating the sound and the action, reacting, dropping, shoving with my feet even as we were on the way to the floor.

We landed hard, my left arm and her right taking the brunt of the fall. I heard her grunt, felt pain lance upward from my elbow joint.

I broke free and pointed. "Against that wall."

And then I was rolling, clawing frantically for the .243 at the door and cursing, my mind working again, measuring, evaluating, deciding even as I yanked the gun out of the case and fumbled in the pocket for bullets that the shooter had to be somewhere in the brush along the county road four hundred yards away. There was no other place. The bullet had come straight between us and there was no cover elsewhere in the small valley or the rolling fields beyond.

I snapped a loaded clip into the gun and jacked a cartridge into the chamber. Only then did I look at Susie. "You okay?"

She nodded, curled against the inside wall, rubbing her elbow, her dark eyes watching me almost calmly. She leaned sideways and spat out a mouthful of banana. She looked back at me and tried to smile, then covered her quivering lips with fingertips that trembled.

I grinned and bobbed my head. "You're doing fine, honey. Don't worry about the bastard. He's in that line of brush down by the county road and you can bet he won't try to cross that open ground. Chances are he's already gone. Besides, it was probably a stray bullet. Some idiot shooting at a tin can down on the road." Even as I spoke the faint sounds of a throbbing motor came through the open doorway. I stepped to the window and flattened against the wall beside it. I poked a finger behind the shade and pulled it away from the frame. The sounds of the motor were winding down and I could see a long trail of billowing dust inside the curving avenue of trees.

"He's gone, heading west toward Interstate 45." I leaned the gun against the wall and helped her to her feet, folded her in my arms and discovered I had a lump of banana in my cheek. I jacked it out with my tongue and swallowed it.

"It's okay, honey," I said, smoothing back her tousled hair, kissing the banana-flecked lips. "Just like I said, some idiot trying out his deer gun. I should take your car and run the bastard down."

"You really think so, Danny?" Her hands clamped down on my forearms, her eyes scanning my face. "You don't think . . . you don't think it was someone trying to k-k-kill me?"

"Of course not," I said with more assurance than I felt. "He had plenty of time to get off another shot if that's what he was trying to do. No, babe, it was some stupid amateur. After he fired he probably saw the cabin and decided he'd better scoot." I smiled and hugged her again, not telling her that most high-powered deer rifles in Texas have scopes, not pointing out to her that the cabin perched on the brow of the long slope was visible for miles from either direction, that to hit a two-inch section of a banana at over four hundred yards would tax the most accurate deer rifle ever made, not to mention the abilities of the shooter, not telling her that the odds against a stray shot, or a ricochet, hitting that same banana were probably a million to one.

We broke apart and she held up her hands. "God, look at me, I'm still shaking."

"It's a scary thing. I feel a little shaky myself. Do you think you'll feel like driving home?"

She took a deep breath and nodded. "I'll be all right. Just give me a few minutes."

"How about a beer? That should help."

She nodded and rummaged around in her purse. She found a Kleenex and wiped her mouth.

"Lord, I don't think I'll ever be able to eat another banana."

I opened the two beers I had been saving for the drive home. I gave her one. "Thank God for that banana," I said. "We could have been kissing."

/15/

Five miles north of Corsicana Susie's light blinked on and off in my rearview mirror and she pulled to the side of the highway. I braked, swerved onto the shoulder and stopped. She rolled the low black car to a halt a few feet behind mine. I got out and walked back.

"What's the problem?"

"Engine's overheating," she said, opening the door and climbing out. She slammed the door and tested the lock, then brushed idly at the wrinkles in her skirt.

"Probably the radiator. When's the last time you had it checked? Or you could be low on oil." I didn't mean to sound condescending, but she cut her eyes at me in a sardonic glance.

"No, it isn't low on water or oil. It has all the juices it needs right down to mixes for Manhattans and Singapore Slings. It's in the motor."

"Oh, how do you know that?"

She looked annoyed. "The computer said so, that's why. Come on, we don't have to wait, they're on their way."

"Who's on their way?"

"The agency people. They'll pick it up and take it in."

I looked at the car, then back at her. "That's a pretty expensive piece of machinery to leave on the side of the road. Some thief in a tow truck come along and bingo, your car's on its way to a chop shop."

She shook her head impatiently. "Not unless they're driving a truck big enough to load it inside. All four wheels lock after fifty feet." She gave me an impish grin. "That would make it tough sledding, wouldn't it?" She patted the glossy hood and started toward my humble Dodge. "Anyway, it's fully insured."

I lit a cigarette and followed her. "I'm just an old country boy, but how did you get in touch with the agency? Mental telepathy? I didn't see an aerial or a CB or . . ."

She laughed. "Telephone. I have a CB too. The aerial's retractable and the CB's built under the seat . . . or somewhere." She glanced over her shoulder at the car as we pulled into the traffic. "It's a beautiful car, Danny. You should get one."

"Yeah, just what I need to take deer hunting. I could sling my deer across the hood, I guess, or put it on top. Might scratch it up a little, knock off a few thousand in value when I got ready to trade it in on next year's model."

She shrugged. "It's only money, Danny." She propped an elbow on the armrest and cupped her chin, staring at the monotonous countryside, her face serene.

I stubbed out the cigarette. "My, my, how quickly we forget, how blasé and sophisticated we become at the drop of a few million bucks. I can remember when you agonized over a dress that cost forty-nine ninety-five. I can remember when you bought your first car, a Plymouth Duster, how high you were riding, how excited and thrilled you were."

"It's all relative," she said a little stiffly. "It was all I could afford then."

"And it's not only goddamned money. For some people it's food and clothing, a roof over their heads; it's education and medical care and living without constant fear—"

"Hey," she said softly, scooting across the seat, her left hand going to the back of my neck, her right to my thigh. "I didn't make the world, Danny, don't lay it all on my frail little shoulders. I just got lucky, is all."

I breathed deeply for a moment, then lit another cigarette, feeling the unexpected swell of anger bleed into her caressing fingertips. I smoked in silence for a while, then turned my head and looked at her.

"How much does it mean to you, Susan? We haven't really talked about that. The money, I mean. The big house, the

fine cars, the ... oh, whatever the hell else there is?"
Her face puckered for a moment, then smoothed into a firm
noncommittal mask. She sighed and moved back across the
seat. She looked through the side window, nibbling at a ragged cuticle on her slender, short-fingered hand. Her brow
wrinkled once as if stung by a thoughtless bee, and then she
was talking, that dry flat monotone she had used once before.
"It means freedom, Danny, freedom and prestige and respect. And power, too, I suppose. A kind of power over people.
It means going into Neiman-Marcus and having them know
you, cater to you, invite you to exclusive showings, treat you
like you're somebody. And I'm not rich rich. I'm poor boy rich
compared to Clarice Doheny. But I've been in Neiman's with
Clarice and they don't treat her any better."
"That's important," I said.
"It means going anywhere you want to go. We've been
married a year and we've been to eleven different foreign
countries. Weekend trips mostly on chartered jets. Two months
ago we flew to Las Vegas for three days. We stayed at the best
hotel, saw all the best shows, gambled a lot of the time. We
spent thirty thousand dollars and I didn't give it a second
thought. A month ago we flew to Los Angeles and went by
limousine to Rodeo Drive in Beverly Hills. I spent eighty
thousand dollars on a new fall wardrobe, and not a complete
one at that—"
"I certainly wouldn't think so, not for only eighty thousand."
She smiled wanly. "I know you think it's funny—"
"Not funny, never funny. People are starving."
"All right then, a bad joke. And maybe it is. But that's the
way of things, Danny. I give to charity the way everyone else
does. I went to a charity fund drive at Clarice's a few weeks
ago. We gave ten thousand dollars. Clarice started it off with
fifty. Jack gave another five thousand before the night was
over. Senators and congressmen and a few movie stars—even
an ex-governor—and none of them gave more than we did.
We're not stingy, Danny. We tip a lot, a lot more than we
should probably. We've found the more you tip the more they

expect, and the next time you go in if it wasn't enough they get surly and do little spiteful things—" She broke off and looked straight ahead for a second, then turned to face me with a rueful little smile. "That sounded awful, didn't it?"

"Pretty awful," I agreed, gunning the Dodge around an ancient Chevrolet that had kept me bottled the last three miles. It was driven by an old man in bib overalls and a tattered western-style straw hat. An old woman perched beside him, peering anxiously through the windshield, an Aunt Jemima scarf halfheartedly restraining thin gray hair, knotted beneath a wrinkled pointed chin.

"Poor white trash," I snarled. "They should keep poor old farts like that off the highways." I tromped the accelerator savagely.

"All right, Danny, you've made your point. Like I said, I didn't make the world or the rules. I just try to get along."

"But you love it, don't you? Neiman-Marcus and Rodeo Drive and all the rest of it."

"Yes, I like it," she said evenly. "More than I would have thought possible before Mother died and left me the money. It gets in your blood. I—I know it's hard to explain . . . but dammit, you know, you've got a lot of money. You don't have to worry—"

I barked a harsh biting laugh. "You're not dumb, Susan, or naive. Don't talk like you are. A couple of hundred thousand dollars is a hell of a long way from being rich . . . or even well-to-do, for that matter. You're trying to compare mudhole crawdads with lobster, peanut butter with caviar." I flipped the cigarette butt out the window. "The way I see it, I could afford you maybe four months at the outside."

I could see her bobbing head from the corner of my eye and the chasm that I had foolishly thought was gone yawned wide and deep and went all the way to the horizon. I stuck another cigarette in my mouth and punched the dash lighter.

"But what the hell, I had six days I hadn't planned on. And that's a lifetime, as they say." I lit the cigarette and turned on the radio, feeling her eyes on the side of my face, a palpable force, warm and tingling.

She snorted and turned off the radio. "Not yet, old man, I haven't finished talking." She reached out and tugged at my right hand on the wheel. When I resisted, she yanked it free and held it between both of hers. She laid it on her thigh and spread my fingers, one by one. She rubbed her palm across mine, traced my lifeline with a slender forefinger.

"You have such big hands," she murmured, her head slightly bowed, glossy hair spilling across my arm, tickling, her voice querulous as if arguing with herself. "So big and rough-looking . . . and yet . . ." Her voice trailed off and she canted her head to look up at my face.

I stared straight ahead into the rear end of a dirty eighteen-wheeler where someone had written in big capital letters LIFE SUCKS, BUT THAT'S OKAY, SO DOES DYNAH ROTHCHILD.

"And yet," she went on dreamily, turning my hand over, sliding her skirt upward and placing my hand on the bare flesh of her thigh. "And yet so gentle . . . so tender . . ." Her eyes widened, grew darker, almost closed again. "And they turn me into mush, Danny, dissolve me inside, make me wet." She pressed my hand against the pliant muscle of her thigh, rocking gently, her eyes tightly clenched, a sibilant whisper escaping gritted teeth. "You make me crazy, damn you, you and your hands and your wounded eyes. You always have. Even when I was eighteen I had feelings I didn't really understand and was afraid to think about. I knew only that I trembled and grew weak inside when you looked at me. I used to wish I was younger so I could sit on your lap, older so I could . . . I wasn't sure what. My favorite fantasy—oh, God, I shouldn't be telling you this—but my favorite fantasy was being kidnaped by someone—boys—stripped naked, and tied to a bed. Then you would find us, destroy them, and see me there so beautiful, so helpless, and be overcome with love and . . ." Her eyes slowly opened and she smiled. "I never went beyond that . . . not for a long time. Not until I knew for certain what men and women did." She lapsed into silence, staring straight ahead into the distance, not reacting at all to my quick side-long glances, her face set and pale, her eyes quiet and glistening.

A mile inside the city limits of Midway City the right front tire on the Dodge gave up the ghost with a loud explosive crack. I discovered to my disgust that my spare was flat and we spent an hour waiting on the side of the highway for a clown in a tow truck who charged me forty dollars to tow us six city blocks to my favorite service station.

We lost another hour drinking coffee in a small café across the street from the station watching the young attendant wander back and forth between my car and the gasoline pumps, stopping often to stroke his sparse scraggly beard and gaze into the distance, making sharp decisive gestures with one sunburned arm, solving, no doubt, some weighty world problem, or, more likely, plotting his latest assault on the virtue of some timorous maiden.

When we finally reached my house, Susie's sleek Maserati sat sedately in the driveway, an envelope tucked discreetly behind the sun visor. It contained an effusive note assuring her the car was now in excellent running order, thanking her profusely for the opportunity to be of service, and tendering a modest bill in the sum of five hundred fifty-nine dollars and fifty cents.

/16/

"Two hundred and fifty thousand," I said. "That's about what I have. Put it with mine and we'll have almost a half million. A half-million dollars, Susie. That's a hell of a lot of money. Even if this depression gets worse we can always squeeze fifty thousand a year out of that. Add to that what I make out of my job and we'll have seventy or seventy-five thousand a year. I think we can manage."

She swallowed hard and smiled bravely, the sunlight beaming through the bay window highlighting the umber tones of her skin. "My car? And my clothes?"

"Of course you'll keep the car if you want to. The clothing . . . it's up to you. But I'm afraid as my wife you won't be going many places you can wear a Dior gown. Remember you only get half the closet space."

She shook her head, a woeful expression tugging down the corners of her mouth. "You strike a hard bargain. You're a worrisome man, Dan Roman."

"I'm not bargaining, Susie. It's the only way it can work for us and you know that. I'm as close to being rich as I can stand to be. And having a rich wife would be almost as bad. Even the simplest life is too complicated without worrying about a pile of money too big to stand flat-footed and jump over."

"All right. If I give up the money, will you promise not to be gone so much?"

"I have to work."

"Not really. Not if you don't want to. Will you promise?"

"Okay. That's fair enough. And maybe some of the easy runs you can go with me."

"I don't know about that," she said dubiously, turning to

look out the window. "Who'd take care of the babies?" Her gleaming eyes swung back inside and found mine.

"Babies? What—my God!"

"Babies," she said firmly, then broke into a lilting laugh, a blush spreading upward from the upper slopes of her breasts. "Isn't that what we've been working on so hard these last six days?"

"Babies! Jesus Christ, Susie!"

"Don't act so shocked. I didn't see you taking any precautions. I have a feeling I got pregnant that first night. A woman has intuition about things like that."

"What about your pills?"

"I didn't take any pills. I went to the cabin to get away, remember? I didn't know a sex-crazed maniac was going to follow me down there and seduce me." She flipped her head and grinned. "And seduce me, and seduce me . . ."

"I'm too old, Susie, don't you think?"

"Nope, I don't think. Bing Crosby started a whole new family when he was a lot older than you. We've already lost six or seven years when we could have been having a family. And only because you were so stubborn. I was ready to start when I was twenty-two . . . or younger."

She stood up and came around the table. She grabbed my chair and slid me backward far enough to squeeze between me and the table. She plopped on my lap with a melodramatic flounce and kissed me. Then she pressed my face into her bosom and murmured into my hair.

"Don't you like making babies with me?"

"How many are we talking about?" I nuzzled the convenient slopes of her breasts.

"Three . . . or four. I was an only child. I want a big family."

"Jesus Christ!"

"You were an only child too," she went on blithely. "You should hunger for a big family as much as me."

"I hunger for a little peace and quiet in my old age, not shitty diapers and three o'clock feedings, not sickness and tantrums and broken arms—"

"That's my job," she said. "Your job is to teach them to grow up with dignity and honor, to grow tall and straight like their father, to be men in the ways that are important. In other words, to be like you."

I laughed. "What if they're girls?"

"They won't be. You have dominant genes. I can tell." She pursed her lips and sighed, then ran her fingers through my hair. "Were your parents both black-haired like you?"

"My mother had dark auburn hair."

She sighed again. "I'd love to have a little blondheaded boy, but I don't guess there's much chance of that." She pushed and patted my hair, then leaned back to view her handiwork. "You have such nice thick wavy hair. With a little help from me I'll bet it would be curly. Why don't you let me—"

"Two," I said firmly. "No more than two." I kissed her, held it for a moment, feeling a quiver of something that was either triumph or suppressed laughter. Or, more likely, both.

She pulled back, her face flushed, her eyes heavy-lidded. "We could start right now," she said.

"I'm afraid not. I'd probably collapse and crush you. That little dab of breakfast and the bite of banana is long gone. It's growing nigh onto supper time and around the Roman household we pay attention to things like that. And since I don't have a maid or a cook, you must know what that means."

"It means you don't have anything to eat in your fridge, is what it means. I've already looked. I guess it means you'll have to go shopping—"

"I'll have to go shopping. Hah. How quickly one forgets."

"All right, then, I'll have to go shopping." She stopped and wrinkled her short straight nose. "But you'll have to give me some money. I'm broke."

"Okay, but just remember you're on a bologna budget now and not fillet and escargot."

She wrinkled up her face. "Ugh. Jack loves those awful things . . . and candied grasshoppers. He loves all sorts of weird things."

"How is Jack in bed, Susie?" The question came out of

nowhere, out of a cold black place in my mind peopled with dark squirming creatures that left slick slimy back trails, out of lonely nights tortured by bright hot images flickering across an internal screen that didn't have a shutoff button.

Her eyes widened, filled with incredulity. She watched me for a moment, then slowly lowered her lids, her face working with compassion and pain.

"Why, Danny? What does it matter now? It's over and done with. We were married and I slept with him and we had sex and it was fun sometimes and sometimes not. I'm sorry, but I can't call it back, I can't go back and do it over no matter how much I wish I could."

"I know that. I understand that. But that doesn't answer my question."

Her low laugh carried a thread of hysteria. "My God. How can I tell you that?"

"It's easy, Susan. Just say it, just come right out and say it. Was he good, fine, bad, indifferent . . . what?"

Her eyes opened slowly, gleaming. "No, that's not what you want to hear. You want me to compare. You want to know if he's better than you."

"All right," I said evenly, "maybe I do."

"Danny!" Her face seemed suddenly stricken and my heart began a long sickening slide toward my stomach, remembering that she had never lied to me. Not once. Not about anything. All at once I wished I could recall the question, go back to babies and kissing and plans for supper. But it was too late, she was already talking, her voice low and intense, her face downcast, her eyes hidden.

"He was very good. Expert. He knows all the right moves, all the right places to make you tingle, all the right words to make you shiver and melt. He's as expert at making love as he is at making money." She stopped and raised bright shining eyes to mine. "And he goes about it the same way, with logic and precision and cold efficiency."

"Sounds like a winner," I said, determined not to clear my throat or blink.

"He could make me soar, Danny. Like one of those rubber-band airplanes the boys used to make when I was a kid. He could wind me up and make my body fly." She studied my face for a long moment, her lips curving. "But not like you, my love. Never like you. He was almost not a part of it. He could play me like an instrument, make me simmer and then boil . . . but you make me burn, Danny; you turn me into a dancing blue flame. And you're the fuel, my darling. Without you the flame could not exist."

"That's damn near poetical," I said, laughing a little to keep from crying with relief, hugging her, the bleeding hole in my machismo closing with a tiny fluid snap.

"You're damn right it is," she said fiercely, squeezing my neck until it cracked. "And don't you ever ask me such a damned stupid question again."

"Not stupid," I protested, "but I'll own up to foolish."

I called Homer Sellers the moment she left for the supermarket, listening to the ringing phone and wondering if jeering fate had grown bored with mauling me at last, had, in jovial capriciousness, adjudicated my inept flounderings, my constant jousting with life, and decided to give me another shot at the wheel, another roll of the dice . . . or what was more likely, a baby step forward before two giant steps back.

"Sellers."

"Hi, Homer, I'm back."

His answer was a surly grunt. "Terrific. I'll send out the town crier."

"Thought you might want to know, buddy. She came back with me. We're . . . well, we're . . . well, we're back together."

"All three of you? That must be cozy."

"She's not going back to him."

"He might have something to say about that. He's hot at you, buddy. He was in here waving his arms and making threats. I finally had to set him down and talk to him like a Dutch uncle."

"Homer? You didn't tell him where we were?"

"That's a stupid question, Dan."

"Well, did you? Dammit, I have reasons ... I need to know."

"Hell no, I didn't tell him! I didn't tell you either and you make sure she knows that." He sniffed wetly and I held the receiver away from my ear while he blew out his sinuses. "And you lied to me, boy," he added tiredly, as if that was just one disillusionment too many, one betrayal too much.

"It wasn't a big lie, Homer," I said humbly, not feeling contrite at all.

"You useta not do that. Not to my face. Not looking me in the eye thataway."

"I'm sorry," I said, thinking he had been a cop too long, seen too much of the shit side of life, the vicious things people do who are hurting beyond relief, who pass the hurt along in the desperate belief that it will somehow help. But it never does.

"Yeah, you are," he said, and hung up the phone.

I put down the receiver and lit a cigarette, feeling a vague sadness. Not about Homer. Homer would mend. I had stretched our friendship to the breaking point too many times before. And like a broken vein, it had always slowly welded itself back together, the bond stronger than the original. But something was nagging at me and I couldn't pin it down. I was shrugging it away and turning when the phone rang. I yanked it up.

"Your friends the Wagermans," Homer said, his voice flat and harsh, "were dumped on four days ago. Two black men ... one big, big mother and a little guy. Did a damned good job of it. The oldest son, Tony, got a dislocated shoulder, the old man a broken leg. They all spent a day or two in the hospital. What do you know about that, Dan?"

"Only what you've just told me. I was up with—"

"I know where you were. But we both know who the big black man was, don't we? Dan, if I find out you had any damn thing—"

"Sorry, Homer, the doorbell is ringing." I hung up on him,

smiling, but taking no pleasure from the act. Besides, the doorbell was really ringing.

It was Jack Farley, handsome and natty in a lightweight blue silk suit, his face pale but determined, auburn hair neatly combed, eyes glassy and cold behind pale amber sunglasses, but not nearly so cold as the gun in his right hand.

"It's loaded this time, old man," he said almost gently, nudging me backward with the edge of a battered briefcase that swung from his left hand. "I hope you think it was worth it."

/17/

"This is crazy, man," I said, stepping through the gate into the narrow space between my neighbor Hector Johnson's cyclone fence and the side of my garage. "Susie's gone—"

"I know she's gone. I watched her go. And she won't be coming back. Not to you. She won't like what's gonna be left of you." He shoved me forward, past the pile of split oak logs stacked against the brick wall, past my riding mower and the Rototiller that Hector and I owned jointly. I reached the six-foot-high section of cedar fence that hid the clutter from the street and stopped. To my right I could see Hector's German shepherd, Rowdy, watching us with alert brown eyes, his long tail waving gently. He had woofed once when we came around the end of the garage, wagged his tail and grinned happily at this diversion in his long and boring day. I doubted that he had ever seen a gun, although he had heard them often enough.

"This is plain damned stupid, Jack, plain dirt stupid, and if you weren't in outer space you'd know it. You've already done enough to put your ass in the pen just waving that thing at me, threatening my life. And it ain't gonna do any good. Susie's—"

"Susie's gone home, hotshot. I saw the way she left. That's where she's gone to and that's where she's gonna stay. I'll do all the protecting that's needed." He took a deep breath, his eyes opaque in the shadows cast by the oaks, so pale in color they looked almost white, dead-fish white. "Back against the wall, Dan. Lift your pants legs one at a time."

I stared at him, uncomprehending.

He gestured impatiently with the gun. "The gun, man. The

little one you carry in your boot. I don't remember which one, so lift them both."

"I only carry that gun when I'm working, Jack. I don't work in my own home."

"Lift them, goddammit!"

I lifted them.

"Turn around, face the wall."

I shook my head. "If you're going to shoot me, you'll do it to my face."

"I don't plan on killing you, Dan. But I will if I have to." There was a cold crisp edge to his voice that made something inside me shiver and slide. I realized with a small thudding shock that what I had thought was determination was something else altogether: the glacial indifference of insanity or a man stoned out of his head. And Jack Farley wasn't insane. Not that I knew about.

"Turn around, man," he said, "or I'll shoot you in the balls." A small thin smile creased his impassive face. "That would be fitting." He pointed the gun at my groin and I saw his finger whiten around the trigger.

I turned around, my genitals shrinking, wondering if he knew how little pressure it took to fire an automatic. I was still wondering when he hit me on the back of the head with a stick of firewood.

Stars blazed: a dark velvet cloud pin-pricked with sparkling diamonds. Consciousness sagged along with my knees, and the second blow, high on my shoulder, probably meant for my back, missed its mark only because I was falling.

I swung on my hands and knees, my head pushed into the corner. I ducked as I glimpsed a moving shadow on the wall and only partially suppressed the scream that tried to rip through vomit clogged in my throat. The toe of his boot snapped between my ribs and hipbone and once again pain dominated my life.

"You son of a bitch," he said, grinding his boot heel into my calf. "I'm going to stomp your goddamned dick off. You won't use it on her again." He drove a toe into my thigh. "Turn over on your back."

I hung with my head pressed between the brick wall and the wood fence, watching the velvet darkness and twinkling lights recede down a long dark tunnel. I began shaking my head, more to help clear it than to deny his command.

"Turn over, man," he said quietly. "Better to lose your love stick than your life."

I kept shaking my head, the shimmering fog almost gone, the ground fading in and out, but ground again instead of blinding darkness.

"So far, Farley, it's still just between me and you. Any farther and it'll be the law, the whole state of Texas on your ass. You can still stop now, right now, and I'll let it go."

"Turn over, wife-stealer." He planted his foot on my hip and shoved savagely. "I won't tell you again."

"You have to know I'll kill you, Farley. You can't be that stoned, man." I was watching ants scurrying frenziedly between my hands and the anthill in the corner. A shadow danced on the brick near my head and instinct more than anything brought my rear end twisting into the cedar fence, feeling with infinite gratitude the exquisite pain of his boot smashing into my buttocks instead of my dangling genitals. I hunched forward, trying to blend into the brick wall, smothered in blinding paralyzing agony. His boot rocked me again; I wasn't sure where except to know that once again my genitals had escaped. For the first time I began to feel fear. I took a deep breath, let it out, then took another. Then I rolled over on my back.

I could see his face, six feet away, smiling. "Sensible," he said, his voice almost crooning, seductive. "Open up, little flower. Let's get this over with."

"No," I pleaded. "No, I can't." I drew up my legs protectively and threw an arm across my eyes. "I can't . . . I can't!"

He took a step forward. "If you make me shoot you, the

bullet won't stop. You may end up dying." He stepped closer. "With my boot all you'll lose is some meat. Think it over, man. Muscle and gristle, man, and balls are tough. Who knows?"

"Only once . . . only one time . . . please . . . just one lick . . ."

"Maybe," he said, the smile almost kindly, "we'll have to see." He took another step forward, then another. "Spread them wide, big man," he said softly.

"Jesus . . . just once . . . only one time . . . all right?" I didn't have to work at it to put a quaver in my voice.

"Open," he said, and pointed the gun at my face. "Last chance."

Staring at him as if mesmerized, I put a hand on each knee and slowly drew them apart. His head bobbed encouragingly. "Please . . . don't . . ." I let it trail off into a muffled sob.

His lips thinned over strong white teeth. "You're not so tough after all, wife-stealer," he said, and took a swift step forward, his right foot coming up, poising at the zenith of its swing, his face twisted, the upper lip curling, the opaque eyes unchanging. For one long second he seemed to hang there suspended, the lightweight material of his pants pulled tight across his crotch.

I roared a curse and kicked him, kicked him so hard between the legs that it lifted him off the ground, sent him windmilling backward, his arms flailing, his right wrist striking the top rail of the fence, breaking his grip on the gun and sending it sailing across Hector Johnson's patio.

Farley hung against the fence for a moment as if gathering his strength, his face dead white in competition with his eyes. His mouth worked, but there was no sound, no movement for that one second in time except his eyes rolling back into his head. While I watched, he slid down the wire fence to his knees, then rolled limply forward, his body slowly curling into a fetal ball, hands cupped tenderly at his groin.

"How's it feel, you son of a bitch?" I said, stretching my legs and lying flat on my back for a moment, waiting for the world to stop spinning. I eased a hand between my battered head and the ground and brought it out again. No blood. That was something at least. I moved my leg and felt an agonizing stab in my side, another in my left buttock. My right thigh felt as if a giant hand had reached in and plucked out one of the larger muscles, left nothing but raw jangling nerve ends. I breathed deeply and shaded my eyes from the bright September sunlight.

Goddammit, this kind of shit had to stop.

Using my other hand, I reached down and cupped my genitals gratefully, feeling an instant swell of relief, an even swifter rush of anger—and hearing noises.

I raised my head and looked at Farley. He was moving, bent double, hands between his legs, sliding along the brick of the garage, slow faltering steps on rubber legs that threatened to buckle at any moment.

I sighed and rolled over on my stomach, hoisted myself painfully to my hands and knees. I crawled to the fence and pulled to my feet. I looked at Farley again. He was at the gate, peering wildly over his shoulder, the pale eyes glaring. I grinned wolfishly.

"Leaving so soon, Jack?" I asked politely, watching him hitch himself through the gate and disappear around the garage after one last frightened glance. I lit a cigarette and followed him, bracing an occasional hand against the fence.

Rowdy was standing over the gun, looking at me and wagging his tail as if this were some new game and he were waiting for me to explain the rules. He looked down at the gun and extended an inquisitive paw.

"Leave it alone, boy," I said. "The son of a bitch said it was loaded this time."

Rowdy gave me a low gruff bark and sat down beside the gun. I made a mental note to retrieve it as soon as I had tended to Farley.

He had made it as far as the redwood patio table, and sat swaying on its edge, his feet widespread, hands hidden between his legs. I walked up beside him.

"Hurts, don't it?"

He raised his head slowly and looked at me. His eyes looked different; better, clearer.

"Stupid move, asshole," I said. "I thought you were smarter than this."

"Go to hell, cocksucker."

I reached out and rapped him lightly across the face with my open hand. "Dirty mouth too."

I started to grin, then changed my mind and shook my head. "Look, Jack, I know how you feel, or think I do. But she's made up her mind, man. And it's nothing against you. She says she loves you and I believe her. But not enough. We go back a long time and what's between us is never going away. I know that now and, what's more important, she knows it. Words of advice are empty things at a time like this, but take it from a guy who's been there, make the break quick and clean. It's easier that way for both of you."

His face had made a raid somewhere and picked up a faint tinge of color, but his expression had changed little except for the sickness of defeat around his eyes. We stared at each other in silence while I finished the cigarette. Then I shrugged and turned away.

"Hey, Dan."

I turned back. His hunched figure had straightened a little, his eyes glowing like pale cold fire.

"You were my hero. Did you know that? When I was eleven and my daddy wrote home about you from Vietnam. He sent pictures of him and you all the time. Did you know that? You ranked up there with Alan Shepard and John Wayne. I couldn't make a hero out of my daddy because I knew too much about him, you see. But I could with you, and I did. And then I came here. You took me in like your own son. That was great. I never told you, but it was great. But then I saw how you treated her, found out most of the situation, guessed about the rest, watched her when you were gone, listened to her cry sometimes late at night. I began to love her, and to hate you. But she wasn't having any part of me. I turned down jobs because that meant I'd have to leave her sooner. I tried her all the time, in every way I knew how. But it wasn't any good until that night. That one night." A shadow of pain crossed his face and he rocked gently, his eyes almost closing. He opened them again and blinked, then resumed talking, his voice steeped in scorn.

"You only want her money. Like everybody else. You had her for years and you treated her like shit and the first, the very goddamned first time you had a chance you run her off. And now she's rich and all of a sudden you want her back, you and your great undying love. Bullshit, man. You want her money and not her, and I think you're shit."

"You're wrong about the money, Jack." I took out another cigarette and watched his handsome sneering face, saw the loathing and realized I was talking to stone. I shrugged and fired the lighter, and it would have ended then if he hadn't decided to make one more try for my manhood.

I bent forward into the lighter's flame and heard the snick, saw the gleaming blade and knew instantly that if he wanted it I was a dead man. But he chose to go for my genitals again instead and he had to lunge for that.

I bowed, chopped viciously at his neck as his long arm went in under my torso. I felt a numbing jolt in my groin, cold fire along the inside of my thigh. Panic ripped through me in a paralyzing wave, and I watched him sprawl on the concrete with no thought of retaliation until he looked up at me and laughed.

I yelled a curse and stomped the knife out of his hand, kicked it spinning into the shrubbery at the end of the patio. I jerked him to his knees using a handful of curly auburn hair and hit him in the face.

Again and again, short, twisting, snapping blows meant to maim and not destroy. I felt a fierce soaring exultation, my own wound forgotten in the icy rage that fed my mindless frenzy, demanded retribution, gloried in the feel of hard bone on soft flesh, the warm slick smear of his blood on my hand, the primal rush of a just and easy victory.

I was launching one last blow at his fine aristocratic nose when I heard Susie screaming. But I couldn't call it back: watched helplessly as his nose collapsed beneath my fist, spouted blood, and he rolled moaning on his side.

"Danny! Oh, my God! What are ... oh, my God!" She dropped to her knees beside him, hands fluttering, tugging at his shoulders, wrenching his fingers away from his torn and bleeding face. Her hands flew to her mouth, her eyes dark seeping wounds in a field of white. "Oh, Jesus, Danny, what have you done? Oh, God, Danny, you've killed him!"

I shook my head numbly, unable to speak, a crushing pall of weariness and pain crashing down on me, leaving me teetering on my heels, helpless before my own guilt and her fury.

She helped him to his feet, urging him on with soft exclamations, taking his stumbling weight on her slender shoulders, looking at me only once, her eyes blazing with brightness I couldn't face. "You ... you ..." Her voice choked, and she turned and led him tottering around the corner of the house. I heard the clang of the gate and stood there unmoving, heard the roar of her car engine and stood there still.

And then a car door slammed, a rapid tattoo of heels, and she stood at the corner of the house, her face white but determined, wild-eyed and anguished.

"I—I can't ... not now ... I—I ... oh, God, Danny, what were you doing?" And she was gone, the sounds fading in the distance, blending with other sounds, with the noise inside my head where the dying cells were groping to find an answer to her question.

I found it hours later, on my knees before the commode, watching the swirling water, wiping my mouth on toilet paper and grinning at my own cleverness:

"I was jousting for my maiden, babe."

And in that moment of cold desolate loneliness came the most bitter of all epiphanies: I had lost her, again.

/18/

"Well, what do you think?" Big Boy Doheny stood waiting as I stepped down out of the thirty-two-foot motor home, grinning happily, his huge muscular frame resplendent in yellow shorts and a black tank top.

"It's yar, Big Boy," I said.

He cut his eyes at me. "What's that mean?"

"It's an old nautical term us honkies use. It means good, fine, great, okay—take your pick. I heard it in an old Jimmy Stewart movie once. First chance I've ever had to use it."

"Yeah, well, it's yar all right. Man, you oughta tool that baby around a little. Drives like a sports car."

"Yeah, I can imagine."

"No kidding, man. It handles great. I don't see how in hell I got along with that old camper I had. Damn bunks were all too short by about a foot. I got a super-king-sized bed in this sucker." He paused and looked at the big vehicle reflectively. "Maybe it was nostalgia."

"What was nostalgia?" I asked, leading the way down the walk to the house.

"Keeping that old pickup camper all them years like I did. I humped old Clarice the first time in that little doodad."

"That's fascinating." I closed the door behind him and made sure it was locked.

"It is to me. Man gets sentimental about a thing like that."

"Yeah, ranks right up there with your first hangover and your first case of clap."

He looked at me across the table, his broad face creasing in a worried scowl. "Man, you're down tonight." He sat down abruptly and picked up the drink he had made before our excursion to see his motor home. "What's the matter, old buddy, it didn't work out with Susie, huh?"

I paused with my drink at my mouth and put it back on the table. "What do you know about that?"

"Aw, come on, man. Her husband's my damn investment man after all. You know how he is. One night last week we had a few drinks and he was crying on my shoulder again. Telling me what an asshole you are. Hey, man, I don't pay any attention to that little turd. He's sharp as a pin with money, but he don't know shit about living, about hanging on to a beautiful woman."

"He's doing a pretty damn good job so far." With a lot of help from me, I added silently, feeling a dull ache as I thought about the last time I saw her, her face stricken and filled with anguish.

"I've seen them at parties. He gets a few drinks and he embarrasses her. I guess he resents her having the money. Maybe that's why he's trying so hard to make it in that investment business of his. And judging from what dealings I've had with him, he's doing great. I went in with a million, man, and in less than three months he laid a hundred grand on me. That's twenty-five percent a year any way you add it up."

"Is that good?" I asked, only half listening, remembering the dark tragic eyes seeping tears over the battered bleeding face, remembering it had been three long days and I had heard nothing from her.

Doheny barked a satisfied laugh. "You kidding, man? With guaranteed principal? It's unheard of." He twirled the glass on its edge. "Even old tightfisted Clarice is getting interested. She goes in, man, he's got it made."

"So what? I get a guarantee on my money market funds, too. He's probably got some kind of insurance."

Doheny frowned and raised shaggy brows. "I don't think that's how it works. Anyhow, I can't lose, and he must be pretty damn sharp to make that kind of return."

"So what?" I said again, tired of the subject, tired of money talk and of hearing about Jack Farley, boy wonder. "I wish him a long prosperous life and much happiness."

He shook his big head and leaned forward earnestly. "Don't sweat it. It'll screw you into the ground if you let it. Hell, I've been hurt by women so many times I'm thinking about having my middle name changed to Pain."

"Speaking of pain," I said, "I understand somebody laid some on some people named Wagerman out in the county. Two black men, they say."

"Only one black man," he said, grinning hugely. "Clarence is my chauffeur. He just likes to watch, hold my hat, like that."

"Dammit, Big Boy, don't you know things like that are against the law, that you can get your big ass in a crack?"

"Them assholes put a stain on my pride coming in my house that—well, your house—thataway and gang-banging you right under my nose."

"Okay, Hank, I appreciate the thought, but I can fight my own battles."

"Hey, I know that, but I don't see why you should have all the fun. Anyhow, you was all busted up. Ain't no telling how long before you coulda got around to them. This way everything was still fresh in their brains." He emptied his glass and grinned. "What they had left."

"You took all three of them, huh? I've never seen the oldest son, Tony, but the old man and youngest boy looked pretty stout."

He screwed up one eye and carefully measured whiskey into a glass. "Yeah. Funny thing, though, they didn't much want to fight."

I laughed. "Shit, I wonder why."

"Naw, I don't think they was all that much afraid of me. I wasn't carrying a gun or anything and they could see that. Even when I said your name real sweetlike they just looked at one another. I had to get high-handed and low-down mean before I rattled their chains enough to get them excited. Them bastards don't fight fair, neither. That youngest shit almost took my head off with a round rod with a hole in it."

"Well, all the same I think you took a big chance. That old man would open you up just to see if he could fit all the pieces back together again. And I've heard Tony is even worse."

He nodded. "He's mean. That old sucker never did say a word, he just come in swinging a pipe wrench as long as my arm."

"You don't look marked up any."

"That's the first thing you learn as a black kid in South Dallas—how to duck."

"Yeah," I jeered. "Now I guess you're gonna tell me about your deprived childhood."

"Man, it wasn't depraved, it was just poor."

"Not depraved, deprived," I said, not realizing until I finished that I sounded condescending.

"Yeah, man, I heard you the first time. Deprivation generally leads to depravity sooner or later, in one form or another."

"True," I said, a little surprised, then realizing that being surprised was condescension of a sort. I looked up to find his eyes on me, bright and shiny.

"Hey, man, I went to college. I even studied some. I know some words besides 'hut' and 'honky' and 'motherfucker.' "

I laughed and took a sip of my drink, watching a squirrel scamper along a high wire toward the giant oak in the center of my backyard that contained his home high on a forked limb, wondering about its predecessor, a bobtailed male who had lived there for five years. More friendly than the rest, as agile and bolder than his tailed brethren, he had been a victim, in my mind, of some old buck's burning zeal to castrate the competition, in his haste missing the tiny balls, severing instead the baby tail.

"Hey, man, did you see them license plates on my new machine?"

I shook my head. "I guess I missed them."

"HONKY 1," he said, and bellowed a laugh.

"I hope you're not planning on taking that thing through Mississippi or Alabama."

"Aw, man, that redneck shit don't go no more. Things has changed. Look at me and you. Ten, fifteen years ago we wouldn't be here drinking whiskey together. Man, I had some good honky friends back when I played ball."

"They weren't your friends, Big Boy, they were your teammates. There's a difference."

"You saying a black man and a white man can't be friends? Man, look at us. We're friends, ain't we?" An edge of belligerence had crept into his whiskey voice.

I gave him a sardonic laugh. "Shit no! I'd turn on you in a minute if you wasn't so damn big." I sneered and took a drink. "Or so rich," I added succinctly.

He stared at me—hard—and I began to wonder if maybe I hadn't gone a little too far, tweaked the grizzly's nose once too often. Simple perversity or a secret death wish? Probably the same thing that had made me want to be a bullfighter at fifteen, a high-wire acrobat at twenty, and a jet test pilot at twenty-five. Fortunately, I decided too late in life in all three cases.

I looked back at him and grinned. "Don't mind me, man. I'm shedding my skin."

His broad face smoothed and he bellowed a laugh. "You son of a bitch, you had me going there for a minute." He slapped the table. "Damn, you a mean sucker."

I nodded morosely. "It's the goddamned time of year. Can't make up its mind whether it's winter, summer, or fall. Early northers and thunderheads. Hot as hell one day, cold and blowy the next." I drained my glass and lit a cigarette with unsteady hands. "September's got a weird song this year, and man, it's a bitch," I added, hearing the high keening in my chest, remembering the taste of sun-heated flesh and hickory nuts, the mournful dirge of a lonely coyote, soulful sighs by a babbling brook. "But maybe it's who you hear it with."

"Shee-it, man, that's almost poetical," Big Boy said, lifting his glass, his eyes gleaming like polished jade in the failing light.

"Shee-it yourself, big man," I said, pounding my glass on

the table. "I feel the need for music, wine, and women, and not necessarily in that order."

His face lit up. "Damn, I thought you'd never ask."

We flipped for east or west, but I think Big Boy cheated. He looked too pleased when he announced that "Fote Wuth" had won and that we were going to his favorite of all favorites, the Sow's Belly Inn, Number Two. When I asked him about Number One, he said it had burned down during his last visit.

/19/

Despite Big Boy's urging, I refused to drive the mammoth machine, accusing him of wanting me along only to chauffeur him so he could ride shotgun like the boss nigger in a Georgia chain gang. Growling obscene suggestions involving impossible physical contortions, he wheeled us more or less in a straight line across Midway City and south on Highway 157 to the old turnpike.

We had the wine, or whiskey at least: a road bottle of Jack Daniel's he dug out of a secret compartment in the floor near the driver's seat. We had the music: country pop I think they called it, melancholy stuff about losing men and chasing women, lonely roads and empty beds. Music for the never-hads or the couldn't-keeps. Fitting music, I thought, for a melancholy September night.

And Doheny almost caused a forty-seven-car pileup trying to get us the women: two hitchhikers somewhere near the Beach Street exit. He tooled across three lanes of traffic to get to the shoulder, horn blaring, emergency lights blazing, finally coming to rest fifty yards ahead of the girls, two young-looking things in country western attire complete with white cowboy hats and cute little orange boots.

While we waited, I argued with Big Boy, telling him I had really meant only wine and song in convivial surroundings, that I had been talking about women only in the abstract.

He took his eyes off the rearview mirror long enough to give me a snaky grin. "Man, it don't make no difference what they're wearing, they won't have it on long enough to matter."

"Shit, Big Boy, you're fixing to get our asses sent to the pen. They didn't look a day over eighteen."

"Yeah, man," he said, and pressed a button on the dash. The rear door swung open with a pneumatic hiss, and the girls clambered inside out of breath and giggling. Big Boy met them, courtly and elegant in the blue blazer and white pants he had donned before we left my driveway. A yellow silk ascot and ostrich boots completed the ensemble, and I was certain he would have worn the new pearl Stetson if his head hadn't already been scraping the ceiling. He carried it in his hand instead.

"Welcome, ladies," he rumbled, his voice two decibels lower than before, stopping three feet away from them and bowing, giving them time to assimilate his blackness, his bulk, his obvious wealth, and the ingratiating manner reminiscent of a boss pimp at a New York bus station. He wagged a sausage finger at them. "Don't you ladies know it purely ain't safe for ladies like yourselves to be out alone on the highways at night?"

"Our car broke down." The taller of the two, a cool-eyed willowy blonde, tilted a hip against the edge of the dinette booth and crossed her arms under ample breasts while I revised my age estimate upwards by ten years.

She smiled wryly. "I guess it's the outfits. No one seemed to want to stop and help us out." She leaned slightly farther to the right and looked around Big Boy at me. "We certainly appreciate you gentlemen stopping."

"We was just talking about that very thing," Big Boy said exuberantly. "Outfits, I mean. How they don't matter nowadays. But only in the abstract, of course." I could see his wide grin bunching his cheek.

The other girl, shorter, plumper, prettier, giggled and waved a flirtatious hand. "My, you're the biggest thang I've ever seen up close." Her voice rang with the soft nuances of the South, the silky resonance of attenuated consonants and elongated vowels, a voice that brought to mind corn bread and milk gravy and fried quail, murky hollows and sharp ridges thorny with steepled pines. She had creamy skin and dimples, freckles across her nose, and an air of sweet innocence that lasted only until you reached snapping brown eyes that glowed with old knowledge and outrageous lust. She blinked up at Doheny slowly in a look that spoke more than a bared bosom. She raised a pretty, short-fingered hand to poke at red ringlets bunched beneath the rim of the hat.

"I'm Clara," she said, "and this is Jill." She lowered the hand and held it out to be shaken—or kissed or sucked on— her eyes said she didn't much care which.

"I'm Big Boy Doheny, late of the Cowboys," Big Boy said fatuously, "and this is intrepid manhunter Dan'l Roman, the last of the rugged individualists." He took Clara's hand.

Jill leaned to look at me again, her eyebrows raised. She had a narrow face that just missed being lovely and wide-spaced gray eyes that quietly scanned without apparent movement. Her mouth was generous, well shaped, and she had an air of reserve that could have been shyness or distrust. Considering the times we live in, I opted for distrust.

I nodded without smiling and she did the same, then shifted her slender body back out of sight behind Doheny.

"Where in the world could you nice ladies be going all dressed up like that?" Big Boy was drooling, the redhead's hand still clutched in his mammoth paw.

"Barney's Barn," Clara said coquettishly, making no effort to retrieve her hand.

Big Boy flipped his Stetson onto the dinette table and whirled, changing the redhead's hand from his right to his left. He slapped his hand against the wall of the motor home with a hollow boom that made Jill jump and look at him uneasily.

"By God," he bellowed. "Dan'l, can you believe that? That's where we was going, ain't it?"

I shrugged. "If it's in Fote Wuth, I guess so," I said, glancing at Jill and grinning at her cynical expression. "He's driving," I explained.

"Well, hell," Big Boy gushed, "whyn't we just take you ladies on over there with us?"

"What about your car, Clara?" Jill asked coolly as the chubby redhead's head began bobbing at Big Boy's suggestion.

"Oh, that old thing. It's just that silly old fuel pump again. I'll have Joey pick it up tomorrow." She pursed Kewpie doll lips and smiled up at Big Boy, her eyelids drooping again. "Joey's my brother."

Big Boy released her hand and slapped his own together. "Well, by God, now that we got that settled, whyn't I just whip us up a little drinkie. Just name it, ladies, and old Hank'll whip it together."

Clara looked confused. "Who's Hank?"

"That's me. Big Boy's just what the fans and groupies call me. My good friends call me Hank. You can call me Hank."

"Why, thank you, Hank. That's a pretty name. Better than Winslow."

Big Boy stared at her for a moment, then slapped his hands together again. "Okay, what'll it be, ladies?"

"Big Boy," I said, "I hate to bring this up, but we're parked on the freeway. Cops might take a dim view of that. Not to mention we could get creamed at any second."

"Hey, that's right. Well, look, man, why don't you just drive us on out of here while I slap some tonic together and show the ladies my little home here."

"That's cool, but I don't have any idea where Barney's Barn is."

"I thought that's where you were going," Jill said, the cynical expression back in place. She pushed by Big Boy and Clara and leaned on the back of the outrider swivel chair. "It's out on Highway 199," she added with only a small trace of irony.

"He was driving," I said, shifting the still-running motor, gaining a little speed on the shoulder, then bulling my way into traffic. An eighteen-wheeler whistled by only inches away and the big vehicle rocked gently. "It's his party. I'm just along for the ride."

She moved over into the passenger's seat. "This is a beautiful motor home," she said, running a slim hand along the soft leather padded dash. She trailed a finger along the juncture of the dash and the windshield. "Good detail work. I know, I used to do this kind of work."

Behind us Big Boy laughed and a mixer whirred briefly.

"Cossack's Kiss! By God, that's a lot of drink for such a little thing like you."

"I might be little, but I'm—" The rest of it was lost in Big Boy's bellowing laugh.

"Your friend certainly is full of . . . life," Jill said dryly.

"Yeah, he's full of it, all right." I took out my cigarettes and offered her one. She took two and lit them from the dash lighter, then handed me mine with a small smile. "I hope you don't mind. I'm not wearing lipstick and I don't have herpes."

I laughed. "That's an accomplishment these days. All it takes is a casual kiss."

"Then it's simple. Don't kiss casually."

She leaned forward and raked her cigarette across the tongue of the ashtray. She sighed deeply. "Sometimes it's not all that simple."

I glanced at her ringless hand. "You're not married?"

She shook her head. "No. Divorced. Are you?"

"No."

"I didn't think so. It would be difficult to be a rugged individualist and be married." I could feel her eyes on me. "You have been married, though." It was more of a statement than a question.

"Yes."

"I thought so. You have the look of sad disillusionment about you."

"Sad decrepitude is probably more like it. I'm getting old and wearing thin."

"You don't look all that old. Forty-seven or -eight, maybe."

I looked at her and grinned. "Forty-five, but who's counting."

"I'm sorry," she said, smiling, really smiling for the first time, a wide smile that eased her gently from almost lovely to damn near beautiful. "I'm lousy at ages. I'm thirty myself and that's a dangerous age for a divorced woman."

"How so?"

I could hear the shrug in her voice. "Still young enough to dream that something wonderful will happen, but old enough to know it won't."

"What makes you think us old folks don't dream once in a while? Without being asleep, I mean?"

Her hand came out impulsively and covered mine on the wheel. "Oh, I'm sorry, I didn't mean—"

"Hey, you two," Big Boy bellowed. "Name your game. We're already two ahead of you."

"I'll take a rain check," I said. "I'm driving."

Jill swiveled sideways in the chair. "I'll have a Tom Collins if you have—"

"Tom Collins coming up!"

Bottles rattled and clinked, and a moment later he lumbered up the aisle, smothering a curse as his head cracked against a dome ceiling light. "Here you go, little lady, just happened to have the fixin's handy." He stood swaying, grinning. "Just sip on that, see if she's all right."

Jill tasted the drink and smiled at him. "It's fine, thank you."

"Right on! You two getting along all right up here?"

"Yes. I was telling Mr. Roman what a lovely motor home you have."

"Don't it shine! I was just fixing to show Clara the rest of it." He leaned down and looked through the windshield. "Hey, man, it's early yet. They don't get to humping out at Barney's until eleven or so. Whyn't we hook a left up here and drive out along the lake? That all right with you, Jilly?"

I could see her looking at me in my peripheral vision, then down at her drink. She ran a slender finger around the rim of her glass. "Yes, I think that would be fine."

"Hey, great!" He turned and pounded back up the aisle. I heard something that sounded like a slap, a high-pitched giggle, a squeaking door, then silence.

Jill sighed and swiveled to face the front. "Clara. She's a little . . ."

"Flaky," I said.

She laughed softly. "That, too, I guess, but she likes to . . . to ball."

That didn't seem to need a comment from me, so I lit

another cigarette and kept my eyes on the traffic. The silence grew until it became awkward, then impossible.

"Nice night," I said finally, then gave up when she still did not reply.

It wasn't until we were turning into the threadbare Lake Worth park that she stirred.

"I guess I do, too, Dan," she said, from her end of the silence. "Ball, I mean."

/20/

"I'm sorry, Jill," I said, moving away from her, standing up beside the dinette bed and slipping into my Levi's, more embarrassed than frustrated. I sat down on the edge of the bed and reached for my boots. "It has nothing to do with you. I want you to know that."

"Hey, man, it's all right, okay? It happens. Nobody's ready all the time. The only difference with us women and you men is we can fake it and you can't."

I slipped into my shirt and took out my cigarettes. I lit two and handed her one. "I don't have herpes either," I said, grinning.

She smiled wanly. "It would be a little late, wouldn't it?" She puffed on the cigarette and eyed me, her expression speculative. "You didn't have that much whiskey, and it's certainly not your age . . . What is it? Your ex-wife?"

"Maybe. But I'd really prefer not to talk about it, if you don't mind."

She sighed, spewing smoke. "A torch, huh? Well, I can give you lessons in that. I don't know if you'll believe this, but you should feel honored. You're only the second since my breakup two years ago. The first one was a bouncer, caught me on the rebound, balled me on the fly, you might say. I don't really count that one. This is the first time I've really been . . . oh, what the hell, back to the vibrator." She scooted across the bed to her feet, tall and slender with breasts a tad too heavy for her body.

She started past me toward the front, then stopped, her gray eyes shining, almost a burning blue. She leaned into me for a second. "You had me going, sad eyes. Too bad, sad blue eyes like yours make me a little crazy. I'm really great when I'm crazy." She smiled a thin warm smile and weaved away toward the front.

"I'm sorry, Jill. . . . I don't know what else to say." I sat back down on the edge of the bed.

"Don't say anything, honey," she said, leaning forward to stub out her cigarette in the dash ashtray. She straightened and came to stand in front of me. "Just tell me you won't think I'm a . . . a . . . well, whatever, if I go in there and join them." Her eyes blazed defiance, but there was an edge of pleading in the small wavering smile.

"I haven't heard anything for a while. I think they're finally asleep, or dead."

"I'll wake them," she said succinctly. "Tell me, old man, what do you think?"

I smiled and nodded. "You're thirty and full growed."

She leaned down and kissed me. "I won't tell him. I'll say I wore you out and you're asleep."

"That part don't matter a damn. You don't have to lie."

"I know, but I will." She smiled the wide-open smile again. "I really need to, Dan."

"Then don't look back," I said.

I found a beer and walked along the lake. But not before I heard the surprised grunt and then the rumbling bellow of pleasure. Excited voices and tinkling laughter; I walked away listening to the jeering twitter of gossipy nightbirds, the heavy moan of the malicious wind. I kicked rocks into the placid water, swatted viciously at buzzing mosquitoes, and with malice aforethought tried my damnedest to stomp the life out of a small black snake I found sliding across my path. None of it helped.

Dreams are sometimes like people; they hang around long after the party's over, making an ass out of themselves, being a nuisance in general, boring the host out of his gourd. Not that my dream was boring: it's difficult to be bored with a two-hundred-and-fifty-pound black snake coiled around your body squirting globules of Jack Daniel's at your parched and aching throat, bellowing sonorously that it's good for what ails your whanger, honky, growling hideously and sinking great white square teeth into your shoulder, squeezing painfully, shaking viciously when your breathing interferes with the rhythm of your intake.

But dreams are sometimes born of reality, and the stabbing pains in my shoulder were real enough, as were the dry throat and growling sonorous voice.

"Come on, Dan, dammit, wake up!" Homer Sellers's blunt fingers bit down again, sinking into flesh still yellow-green and tender.

"Shit, Homer, cut it out!" I tried to raise my arms and found that I was securely bound in a rolled and twisted sheet, mute evidence of a wild nightmarish night I gratefully couldn't remember beyond the somehow poignant dream about the snake. I rolled over on my stomach and felt my bonds loosen. I thrashed and squirmed until I was free, then lay blinking up at Homer's florid face, trying to understand what was going on.

"How did you get in?"

He waved a beefy arm, his voice disgusted. "Damn, I lost that one. I bet myself you'd ask what time it is."

I yawned. "I don't give a shit what time it is, and I do care how you got into my house."

"I have a key, remember—somewhere. But I didn't have to hunt for it. Your door was unlocked."

"Oh, hell." I swung my feet to the floor and reached for a cigarette. A tiny dibble of pain hit me squarely between the eyes. I gripped the lighter with both hands and waited until the flame came back into focus before searching for the end of the cigarette.

"Look at you. You're shaking like an eighty-year-old man."

"I was born an eighty-year-old man."

"Where the hell you been the last three days?"

I shook my head and massaged the bridge of my nose. "What've we got now, Homer, a police state? I have to check in and out with you when I go somewhere?"

"I was by here Saturday afternoon," he said, his voice suddenly gruff. "I saw that big-assed motor home parked in your driveway. Belongs to that big black mother, I guess. You been out catting around with him, I reckon."

"Why didn't you stop?"

"Naw, he's not my type."

"You getting prejudiced in your dotage, Homer?"

He rolled thick shoulders beneath a lightweight tan sport coat. "Not much in common, is all."

"How do you know until you meet him? He's not all that much different from us, Homer; he laughs, drinks whiskey, and tells dirty jokes the same way we do. He even stands flat-footed to piss the way—"

"I didn't come here to get no damn lecture on race relations." He pushed away from the wall, his red-rimmed eyes scornful. "You stink. I'll wait in the den while you take a shower."

"Yes, Daddy," I said, grinning a dry cracked grin at his indignant back as he marched solidly out of the room.

"Little early for you, isn't it, Homer? Middle of the afternoon on a working day? You know what they say about the perils of loose companions and booze and ladies of easy virtue."

"I don't see no ladies," he said a little shamefacedly, chucking the rest of the scotch into his mouth and smacking his lips. "A little pick-me-up never hurt nobody. Besides, I don't get by so much anymore and I miss this good scotch of yours. I wish I could afford it." His blue eyes glinted wetly. He took a handkerchief from his jacket pocket and blotted them carefully, then unfolded the cloth and bunched it around his nose. He blew lustily.

"Damn sinuses and these stupid contacts. I don't know

which is worse." He watched me slosh vodka into a glass and curled his lip. "You drinking your breakfast now, boy?"

I shrugged and lifted a bottle of orange juice from the small refrigerator under the bar. "Vitamin C, Homer, best thing in the world to start off the day." I dribbled a spoonful into the vodka and put it away. I grinned at him until he looked away, then quickly raised the glass with both hands.

"What're we going to do about Susie, Dan?" he asked quietly, taking a plastic-tipped cigar out of his coat pocket. "I thought you told me you had her back."

"The best-laid plans of mice and men," I said, using only one hand to raise the glass. To hell with him, he'd seen me shake before.

"Don't get cute!" he shouted suddenly. "Goddammit, Dan, this is serious!"

I studied his flushed face, the blue eyes that had turned as dark as gunmetal. He had snapped the cigar in half and he stared at the pieces helplessly for a moment before throwing them into the ashtray.

"I'm sorry, man," I said, realizing all at once how often I was apologizing lately, "I know you love her too, but it's your problem—or was—now it's just mine."

"I'm not talking about that," he said, his voice reduced to an impatient rasp. "I'm talking about the Wagermans, the pig they left on her doorstep."

"Pig."

"Yeah, pig, as in ham and bacon. A little pig. Hanging on that big beam that holds up their little front porch. A little pig, gutted and skinned and its throat cut."

"Jesus Christ!"

"And a sign that said THIS LITTLE PIGGY SQUEALED." His face had changed color, pendulumed to pale.

I stared at him silently, the slowly spreading warmth from the whiskey arrested by sudden jolting shock, my face tingling with heat. I drank the rest of the vodka, mildly surprised to find my hands were no longer shaking. I reached for the bottle mechanically, my mind's eye suddenly alive with images of her: wide-eyed and frightened a few seconds after the banana exploded.

"Well?" His face was bunched, impatience battling with contempt. "You just gonna stand there swilling booze or are we gonna talk about it?"

"What's to talk about? She made her choice. She has a husband. Let him protect her if she needs it. Which I doubt. Wagerman would have to be a stone idiot to do anything to her after all the bullshit that's gone down. Dammit, he's still on parole. You could probably get him sent back for consorting with a known criminal, his son Tony." I lifted my glass and gave him a mocking smile. "Anyhow, partner, you're the cop here. I'm just a saddle tramp passing through. I've had my charity handouts and a few nights' lodging. Now it's time for me to ride off into the sunset, as they say."

He stood up, tugging his jacket together in front and buttoning it, his hand reaching to straighten a nonexistent tie. His eyes burned with scorn. "You make me sick," he said. "You useta be a hell of a man, buddy. Steady, sensible. I'm older than you, but if I'd been the kind to have a hero—"

"Don't lay that hero shit on me. Last guy who did that tried to cut off my balls."

"But now you're a lush," he went on as if I hadn't spoken. "And even that ain't so bad. I know some nice guys who are lushes. But you just don't give a damn. You don't care about anything or anybody, least of all yourself. Just because your daddy died a drunk—"

"That's enough, man. I got enemies for this kind of shit. I don't need my friends dumping on my ass."

He shook his shaggy head, his eyes holding mine, deep-set and darker again. He walked toward the door. "I don't think you have to worry about your friends any longer, Dan. Friendship is like taffy candy. It'll stretch and draw thin and hang together a hell of a long time, but finally, buddy, it'll break."

"Is that a threat or a definite commitment?" I heard the sneering words and a small part of me wept silently, with no thought of tears.

He went out without answering.

"Home team zero, visitors one," I said aloud into the empty room. I trickled the last few drops from the vodka bottle and searched the back bar.

"Johnny Walker, where are you when I need you, babe?"

/21/

Maybe it was my alleged death wish that made me more or less dash to open the door when the chimes began chiming, or, more likely, the sudden swelling images of Susie standing there sad-eyed and penitent, sweetly begging forgiveness. Whatever the reason, I wasted no time peeping through the peephole, just threw the lock and yanked it open, fully expecting to see her dark eyes beaming at me like tomorrow's sun.

I saw instead the dark yawning holes of a double-barreled shotgun, twelve gauge.

I stared dumbly, looked along the barrel at heavy brows and a wide forehead, pale nondescript eyes that glistened like raindrops on cold metal. A strange face, heavy and square, but oddly familiar.

The gun moved forward and I backed up.

"Search him." This from lips hidden behind the stock of the gun, a voice guttural and harsh.

Another face appeared at his shoulder, slipped past him, another face heavy and square with long hair that I recognized. Karl Wagerman.

"This is plain damned stupid," I said, feeling the young man's hands slide down my thighs, trying to remember when I had said those words before, wondering vaguely about my intense feeling of déjà vu. "You're the Wagermans," I said, "and I've got no fight with you."

Tony Wagerman laughed harshly. "It don't work that way." He gestured with the short-barreled gun balanced across an arm bound tightly with tape and white bandages all the way from his elbow to his neck. "Move it, cowboy, you've got a date."

I shook my head. "I'm not going anywhere with you."

"Bring him, Karl." Tony Wagerman backed toward the door.

I glanced over my shoulder in time to see the stocky figure squat. I felt thick arms encircle my hips, pinning my arms and lifting me a foot off the floor. We lurched forward and I had to duck my head to keep my brains away from the top of the door. Two-hundred-odd pounds and I had the feeling he could have carried me around the block at a loping run if need be.

A white van had been backed into my driveway, the rear doors gaping open. I looked at the dark silent houses around me and wondered until I realized it was almost midnight and all the righteous hardworking citizens were safe in their beds. I heard Rowdy bark and thought about screaming, but by that time we were at the van and I was flying through the air into darkness.

My knees and elbows made hollow clanging sounds on the metal floor covered with a thin sheeting of carpet. I rolled on my back and heard the click of the lock on the rear doors, then their footsteps and voices as they came toward the front.

"Are you going to tie him up?"

"No need," Tony Wagerman said, climbing into the bucket seat and swiveling it to face backwards. "There's a chance Pa may not kill you, asshole, but if you try any shit, I goddamned sure will." He reached behind him to the dash, flicked a switch, and a dim light came on over my head. "Just lay down, cowboy, and enjoy the ride." The motor came to life, and the van eased forward to the street. It turned right.

I scooted until my back was against the metal wall. "You ever hear the story about the Hatfields and the McCoys, Wagerman? That went on for years. I figure we're about even. Don't tip the scales."

His laugh was almost genial. "Whose idea of even, cowboy? You come into our place of business, stick a gun in my old man's face, scare him half to death, then send your nigger friends to finish the job. Man, you got some idea of justice."

"I got in one good lick," Karl said. "I slammed that big black mother's jaw with a piece of bar stock."

I tried again: "I had nothing to do with that."

His thin lips drifted apart in a sneering smile. "I hear you, cowboy. We'll see if you can take it as well as we can."

"Cops," Karl said tensely.

"Get down!" Tony jabbed me with the gun menacingly. "Down flat! And stay there. Keep your damn mouth shut!" He stretched out his right leg, held the gun alongside, the barrel never wavering from my face.

The van turned sharply and speeded up. Karl craned his neck to look in the rearview mirror. "Okay," he said. "They're not following us."

"How about the night you came to my house—" I broke off as Tony jabbed me again.

"I told you, goddammit, to shut up!"

I shrugged and took out my cigarettes. I had been trying to maintain some sense of direction, but the sharp turn and the subsequent ones had me disoriented. Not that it mattered a hell of a lot. I would know where to find them when the time came—if it ever did.

"There's a car over there on Chester Point," Karl said, confirming my suspicion that we were somewhere near Midway Lake, a three-thousand-acre man-made reservoir at the eastern edge of Midway City. During the hot summer months the small lake had a tendency to smell like rotten cabbage and putrefied fish, and I had driven the ribbed, rutted road that crossed the dam enough times to recognize its peculiar rhythm.

"It's okay, it's empty," Tony said. "Probably some fishermen. I don't see any lights down on the bank, so they must be on the other side of the point."

Thirty seconds later the van rolled to a stop. Tony gestured with the gun. "Now you can tie his hands. In front. There's rope in the side pocket."

Karl grunted and crawled around his seat. "How about his feet?"

"No. We don't want to have to carry the son of a bitch."

"Do I get a blindfold too?" I mashed out the cigarette on the carpet, thinking about the empty elastic pocket in my boot, the little .32 automatic on the closet shelf at home.

Tony watched alertly while his younger brother tied my hands, the pale eyes glittering, the mocking smile challenging.

I winked at him over Karl's shoulder with whiskey bravado that was rapidly wearing thin. "All trussed up and no place to go."

Tony chuckled. "I'll say this for you, cowboy, you ain't lacking in guts. We'll see how long they hold up. Now move back to the rear doors. Karl, you go let him out."

Karl opened the doors from the outside. I scooted across the greasy carpet that had the same odors of burned oil I had noticed at the machine shop. Karl helped me along the last few feet by closing a big fist on my shirt front and yanking. He put me down and pointed to the front of the van, his flat pallid face expressionless.

As I had suspected, we were on the rutted gravel road that crossed the Midway Lake dam. Established for use by maintenance crews only, the road had off and on over the years been a lovers' lane of sorts, a shortcut for fishermen, and, before the public rest rooms on Chester Point burned down, a cruising strip for local homosexuals. The chains strung between metal posts at each end had been cut and stolen so often the city fathers had finally given up.

But there were no lovers tonight, no fishermen, and no homosexuals that I could see unless my captors had interest beyond incest that I knew nothing about. Fifteen feet below us the dark water lapped and gurgled fitfully against the rip-rap, affected little by the stiff western breeze that whipped my hair across my forehead and dried my mouth. A sour taste boiled up in my throat and I hawked and spat toward the water.

"Son of a bitch!"

I felt a sharp blow to the center of my shoulders and stumbled forward into the dim glow of the van's parking lights.

"What's the matter?" Tony's voice came from in front of me, out of the shadows around a pickup truck parked fifteen feet away. A bulky figure with one white leg loomed at the rear of the pickup, leaping into sharp definition as Tony switched on the truck's back-up lights. Dalton Wagerman, his lined face revealing no more than it had in the dim light of his office, leaned against the truck's tailgate, his left leg bound in a gleaming white cast all the way to his hip.

"The son of a bitch spit right in my face!"

I glanced over my shoulder. Karl Wagerman scrubbed furiously at his skin with a large red bandanna, his face writhing with loathing. "Shit, man! I oughta stomp your nuts. Goddamn spit in my face!" There was an edge of shrill hysteria in his voice, thick with horror and revulsion.

"Come on, Karl. A little spit ain't gonna kill you." Tony appeared beside his father, handed him the sawed-off shotgun, then reached over the tailgate and brought out a long narrow bundle wrapped in a burlap sack. His mocking eyes on me, he unrolled the bag and brought them out one at a time: short slender baseball bats brightly gleaming with newness.

"Bought 'em today," he said matter-of-factly. "Little Leaguers. Got a nice heft. Oughta bust a few corpuscles." He handed one of the bats to his father and took back the shotgun. "Okay, cowboy, let's play some ball."

I cleared my throat, feeling Karl come up behind me, the last vestiges of the whiskey fog draining out of my brain like hot water through a sieve. "Mr. Wagerman. Unless you're planning on killing me, which I doubt, you must know this is the craziest thing you've ever done. I let you get away with it the other time because maybe I deserved it a little coming at you like I did, and you didn't do any major damage. But if you use those things you're going to break something I won't be able to overlook—"

"That's the idea, cowboy!"

"And as far as the girl is concerned, she's being well protected. The police are aware of what's going on and anything, any little thing you do to her—"

"This is bullshit, man!" Tony Wagerman swung the bat

into the pickup's tailgate with a hollow bong. "You're talking bullshit, cowboy, and it won't do you any good. The old man can only barely hear you and can't talk at all. They cut his tongue and busted his ears in the joint. And the police can go suck, man. Our sister's of age and she's living with us because she wants it that way. And she's got all the protection she needs." He paused, breathing hard. "Get him over here, Karl!"

I felt myself being lifted again, hard steel bands that squeezed mercilessly, bringing forth old, almost forgotten pains from my yellow-green bruises. My head finally clear, I realized that I had lost whatever chance I might have had and wondered dimly what James Rockford or Magnum would have done. Something, certainly. Intrepid heroes that they were, they would never for a moment submit docilely to a senseless maiming at the hands of cretins only one small step above morons—

"Stand him here," Tony ordered, and I felt his hands at my belt, felt a wash of cool air as my pants dropped around my ankles, followed by my shorts.

—A flashing attack with educated feet, perhaps, gross features smashed and torn and bleeding, pummeled into insensibility by clubbed righteous fists—

"Put him here," Tony said, and I felt myself being lifted once again, slammed across the sideboard of the pickup, the metal cold against my stomach, balanced there by a horny hand on my neck while Karl clambered into the pickup's bed. Karl hooked a booted heel between my bound hands and stretched my arms, dropped to one knee and grasped my triceps with hard bruising fingers. He pulled forward and my feet left the ground.

Tony patted my bare buttock and I saw the old man's head and shoulders at the tailgate, the bat held at port arms.

"I'm gonna pulverize your ass, cowboy," Tony said almost gently. "And then Pa here's gonna break your legs, one at a time." He rapped me lightly with the bat.

"I get my licks," Karl said, his breath stirring the hair dangling on my forehead.

"That's the game plan," Tony said, rapping me a little harder. "Anything else happens, it'll probably be your fault."

"You can stop now, Tony, and I won't kill you."

He laughed and hit me again—hard. Bright blisters of pain brought a groan through my clenched lips and a flood of saliva into my mouth. I swallowed convulsively and clenched my teeth again, closed my eyes as the time for the next blow neared, feeling the swell of saliva and holding my breath.

But time dragged on and nothing happened. I heard Karl grunt and was suddenly aware of shrill cacophony, of bright lights against my eyelids and screaming voices:

"Hey, lookit the queers!"

"Hey, you fruity assholes! You guys taking turns?"

"Goddamn fags!"

"Lookit that guy's ass!"

"Hey, you wanta bite on this . . . ?"

"Shit," Tony snarled, his feet grating on the gravel. "Goddamn kids. Musta been in that car—"

"Hey," Karl bellowed in my ear. "You goddamned kids turn off that light! Get your asses out of here."

"Go to hell, fairy!" A young voice, high and shrill with defiance and excitement.

"Robbie Williams!" Tony yelled. "I know your father, man." He moved again and I felt him brush against my feet. "He'll bust your ass for being out here this late."

I raised my head and looked over my shoulder. Tony was standing directly behind me, thick-shouldered, his head high and cocked with anger. He raised the bat and hit the guardrail for emphasis, and I drew up my legs, arched my body in an impossible arc, and kicked him squarely between the shoulders.

I heard his yell, saw the bat go into the air, his arms windmilling as he sailed forward, diving headfirst into the jagged riprap below.

"Hey!" Karl was yelling, his mouth open.

I hawked and spat a mushy globule of saliva and phlegm into the gaping orifice.

He screamed hoarsely, wetly, turned me loose and lunged to his feet, gagging, spitting, trying to retch.

I squeezed my wrists around his heel and jerked savagely. His hands fled his mouth as his arms scrabbled frantically for balance.

I yanked again.

He fell backward across the sideboard of the truck; a startled grunt, and something banged hollowly against the sidewall as he dropped out of sight.

Out of the corner of my eye I saw Dalton Wagerman lurching around the end of the truck, the other bat gripped in both hands high above his head, hoarse animal grunts and a pallid face working with a madman's rage.

I shoved with my bound hands, dropped free of the truck, and leaped clumsily toward him. The pants tripped me, but my momentum carried me inside his swing; his wrists chopped my shoulder and the bat flipped almost harmlessly against my hip.

But the move had cost him his balance, and I stepped back and watched him tumble helplessly forward, sprawl into the gravel and dirt, a choking scream burning his throat as the broken leg banged against the metal guardrail.

I stood breathing heavily, sucking the air in huge gulps, barely aware of a car motor coughing to life and a high thin voice:

"Hey, man, right on!" Lights flashed across my eyes as the car spun in a tight circle, roaring away into the trees behind Chester Point.

I awkwardly pulled up my pants and walked around behind the pickup. The shotgun was propped against the bumper and I grabbed it without stopping. Karl was on his hands and knees, shaking his head and retching dryly. I stepped forward and hit him behind the ear with the stock of the gun. His shoulders hunched and he groaned, his head going almost to the ground. I hit him again. He fell forward on his face without a sound.

Dalton Wagerman was where I had left him, his face milk-white and his eyes closed in agony. I poked him in the cheek with the gun barrel until the dark eyes opened. There were tiny slits, but enough to let me know he was conscious. To my left I could hear a monotonous drone of cursing, a rattle of rocks as Tony Wagerman climbed slowly out of the water.

I placed the bore of the gun two inches from his nose. "I told you once, old man, but you didn't listen." I clicked off the safety, the tiny sound amazingly loud in the silent night.

Tony Wagerman had stopped cursing. I could dimly see his dark outline against the pale blur of the rocks.

"Hey, cowboy, listen—"

"You didn't acknowledge me that night, you tough old shit, but if you don't nod your goddamned head tonight, you'll lose it. It's over. All of it. And that includes the girl—especially her. Just nod your head. That's your word and I'll accept it. I'll kill you sure if you don't and I think you know that. So nod your head, old man—or not. It's up to you."

"Hey, cowboy—Pa . . ." I lifted my head and Tony's voice choked off.

With the car lights gone the light was poor, but I could see his eyes, open wide now and gleaming, and my heart sank as they stared up at me balefully, unblinking—raw defiance or pure insanity, I had no way of knowing which.

But a promise is a promise and empty threats have no meaning in the lexicon of an ex-convict or a madman; I tightened my finger around the trigger, closed my eyes and took a deep breath.

Then with a hoarse bellowing curse, I whirled and sent the gun winding into the lake. I stood trembling, staring into the glittering eyes that hadn't wavered. I whirled again, lifted my arms and pointed at Tony Wagerman standing just outside the guardrail, his face jagged with cuts and streaming blood.

"Keep away, man. I'll kill all of you next time."

"You got it, man," Tony said earnestly. "I swear . . ."

I walked stiffly to the van, climbed in, and started the motor. Driving slowly, carefully, I backed the van across the dam until I could turn it around. I sat there for a moment

sawing at my bonds with my penknife, watching the dim
figure of Tony hobbling between his father and his brother.

I drove home crushed with weariness, chilled and shivering
with the knowledge of how close I had come to killing again.

/22/

"Aw, come on, man," Big Boy Doheny said, crunching beer nuts between strong molars with the sound of a boar hog eating a lump of coal. He arched bushy eyebrows in what he apparently thought was a lascivious leer. "Them two ladies, Clara and Jill, are raring to go. We'll make a long weekend out of it, man. Nashville music and maybe some good old Tennessee barbecued pussy. I got Honky 1 all stocked and ready to go—"

"Can't do it, Big Boy," I said. "I've got a job."

"A job? What the hell you mean, a job?"

"A job. You know, where you work, where you earn money?"

He frowned. "Hell, man, you don't need no job. If you need any money—"

"Money isn't everything, Big Boy. I need the action. I need to be moving, hit the road for a while, smell a different wind, see a different face, hear a different song." I gunned the rest of my Bloody Mary.

"Bullshit," he said, looking alarmed. "Hey, man, where the hell is this job, anyway? Hell, I'll hire you myself. I'll pay you double—"

"That's not the point. What I do is find people. You should know that better'n anyone. Somebody needs to be found, and I've been hired to find her, and that's that."

"It's a her, huh? Somebody's wife run off with the church deacon?"

"None of your damn business, Big Boy, but, yeah, something like that. Not a deacon, but a pornography salesman, if you can believe that. Left a good old boy and two small kids.

Left a nice home and a loving husband to run off with some yo-yo who sells smut out of a suitcase."

"If that don't beat all. Where'd a housewife meet somebody like that, anyhow?"

"Who said she was a housewife?" I sighed. "She and her husband run a bookstore in Dallas. He'd been coming in off and on for six months or so pedaling his wares. Then bingo, a month or so ago she left her husband a bye-bye note and they took off for parts unknown."

"Which bookstore?"

I gave him a sardonic smile. "Worst part was she cleaned out their operating expense account, something better than five thousand."

"Jesus! I'll bet he was pissed."

"No," I said slowly, remembering the gangling awkward man with thinning sandy hair and soft gray eyes filled with puzzlement and pain. "He wasn't angry, just confused."

Big Boy snorted. "Damned if I'd want her back, leaving two little kids thataway."

"You never know what you'd do, man, until it happens to you."

"How you gonna find her? How do you know where to start looking?"

"In this case it's easy. She called her husband collect a few days ago to ask about the kids. Collect calls are logged. I know a man at the phone company. All I have to do when I get to Houston is find the address that goes with the phone number. That's no big deal."

"What if she called from a booth?"

I shook my head. "We tried the number from his bookstore. His wife answered."

"Why didn't he just ask her to come back?"

"She wouldn't let him. She wouldn't talk about anything but the kids." I lit a cigarette and shrugged. "He's convinced that if I can find her, he can fly down there and talk her into coming back." I looked through the bay window at the darkening day. "I don't believe it for a minute, but it's his money and his life and I'll give him his chance if I can."

"You won't bring her back, huh?"

"No, that's not what I do. Just like with you, I only find them, I don't go dragging anybody back anywhere. I couldn't legally if I wanted to, which I damned sure don't. It's a sorry way to make a living, but it keeps me out of the nine-to-five rat race."

"You don't have to work," he said, giving me a sneaky knowing grin, "you just like this shit. You're like an old hound that just has to get out every so often, put his tail in the air and his nose to the ground—"

"How the hell do you know I don't have to work?"

The grin widened. "I told you once, man, I ain't fool enough to let anybody who carries a gun go chasing me unless I know something about him. Anyhow, I probably heard that from Susie or Jack."

"Do you see them a lot?"

"Quite a bit. Susie and Clarice are good buddies. Clarice makes sure they're invited to most of the parties we go to and we visit back and forth some, like that." He paused and glanced sideways at me. "We haven't seen Susie since . . . well, since she went back to Jack."

I made another Bloody Mary and watched Rowdy sitting dignified and stately in the corner of Hector Johnson's yard. He was watching the parade of squirrels along the high wire to their home in my big oak tree. He had long ago given up fantasies of pursuit and capture and now often sat and watched their sometimes teasing antics with aplomb and monumental indifference. The bobtailed squirrel, in particular, had delighted in teasing him, running along the top rail of the fence, chattering, swooping low along the wire, dropping to the ground a few feet away. But, to my knowledge, not once had the shepherd's cool reserve succumbed to the primal instincts that must have been raging in his brain.

Big Boy slapped the table with thick, splayed fingers. "Man, I just got me a piss cutter of an idea. You said Houston, right? When you planning on going?"

"I'm not sure," I said cautiously. "I suppose early in the morning."

149

"Right on, man, better and better. Tomorrow's Friday. Them girls can take off tomorrow and Monday. We'll catch us an Oiler game—"

"Hey. Hold it. How do you know them girls can take off? Some people have to work, Big Boy. Otherwise they don't eat. I suppose you're just going to call up their bosses and fix it for them, huh?"

He rubbed a big hand down across his face and followed it with a snaky grin. "No need to fix nothing. Them ladies are working for me."

"Jesus Christ."

"Now wait a minute. It ain't nothing like it sounds. Them girls are upholsterers. We just happen to own a furniture factory, is all. I'm paying them more than they was making in Fort Worth."

"Giving them more overtime too, I imagine." I shook my head. "I'm sorry, man. I'll need my car in Houston—"

"Hell, that's no problem. We'll hire you a damn car. Come on, man, we'll have us one of them tailgate parties that'll blow their minds."

"I think you need a pickup for that."

"We'll get us some of that soul food, barbecued ribs and fried chicken—"

"What? No watermelon?"

"Hell, yes, some of that, too, if you want it. And seafood. Man, I'm partial to seafood. Shrimps and lobsters and them little bits of things that come in little paper cups like candy."

"Diced barracuda hearts."

"Is that what they are? Well, anyhow, man, some of them. What do you say?"

"I don't know," I said, thinking about it, suddenly feeling the need for ribald laughter and dirty jokes, the jaded camaraderie of desperate characters even more insouciant than I. And, anyway, I wasn't looking forward to my brand-new case in Houston, another variation to an old and worn-out theme, a lonely bewildered husband and another weeping woman.

"Well, what about it, bro? Do we taste the sweet fruits of

life this weekend or do you cry in your beer in some lonely bar?"

"Lonely's a state of mind, buddy, not a location, but yeah, you've got yourself a honky."

"Shee-it! Old lucky me." He wagged his head in mock disdain, but his eyes were shining like a three-year-old's on Christmas morning.

"Well," Jill said, popping the tab expertly on a can of beer and handing it to me with a flourish. "Maybe now that it's semiquiet back there we can finally talk." She opened a beer for herself and propped bare feet against the padded dash. She tasted the beer and swiveled a degree or two in my direction. "Well, how's our intrepid manhunter?"

"I hunt women, too," I said, "and sometimes kids. Not often, but sometimes."

"Is it exciting work, hunting people?" She was wearing short-shorts, or today's equivalent, and her slender tanned legs seemed to glow in the sun like molten honey.

"More than a blowout at sixty-five, but it can't come close to pepperbelly food and spring water in Juarez."

There was a huskiness in her laugh I had never noticed before. "Hank said you had someone in Houston you were looking for. Is it a man or woman?"

"A woman," I said, keeping my eyes on the traffic that had become noticeably heavier as we approached the outskirts of the sprawling confusion that was Houston. I had a feeling she knew all about it from Big Boy, but I played it straight. "A runaway wife."

"What makes a woman do that?" she asked, then went on to confirm my suspicions. "Run off with a man who obviously isn't of the same caliber as her husband."

"In answer to your first question, there are probably as many answers as there are women who do it. And who can judge the caliber of a man better than a woman who loves him?"

Her chair swiveled another degree or two. "Do you really believe that?"

"No," I said, smiling. "A woman in love, or infatuated, is

no damn smarter than a man, and that's usually just one baby step above a babbling idiot."

"And you think that's why she did it, because she was in love with the porno salesman, or infatuated."

I shrugged. "I'm just a dog-eared detective and not a psychologist, but I don't have to go to the textbooks to figure out a reason for a thirty-five-year-old woman running off with a twenty-six-year-old man, a handsome, smooth-talking rascal according to her husband."

"Maybe," she said dubiously, and lapsed into silence, nursing her beer.

I lit two cigarettes and handed her one, then turned my attention back to the rumbling, belching monsters around me. Freeway madness. Tiny scuttling bugs and angry behemoths vying for the same space on a treadmill to nowhere. A battlefield without honor, with mechanical drones instead of soldiers.

"I've been thinking, Dan. About the other night." Her voice was small, oddly shy.

"What night?" I asked, for lack of something better.

"You know what night. The night I—we couldn't make it together."

"Not we, babe. I. I was the one who couldn't make it. It wasn't your fault, I told you that."

"Oh yes, it was. My mother didn't teach me much, but she taught me that much. A woman is always the one who makes or breaks it with a man sexually—and you know that." She ran a thumb along her thigh, creating a trough of white that rapidly disappeared behind her hand.

"That's not always true," I said, picking my words carefully. "A man can be tired, preoccupied, nervous—"

"Baloney," she said vehemently, her face resolutely turned toward the bruised western sky. "There were a lot of things I could have done. I was intimidated by you, even a little scared, I guess. Everything went out of my mind. I must have done something stupid."

"You didn't do anything."

152

"That's a fact," she said bitterly. "I hardly even touched you."

"That's not what I meant," I said, not exactly sure what I meant, not sure if I was on the offensive or defensive. "Look, what I mean is that it was impossible not to be aroused by you ... at first. But then other things ... other thoughts intruded—"

"Your ex-wife," she said quietly. "Hank said you were carrying a pretty big torch."

"Hank has a big damn mouth."

"He likes you. He talks about you like you were really something ... you know what I mean, like you're somebody he would like to be, but can't. He says you really shine, man."

"Maybe I'm his hero," I said dryly.

She bobbed her head soberly. "Yes. Something like that. He looks up to you. He says you have a weird code of honor, but he doesn't hold that against you."

I chuckled, then felt it escalate into a smoke-filled, choking laugh. She leaned sideways and pounded me on the back, smiling faintly.

"Watch it, Pedro, you're driving. What's so funny, anyway?"

I shook my head and coughed, then cleared everything out with a wash of beer.

She gave me another light blow for luck, then straightened in her seat. She stubbed out the cigarette and put her feet back up on the dash.

"I don't suppose you'd want to try it again."

"Nothing has changed, Jill."

"I don't suppose you'd want me, anyhow, now that I've slept with him."

"Not because of that, although I imagine he'd be a hard act to follow."

"Yes," she agreed solemnly, "he's pretty fierce. He's going to wonder if we don't sleep together tonight, so I guess—"

"I don't care what he thinks, Jill. I told you before—"

"But we don't have to do anything," she went on hastily. "We could just lie and talk, or sleep. Or maybe if you wanted, fondle a little bit. I don't really want to go back in there with him, Danny."

"Sure, that'll be fine. I like to fondle as well as the next guy."

"Good then, it's all settled." She drew her feet into the seat with her, laid her head on her knees, her face toward me. I could feel her eyes, her smile.

"He's right, you know."

"Who's right about what?"

"Hank. About you. You do shine . . . a little bit."

Big Boy dropped me off at the car rental agency that tries harder and, after hanging around long enough to make sure there were cars available, drove away amidst a clashing of gears and the grinding clatter of the diesel engine. While I waited for the car I borrowed a phone and called the number my Ma Bell contact in Fort Worth had given me.

I gave the guy who answered my contact's name and asked for an address to go with the telephone number I had obtained from Loren Wainwright. But it wasn't enough, and since this world has come to be a dark suspicious place and all its inhabitants are either paranoid or wary, he wanted to know who I was and why I wanted the information.

"I'm Captain Homer Sellers," I said, "of the Midway City Police Department, badge number 302."

"I don't know if that's true, do I? I can't see your badge over the phone. Why wouldn't you go through official channels?"

"I ordinarily would, but you see, it's a personal matter. I wouldn't care for my many friends in the Houston Police Department to know about . . . well, to make it short, it's my mother . . . well, hell, it's hard to talk about, but, you see, she's run off with a younger man, left my daddy flat on his back in an oxygen tent. And that's not the worst part."

"What could be worse than that?"

"Well, we have reason to believe . . . aw hell, reason to know, that the guy she ran off with is a pimp and he's . . . he's turned her out."

"My God! How old is your mother?"

"Well, she don't look a day over sixty. But that doesn't

155

matter a lot; he's got her working them retirement places, you know, like Happy Harvest Village."

"You have my sympathy, Captain Sellers, but I don't know . . ." His voice trailed off vaguely.

"Twenty dollars is the going rate in Midway City," I said.

"Oh, no, I couldn't do that. That would be . . . unethical." He hesitated, a soft whistling sound coming over the wire. "But I am partial to Chivas Regal."

"Shall I bring it to your office?"

"Oh, no! I'll give you my address." He giggled. "If you can't trust a police officer, who can you trust?"

"Certainly not my mother," I said, listening to his loud braying laughter, understanding why Diogenes died a sad and disillusioned man.

The house that went with the telephone number was located in a quiet, well-kept neighborhood a half-hour's drive from the rental agency. And that in itself presented a problem of sorts. Time was a man could sit quietly behind a newspaper on a neighborhood street and not arouse much more than mild curiosity, could expect at the most a polite roust by the neighborhood cops, who would generally leave you alone if you smiled a lot and had an up-to-date P.I. ticket, a logical reason why you needed to be where you were. But times have changed; we live in an aware world. Crime statistics on the six o'clock news have turned us into a nation of Nervous Nellies, the more insouciant citizenry finally joining hands with the timorous old maids in a united assault on the lurks and the moles, the loiterers and would-be Peeping Toms. All of which makes it damn near impossible for a hardworking private detective to do his job.

So I was forced to resort to the oldest ploy in the manual. I made a turn around the block and, half a block from my desired location, opened the hood and crossed two spark plug wires. I coasted to a lurching, backfiring stop across the street and two houses away from the moderate-sized brick house I was interested in. I got out and stood listening to my chugging machine, scratching my head and walking around it. Finally I threw up my hands in disgust, slipped out of my jacket and buried my head beneath the hood.

I worked busily with screwdriver and wrench, withdrawing the coil wire to the point of intermittent contact, creating coughing, sputtering havoc on those occasions when I climbed inside and gave it a hopeful try.

Creeping twilight was rapidly bringing down the curtain on my little charade when the silent gray-brick house showed its first signs of human habitation. The front porch light came on. A man stepped through the door, a tall heavyset man with dark, earlobe-length hair and a heavy drooping mustache. His features were indistinguishable in the growing gloom but I was satisfied I was getting my first look at Archibald Malone, glib proliferator of human smut, stealer of wives.

He was followed almost immediately by a slender, dark-haired woman in a sleeveless summer dress that ended inches above her knees. She waited on the steps while he attended to the door, tugging on the dress with one hand, fluffing with the other the mass of dark auburn hair that looked black in the twilight. A well-formed woman of thirty-five, Meg Wainwright had an air of impudent gaiety that came through in the impish smile, the twinkling green eyes in the photographs her husband had given me.

I watched them walk toward the rear of the house, toward the light-colored sports car I had noticed on my first pass around the block. I uncrossed my plug wires, plugged in the coil, and wiped my hands leisurely on my handkerchief. I was inside the car when they backed out of their driveway, had my own car running more or less smoothly by the time they turned the corner. I followed slowly, memorizing the pattern of tail and stop lights, fixing the silhouette of the low-slung car in my mind. Not that I expected any problems tailing them, but the private eye's handbook preaches diligence, admonishes emphatically to always be prepared. I often wonder if maybe they stole that from the Boy Scouts.

*   *   *

He left her in a small frame house in a slightly seedy section of older Houston called Mulligan Heights. He went inside long enough to turn on the lights, then kissed her at the front door and drove away in his Ferrari, big and bulky and somehow ludicrous in natty blue blazer and white pants, a polkadotted ascot and snap-brimmed Stetson.

I sat and fretted for a while, smoking and pondering. I needed a closer look at her. Reasonably certain she was the green-eyed pixy in the photographs Wainwright had given me, I had to be positive before dragging my client away from his business. Also, I was puzzled. While the gleaming Ferrari could conceivably fit into the modestly plush surroundings of the house on Cantrell Street we had just left, it had no validity here in this area of cracker-box houses, struggling cottonwoods, and transplanted mulberry trees. It made little sense that Malone would maintain a separate residence for his newfound mistress; that she would hold still for it made even less. Unless, of course, he had a wife who had been away, who was due home and was a narrow-minded type who might object to a ménage à trois. But even that made almost no sense. There had been no attempt at furtiveness that I had seen. Malone and the woman had moved openly, almost leisurely across the yard and up the driveway to the car, sitting ducks for nosy neighbors spying on philandering husbands. No, there was another reason for this seemingly meaningless maneuver, and I was still pondering when the green Chevrolet pulled into the driveway.

A dark figure climbed out, stood looking around for a moment, then crossed the short walk to the door. The front light came on and the door opened. I caught a glimpse of a bright red, floor-length robe and my own light came on in my head.

/24/

Somber cynic that I sometimes am, I waited through two more masculine visitations before I would allow what little was left of my belief in the sanctity of marriage, the inherent saintliness of motherhood, go slithering right out the window with my cigarette smoke.

She was hooking. That was the plain and simple truth. Hooking for a sleazy purveyor of filth, and I saw in my mind's eye Loren Wainwright's honest, bewildered face and bled for him, saw smaller faces with red-rimmed eyes that couldn't understand, and wanted to break something, feel the crunch of Malone's porcine flesh and smell the copper in his blood.

Twenty minutes after the third man left, I saw his car turn the corner.

Malone was pulling into the driveway when I got out of my car. I crossed the street swiftly, breaking into a trot when I reached the ankle-deep grass of the yard. Near the porch he heard me coming and turned, instant alarm spreading across a narrow saturnine face with a Zapata mustache and bangs.

I pulled up, breathing hard, let my coat drift open so he could see the gun, lifted the thin worn case from my pocket, and flashed the badge I had worn when I was a cop.

We looked at each other. I smiled and put the case back into my pocket. "You still want to go in?" I asked politely.

His grin was feeble but his voice was strong: "No. No, I had about decided I had the wrong ... you know, the wrong address. I was looking for the ... uh, the Armbrusters." He looked up at the house numbers tacked to the wall. "But no, this ain't their house, after all." He waved an apologetic hand and moved toward his car. "Uh, thanks for ... for your help."

"You're welcome," I said. "Have a nice night."

I watched him back up and drive away, pondering again, already regretting my impulsive action, feeling with resignation the physical and mental interactions that were my own peculiar harbingers of impending stupidity, knowing deep inside that it wasn't going to end here, accepting with something approximating relief that I was going to break Roman's first law of nonintervention, break it and anything else that happened to blunder into my path.

I turned and walked up the single step, crossed the squeaking wood floor, and rapped lightly on the door, watching her come into view through the curtained door glass.

"Oh," she said a moment later, her eyes going past me, a small crooked line slashing across a wide smooth brow peppered lightly with freckles. "Oh, I thought you would be Archie. There were only supposed to be—" She broke off and dredged up a miserly smile, rolling her slender torso in a resigned shrug. She stepped back and opened the door.

"But that isn't your problem, is it?" The smile warmed a little, stopped short of mirth. Her eyes seemed darker, the lucidity missing, the tantalizing sparkle I had seen in the photographs gone. One hand combed through her tangled hair as she closed the door.

"No," I said. "I have a problem, all right, but that isn't it." I grinned tightly and stepped close to her. I linked my left arm around her waist and yanked her against me. I put my right hand on her breast, molded it through the cloth. "I bought you for the night," I said huskily. "Archie said you were the best."

"I—I am," she said, then spread her eyes wide in alarm. "The—the whole night?"

I nodded sagely. "The things I like to do . . . it takes time. I don't like to be rushed."

"Look, I—"

"Perhaps a golden shower first," I said dreamily. "You think you'll be up to that right away? If not we can wait until later. We could start with . . . oh, maybe a trip around the world . . ."

"I—I don't think—" She broke off, blushing, the color draining away as fast as it had appeared. "I couldn't do . . . that . . . those things. I only . . ."

"Missionary freak," I said scornfully. "Don't tell me you're one of those. Archie said—"

"I don't give a damn what Archie said," she said furiously, pulling against my arm. "I told him . . . he promised me—" She broke off as I let her go, stumbled backward, cinching the robe tighter around her waist. "I think you'd just better go."

"Hey, baby," I said. "I can't do that. You're bought and paid for. You're mine for the night. Hey, we've got a lot of time. You'll get used to it. These kinky things kinda grow on you. We'll start off slow with a little head—"

"Oh, God," she said, the flash of resistance disappearing, her face suddenly stricken. "Please, I—I'll give you your money . . . I'm sorry, I just can't . . . can't do those things . . ."

"Why not, Meg?" I asked quietly.

"I just can't—" She stopped, blinking slowly, her eyes staring at me with something like horror. "My—my name is Wanda." She wet her lips. "Who—who are you? Did Archie tell you . . . ?"

"I don't know Archie. I'm that way with pigs. I have trouble telling them apart. As far as I know he's off somewhere rooting for truffles."

"Who—what are you doing here?"

I backed up a step and sat on the arm of an overstuffed couch. I took out my cigarettes. "I don't think I can answer that," I said. "Not with any great degree of accuracy. I know why I'm here, I just don't know why I'm in here talking to you."

"But who are you? I don't understand."

"My name won't mean anything to you. It's Dan Roman and I'm a private investigator. Your husband hired me to find you. Well, I have, and I'm not particularly proud of it."

Her fingertips grouped at her mouth, pressing against quivering lips. "My God, Loren did that? Was—is it the money? I—I don't have it—"

"It isn't the money, lady. He wants you back. I'm not sure why."

Her shoulders slumped, her body swaying. Her hands dropped to do battle near her waist. Her head shook vehemently.

"No! No, he wouldn't. It must be the money. He wouldn't want me . . . me back. He called me a . . . a tramp . . . a slut . . . said I wasn't fit to raise our daughters."

"When was this?"

"A week . . . two weeks before I left. When I . . . he found out I had been . . . had been to bed with Archie."

"I wouldn't pay too much attention to that. It's a stressful thing. A man tends to say things he doesn't mean at a time like that. But the fact of the matter is, he does want you back. If I was doing my job right I'd be on the phone right now telling him where to find you instead of sticking my nose in where it doesn't belong. And I don't know why except it's not often one meets a woman who leaves two beautiful daughters, a good home, and a husband to run away to be a hooker."

Her eyes burned at me, the corners of her mouth turning down. "You think that's why I left? To be a whore?"

"Appearances can be deceiving, but I don't see a manger and those guys I just saw leave here weren't the three wise men."

"I—we were . . . are broke. We needed money. Archie said . . ."

"What happened to the five thousand?"

"We—Archie put it down on his . . . our car." The flat planes of her pale cheeks billowed fleetingly with defiance, the small chin firming up. One thin nostril flared gently as full, almost pouting lips crimped together in a tight pink line. "We have to live . . . eat," she added sullenly. "Archie lost his job."

"What about the place on Cantrell Street? Why do you come here?"

"That's Archie's home. His mother left it to him. We couldn't . . . work there."

"You love Archie, huh?"

She nodded without speaking, her head turned slightly away, the defiance melting out of her features, leaving them soft and unformed. I suddenly realized with a small thrill of shock that she was a beautiful woman, and I wasn't all that surprised when I felt a gentle tug somewhere deep in my vitals.

"Or maybe he's just better in bed than the old man, huh? Trickier maybe? Considerate? Knows just what a woman wants, wants to hear? Knows all the right buttons to push?"

"Why don't you just please leave?"

I sighed. "Nope. Not yet. I've broken the law and I have to pay for it. My own law, but it's binding, nevertheless. Let me tell you, Meg, how this is going to go. I'll call your husband and tell him I've found you. Okay so far? Then he gets into his best suit—which you probably picked out for him—and he comes galloping off down here with flowers in one hand and a box of candy in the other—"

Her hands came up to cup her face. "Oh, God, no! Not now. I couldn't face . . . please, can't you just go away, just say you couldn't find me . . . I'll pay you . . . I'll . . ."

"What with, Meg? You said you were broke. Oh, I see. You'll pay me with the proceeds of your night's work. Or better yet, maybe a nice little roll in the hay."

"You're despicable!" The green eyes were sparking fire, two red spots burning high on her cheeks.

"You meet a lot of despicable people when you're a whore, Meg. You better get used to it. A lot of them are going to be the kind of guy I was when I came in here tonight. Are you up to that? I don't know how long you've been at this—"

"Just two days," she said, her voice low and fluttering. "And I'm not a . . . not really."

"Oh, I see. How many times does it take? Ten? Fifty? A hundred?"

"Would you please leave now?"

I nodded and stood up. "Okay. I guess I'm wasting my time. And I'm damn sure your time is a lot more valuable than mine." I lit another cigarette and stood looking at her downcast face. "It's just that I'm a hopeless romantic. I had this flash, this crazy notion that maybe you'd had your fling, that maybe you'd had it out of your system. Your husband told me how young you were when you married, about the two babies that came along right away. I know he's quite a bit older than you, and I thought maybe you were going through a thing about trying to recapture your youth. I know about things like that, you see. Age and youth. Sometimes they mesh, sometimes they don't. I guess this time they don't." I walked to the door. "I'm sorry to have troubled you. And you don't have to worry, I'll tell Loren I couldn't find you."

"He wouldn't want me now," she said. "Not now. Not after this. Maybe . . . maybe the other thing . . . with Archie he could have accepted. But not this. You don't know him." Her hands ripped apart, fluttering in the air like startled doves.

"You're right," I agreed. "I don't know him. I only met him once and all he did was hire me to find you. He didn't hire me to be the town crier."

She raised her head, the green eyes darker, almost a burning blue. "What are you saying?" Her voice was low and husky, barely above a whisper, her face flushed, contorted with emotion I could only guess about.

"I'm saying that I'm not a blabbermouth. I'm saying that you can leave with me right now and Loren Wainwright will never know what you don't tell him. What you don't tell him can never hurt him . . . or you."

"Oh, God . . . you think I could?" All the blood had fled her face again and she swayed, one hand going out to the wall to steady herself. "I don't know . . . Archie . . . he won't let me—"

"Archie's not even in this. Archie's somewhere peeping around a rock."

"I don't know . . ." Her voice faded, a querulous moan.

"Do it, Meg," I said. "You'll never have a better chance; you may never have another. I can put you up in a motel and you can call him yourself. He can be here in a matter of hours."

"Oh, no, I'd need some . . . some time to . . . to think, to prepare." Her hands flew to her hair, fluffed, combed, came back to her face, rubbed her cheeks the way a man tests his five o'clock shadow. "I'd need some time," she said again in a small hushed tone.

"All right. I'm down here in a motor home with some friends. We're staying over the weekend for the ball game. There's plenty of room. If you want, you can go back with us Sunday evening."

Her face lit up. "You don't think they'd mind?" she asked timidly.

I walked back and sat down on the arm of the couch. "Get your things, Meg, if you have anything here. We can go by the house on Cantrell—"

She shook her head quickly. "No, no. I only have a few things. The new things I've bought are too . . . too—" She broke off and smiled a tremulous smile. "I'll only be a minute."

It took longer than a minute, but I didn't mind.

/25/

Big Boy and Clara welcomed Meg with open arms. Jill nodded politely and watched silently with a small cool smile while I explained that Meg was an old friend who had found herself stranded and needed a place to stay and a ride back to Dallas.

"That's cool, man," Big Boy bellowed exuberantly, his eyes shining, assessing Meg as if she were a delectable little hen and he was the only cock that could crow. "You got good taste in old friends, man."

"I like your name," Clara said, her round little face beaming. "It's better than Lorena." She slipped a short arm around Big Boy's waist and leaned her head into his armpit. "Big Boy has a short one, but I like it," she said dreamily.

Big Boy grinned down at the top of her head and patted her hip with a big leathery hand. "She's talking about my name. It's Hank. All my friends call me Hank. Big Boy's for the fans and groupies."

"They follow him around," I said. "In droves. I hang around to protect him. You haven't seen anything until you've seen a Big Boy groupie in full heat. They'll walk right into a twelve-gauge scattergun."

He reached around Clara and gave me a playful punch that jarred me to my ankles. "You just wait'll we get out at that stadium. You'll see they ain't forgot old Big Boy."

Meg was smiling faintly, staring at him with an expression that wavered somewhere between fascination and fear. "I remember you," she said. "Loren took me to see the Cowboys play on our first date. You were playing the Steelers. I think you lost."

"Nice camping place you've got here," I said, accepting the

beer that Big Boy handed me, walking to the picture window beside the dinette. I looked across a rolling expanse of brownish green grass that had the look of a well-tended fairway. A brace of doves rocketed in to flutter and land in the giant pecan tree that provided the motor home with dappled shade.

"Sorry about the mix-up," Big Boy said gruffly. "But them suckers wouldn't let us into the parking lot yet. Said it was too early to start partying. Hell, I think that is our business, don't you? Anyhow, I left word with the guard there and at the rental place."

I nodded. "The guard gave me your message but he didn't have any idea where the Jesse Coldwater place was. I didn't either."

Big Boy grimaced. "I never thought about that. I thought everybody knew old Jesse. . . . Where'd you bunk down for the night?"

"Small motel out near the edge of town. Everything was filled up around the stadium. Lucky to get what I did. It was the only room left." I took a sip of beer. "It was okay," I added, not telling him about the hours of sleeplessness listening to soft breathing on the other side of the bed, the unaccountable restlessness as my capricious brain brought unbidden images of Meg Wainwright's taut supple body writhing in passionate embrace. Adolescent fantasies prompted by a deep pulsing desire that caught me unaware and hit me like a careless knee to the groin. I lay half the night tensely awake, not trusting myself to move, remembering her incredibly vulnerable expression when she learned we would have to share the same room, the timid submissiveness in quickly downcast green eyes as she realized we would be sleeping in the same bed.

And it was during the small hours of the morning, when I had conquered my demons of desire, that I was able to think about it rationally, put it into perspective, realize that it had been that very air of sweet submissiveness, of trusting acquiescence that had fired my blood and brought the uneasy rampaging lust.

"Well, no harm done," Big Boy's voice brought me back to

dark gleaming eyes and a crooked smile that lifted only one corner of his mouth. "All's well that ends well, as they say."

"Right," I said, tilting the can of beer at my mouth. "No harm done."

Jill sat down at the dinette with me while Big Boy and Clara took Meg on an inspection tour. She picked up my can of beer and took a sip.

"I missed you last night," she said lightly, pinching the corners of her mouth delicately between thumb and forefinger. "It was lonely all by myself in that big old bed."

"It was a long night for me, too."

She created a series of interlocking rings with the bottom edge of my weeping beer can. "Only one room, you said. Does that mean you slept with her last night?"

"I slept in the same bed, yes."

"Were you able to get it up for her?" Still light and faintly humorous, her voice sagged a little near the end with acerbic irony. Color crept across her face like a slowly spreading fever.

"I didn't try, Jill."

She made a face and turned her eyes to the picture window. "I'm sorry, it's none of my business. I only started this conversation to tell you that I slept by myself last night." She laughed softly. "I have the distinct feeling that isn't as important to you as it is to me. One tends to exaggerate the importance of one's own small sacrifices."

"Hey, little lady," I said, imitating Big Boy's rumbling bellow, "that's philosophical."

"Self-pitying is what it is," she said. "I'm not used to rejection. Not sexual rejection, at least." Her expression softened and she touched the back of my hand with one finger. "I'll bet I could make you want me if we gave it a solid chance."

"Hey, man!" Big Boy hove into view, not looking much like the cavalry in his high-visibility yellow shorts and royal blue sleeveless shirt, but a welcome diversion nevertheless. He carried a fifth of Wild Turkey and an empty glass. "How about a chaser for that beer?" A red headband encircled his huge head, with what looked like the tail feather from a tom turkey dangling behind his right ear. Beaded Indian moccasins completed the curious ensemble, and despite the valiant efforts of the small air conditioner, his brown skin glistened like oiled leather on his long, heavily muscled arms. "You way behind already, man," he added, folding his bulk into the seat beside Jill, his legs extended into the aisle.

"Why not," I said.

Jill propped her chin in her hand and swiveled her head toward the window. "You two start now and you won't be worth a hoot by time for the party tonight." There was a thread of annoyance in her voice, but I had a hunch it had nothing to do with drinking.

"Little lady, listen here," Big Boy said ponderously, pausing for dramatic effect as if he were about to disclose some long-withheld bit of esoteric wisdom. "Us old soldiers know about drinking. Right, Dan'l? Drinking is a man's thing. With all due respect to the nobler sex, us men know instinctively what to do when we're getting too much—"

"Yeah, we stick our fingers down our throats and vomit," I said.

Big Boy scowled ferociously. "You ought'n be giving away our secrets thataway, boy," he growled. "First thing you know, they'll be drinking as good as we do and then where'll we be?"

"Right where we are now. Under their sweet little thumbs."

"Yes, Lord," Jill said, shaking her head and smiling reluctantly. "You two are certainly shining examples of subjugated males."

Big Boy squinted at me, his face twisted lugubriously. "Is she talking dirty about us?"

I laughed. "I think she's giving us a compliment of sorts. Maybe not, but I'm going to take it that way."

Jill chuckled and wrapped both hands around Big Boy's biceps. He immediately cocked his wrist and made a muscle, pulling her fingers apart.

"Nineteen inches," he said proudly. "I'll bet you've never had one that big in your hands before." He grinned at me. "And rock hard, too."

Jill released him, the fever spots high on her cheeks again. "No," she said solemnly, "that's the biggest one I've ever seen."

"Biggest what?" Clara's head appeared above Big Boy's. She slipped her hands over his shoulders and splayed her fingers flat against his broad chest. Meg drifted up beside her and I slid toward the window and motioned. She came obediently and sat down, a small fixed smile on her face.

"Biggest roadrunner," Big Boy said. "I was telling them about that dream you had last night."

"It wasn't the roadrunner who was big, silly. I was the roadrunner. It was the coyote who was so big. You were the coyote."

"Did I eat you?"

Clara rubbed her chin in the curly mass of his hair and squinted reflectively. "I'm not sure. I'd say yes and no . . . or are you talking about before the dream or after?"

Big Boy slapped the table and howled; beside me Meg shook her head and covered her mouth with her hand. Jill swiveled to face the window again, her cheek bunching.

"What's so funny?" Clara asked aggrievedly, her young-old eyes twinkling. "It's better than a sharp stick in the eye."

Big Boy's laugh wound down. He turned glistening eyes on Meg. He reached across the table and picked up her hand. "I've been meaning to tell you something, Miss Meg," he said fatuously. "You've got the prettiest little hands I ever did see." There was a proprietary air in the way he held the small hand and I remembered that first time with Clara and felt my hackles rising.

I touched Meg on the shoulder. "If you'll let me out, I think I'll catch a few winks out there under the oaks before we eat."

Without a word, she withdrew her hand from Big Boy's, her face slightly flushed, expressionless. She stepped into the aisle and I scooted out of the dinette booth. "Call me, Big Boy, and I'll help you with the steaks."

"Yeah, man, I'll do that. There's some old blankets and a

170

couple of them folding lounges in the baggage compartment. Help yourself."

I found deep shade twenty yards from the motor home and settled on one of the aluminum lounges. I smoked one last cigarette, shielding my eyes from the glare of the cerulean sky, then turned on my side, forced all thought from my mind, and went to sleep.

"Dan."

The voice was soft, but I awoke abruptly, the way I do on those mornings when my brain isn't fogged with the residue of alcohol.

Jill sat on her heels a few feet away, hugging her legs, her chin propped on her knees. "I didn't know whether to wake you or not. I don't know what's between you and Meg, but I thought you might want to know he has her in the bedroom with Clara."

I swung my feet to the ground. "How long?"

She shrugged and looked toward the motor home. "Five minutes, I guess."

"Thanks." I struggled to my feet, the light aluminum frame of the lounge creaking and groaning.

"You're welcome," she said flatly.

"She's too vulnerable, Jill. Goddammit, right now she's too vulnerable." I turned and stalked across the uneven ground, feeling a rising tide of cold anger. I lit a cigarette and went up the steps of the silent vehicle.

He was seated on the edge of the bed, Meg standing like a penitent child between his widespread legs. She was naked from the waist up, her arms hanging limply, immobile beneath the huge brown hands that moved slowly, reverently across her shoulders to her breasts. Clara sat propped against the headboard, her naked legs drawn up, watching them with bright, birdlike eyes.

Big Boy's eyes swung toward me, hot and dark against a field of marbled white. "Hey," he said, his voice thick and hushed. "Come on in, man."

I stepped forward into the room. "This is no good," I said evenly. "She's not ready for this, Big Boy."

He spread his hands eloquently, returned them to her arms, began stroking again. "She's willing, man. Nobody drug her in here. She said you and her ain't tight, or anything."

"Goddammit, Big Boy, she's not participating. She's submitting. Even you ought to be able to see that."

He bristled. "Hey, man, I ain't stupid. That's just the way some women are. They want to be told what to do."

"No, not this woman. Not this way. I can't let you have her, Big Boy."

"Aw, come on, man. I'm gentle as a baby kitten. I ain't going to hurt her. Ask Clara here. Clara, tell him." The whiskey whine I had heard before was in his voice.

"He's gentle, Dan." Clara bobbed her head vehemently. "Better than a vibrator."

"No," I said. "Meg, get your blouse."

I saw the big hands tighten on her arms, his face darken, closing with defiance, and I felt a sliding lurch inside me.

"Me and you are friends," he said gently. "I can't see us fighting over a woman."

"I wouldn't fight you over a woman, Big Boy, but I'll fight you for this one."

"You can't win," he argued reasonably. "Not unless you shoot me."

"You've probably got that right."

His eyebrows lifted and he stared at me while time ticked by, a long time it seemed to me, watching the dark eyes go from warm humor to cold anger and then to something I wasn't sure about. I thought of the .38 in my overnight bag and wondered why he hadn't noticed that I wasn't wearing it. Or maybe he had.

"Shee-it!" he said suddenly, turning his eyes back to Meg, sliding his hands down her arms to her hands, engulfing them in his. "Too bad, little lady. We could have had us a high old time, I'll bet. This crazy old square shooter here, you can't argue with him when he's on his white horse. He'd just as soon shoot a feller as look at him."

Muttering under his breath, he picked up her bra from the floor beside the bed and held it for her, turned her gently and fastened it in back. He helped her into the blouse, not once looking in my direction.

He still hadn't looked at me when she walked silently past me. I scanned his sharp profile for a moment, then turned and followed her.

"Get your bag, Meg. I think it's time I took you home."

She nodded, biting her lip. "I'm sorry. I thought when you left . . . I thought you wanted me to go with him." She shrugged helplessly. "I thought . . ."

"It's all right," I said. "It's a ten-hour drive home. You'll have your time to think. You can't do it here. Not now."

"All right, Dan."

We stopped at the rental agency and changed the contract. An hour later I left Houston, Meg sitting placidly beside me, the images of taut white breasts thrusting passively into big black hands fluttering in my mind like ticker-tape confetti.

/26/

Although I've always considered myself to be what you'd call a compassionate man, I didn't spend a lot of time worrying about Meg and Loren after I dropped her off at home. I had no desire to hang around and witness the poignancy of their reunion, the hunger in his lugubrious face, the shame in hers. I had my own bittersweet memories to contend with.

There was no Susie waiting, no messages on the telephone recorder. Nothing but an empty house that rang with silence and pulsed with the irony of unlikely dreams, that echoed with the murmur of years gone by, of bright mornings filled with youth and rosy cheeks, long nights singing with easy laughter and careless love.

But I was no longer young and rosy-cheeked, if indeed I had ever been, and neither love nor laughter came easy; I needed sustenance the way a baby needs its mother's milk, and I settled effortlessly into a drunk's nirvana, a dead zone somewhere between simple awareness and total insensibility. A rosy glowing world chock full of high hopes and impossible expectations: not drunk, but a long way from sober.

Two days passed without intelligible input into the uncertain banks of my memory, and once again Homer Sellers's blunt fingers dug meanly into my shoulder, his harsh voice ringing scornfully in my brainpan, shattering my hard-earned edge of sweet contentment, bringing me shivering and quaking into that other world of unrelenting reality.

"You're sorry, boy. I ain't sure just how sorry, yet. But a man is known by the companions he keeps, and that black friend of yours has gone too far this time. He's left a dead man behind. Not much of a man, but that don't matter a damn, and if I had the sense God gave a goose I'd be down at County telling the sheriff what I know about this mess instead of here watching you bleed whiskey-sweat and blowing your stink in my face. If I thought for one minute you knew any damn thing about this, I'd drag your ass down to county jail myself." He stopped, breathing heavily through his mouth, his face rosy but hard. "Look me in the eye, Dan. Tell me you didn't know."

I wavered, then focused on his bright berry eyes, cop's eyes, penetrating and hot.

I shook my head. "Who, Homer, I don't even know who?"

"Dalton Wagerman." He pulled a handkerchief from his jacket and blew lustily, with the thick gurgling sound of heavy mucus breaking loose from inflamed sinus cavities. "Burned to death in that little office of his. That part maybe was an accident. It was late and nobody was usually there at that time. But he had evidently fallen asleep at his desk and when that old building went up he didn't have a chance. They used incendiaries of some kind. They're not sure exactly yet. Grenades maybe."

"What about the sons?" I brought an arm out of my warm cocoon into the artificially cooled air and fumbled for a cigarette.

"Don't know," he said brusquely, turning away. "It was on the morning news and I called County and asked some questions." He stopped at the door, his face still hard, his eyes bright and unrelenting. "Don't bother to get up, boy, I'm leaving. I see you still got more than a half bottle there handy. That oughta hold you for a couple more hours."

"It hurts, Homer," I said piteously, cringing at the whine in my voice. "Man, you don't know."

"So does dying, buddy," he said contemptuously, and disappeared from my view.

I dropped the unlit cigarette into the ashtray and settled back, hearing the muted click of the front door and wondering if I had left it unlocked again or he had used his key. I'll have to ask him, I thought drowsily. I'll have to be more careful now that—that what? Now that what? I couldn't remember. Homer's image drifted across the fuzzy contours of my mind, his voice tiny and far away, his words garbled and meaningless. I sank slowly beneath a warm velvety canopy of darkness, and slipped gently back into uneasy sleep.

When I awoke again it was to the pearl grayness of either dawn or twilight. I couldn't be sure which. My dime store alarm clock had long since wound down and I had no clear idea where my watch could be. I swung my feet to the floor and immediately lost my preoccupation with the time of day as hot spikes of pain lanced across my head and nauseating gases hissed and bubbled in my stomach.

One hand clamped over my mouth, I tried to stand, then slipped resignedly to my hands and knees and crawled the few feet to the bathroom. I dry-heaved drearily for a while, each spasm sending a pang of sickening pain across my brow. Then, in a kind of numb despair, I shoved a finger down my throat, held it there, my back bowing as the convulsions began, spewing a noisome mess across my hand and wrist into the clear unsuspecting water. Shivering, I closed my eyes and held my breath and let my stomach do its accustomed work.

Minutes later, cleansed yet filthy, I walked upright into the shower.

Naked, shaking in the refrigerated air, a bundle of clean clothes on the bar beside the bottle of scotch, I lifted a half-filled glass to my mouth with both hands and held it there, the glass chattering against my teeth until it was empty. Leaning on my elbows, my head bowed above the goblet like a priest paying homage to the chalice, I closed my eyes and waited, sober enough to feel a fleeting wash of shame, too damned sick to care. It was moments like these that could make a man truly humble.

The warm glow spread, teasing my jangling nerve ends, jousting halfheartedly with raging thirst. Not enough. Not nearly enough. I was reaching for the bottle again when the phone began ringing.

I let it ring fifteen times by actual count, then toasted the twanging silence. It immediately began ringing again.

On the tenth ring I began the long trek across the den to the kitchen. If nothing else, you had to admire that kind of persistence. A storm-door salesperson, no doubt, I told myself, or insulation, or carpeting . . .

"Hello, dammit!"

"Oh, God . . . thank God you're there." Her voice was hushed, halting, barely above a whisper, a breathless little-girl quality I had heard only in those precious moments before mind-bending orgasm. But that was damned silly. She had just let the phone ring twenty-nine times, for christ sakes. . . .

"Oh, it's you," I said. "I was expecting an important call, Susan."

"Danny . . . please listen . . . I need you—"

I made a noise that would have been a biting sardonic laugh if not for the whinnying note near the end. "Jackie-boy still out of commission, is he? Well, patience, my love, he'll soon be his lusty ramroding self again. We mustn't be impetuous—"

"Danny, please! Oh, God, honey, someone's trying to k-k-kill me."

"Yeah, I know, you told me that. But Dalton Wagerman's dead, Susie. I don't think he's much interested—"

"No, no, no!" Her voice was high and shrill with hysteria. "Now! I mean now! Just . . . a few minutes . . . a little while ago. Some—somebody shot at me! Oh, God, Danny, he almost . . . he almost . . ." Her voice dissolved into liquid choking sounds.

"Now?" I echoed dumbly. "Susie, are you sure?"

"Oh, Jesus, Danny give me credit for . . . of course now! A little while ago. I called the police but they couldn't find . . . couldn't find anything."

"Where's Jack?"

"On his way to . . . to Houston. Oh, Lord, I don't even remember where he's staying . . . Ramada Inn or . . . I was setting out the roses he bought me ... they were getting brown ... he said if I didn't get them set out today they might die and I was down on—"

I cut into the almost incoherent babble. "Settle down, Susie. Where are you now?"

"In—in the bathroom. I brought the phone in here. . . . Oh, God, honey, I'm scared. I'm here all alone. Our maid doesn't sleep over and Jack is gone and I know I heard a noise."

"How about the police?"

"They've gone. They couldn't find anything and I'm almost sure they didn't believe me ... but he's still out there ... or in here. I swear I heard a noise."

"All right. Do you have a gun in the house?"

"No—no, wait. Jack has a deer rifle."

"Where is it?"

"In the bedroom closet. I know because I put it there Tuesday when it came back from the repair shop—"

"Susan! You're wasting time. Get the gun. You know how to handle it. Lock yourself in the bathroom. Don't come out until you hear me."

"All right, Danny." Her voice was tight, steadier, almost calm. "Please hurry."

"Do it now, right now. Then lock yourself in and wait for me. Anybody comes around that door and won't sing out, blast his ass. You got it?"

"I got it, Danny." Still a little breathless, but firming up, her voice rang with determination.

I broke the connection and dialed Homer Sellers.

"Sellers."

"Homer. Somebody's taken a shot at Susie. I'm on my way over there, but I'm at least ten minutes away and she thinks he may still be around. I need a car, or two, if you've got them handy. Tell them to go in wide open, siren and lights. She's locked herself in the bathroom in the master bedroom. But tell them to stay away from the door until I get there. She won't answer to anybody else and she might just cut loose on them."

"Got it," Homer said, and I heard the click as he cut the connection.

One thing about Homer, I thought fondly as I fumbled through the wad of clean clothing on the bar, he was a man of few words when action was the code word of the day.

I discovered that I had brought two T-shirts and no shorts, but I slipped into my Levi's anyway, taking a tad more care with the zipper than usual, feeling naked and vulnerable, yet somehow flippant.

Unable to remember where I had taken off my boots, I slipped into a pair of deerskin loafers that did double duty as house shoes. I took one long look at the inviting amber bottle on the bar, then forced myself to turn away from its importunate call, found my gun, and pressed resolutely through the door.

Inside the car I was a tight mass of thrumming nerves and muscle, the mantle of whiskey fog beginning to dissipate before the twin forces of hollow fear and helpless dread.

I drove like a madman, running lights, whipping the big Dodge into and through spaces it was not meant to go. I felt scraping metal and juddering tires, heard blasting horns and hoarse screaming voices, and, by the time I reached the foot of Cooper's Mountain, I had picked up two more of Homer Sellers's stalwart centurions screaming in hot pursuit.

/27/

Police Sergeant Leo Halleran, burly, sixtyish, stood with legs widespread, his head bowed over a pad in his hands, writing furiously as Susie talked. They were standing at the end of a long narrow hallway near an arched doorway. As I approached Susie paused and blew her nose lustily into what looked like a crumbled mass of pink toilet tissue, turning her head toward me in that same instant. Her eyes widened and she took a small halting step, her hands falling away from her face. Her lips quivered, then with a tiny inarticulate cry, she threw herself at me.

"Hey, easy," I said, my arms automatically encircling her, my hands beginning the ritual of comforting caresses even before her wet sobbing face buried itself against my neck. "Hey, it's okay. It's okay now."

"Oh, God, Danny, he was here! He was at the bath—bathroom door. I heard him . . . but . . . but . . ." Her voice faded into a snuffing sob, her arms tightening around my neck.

"We scared him off, Dan. That's what it looks like. She said he was trying the bathroom door when she heard the first sounds of our sirens. He must have seen the telephone cord under the door and realized she'd called us." Sergeant Leo Halleran removed his hat and idly rubbed the crease across his florid forehead. He smiled ruefully. "Good we came in the way we did, I reckon."

"No sign of him when you got here?"

He shook his head and replaced the hat on thin close-cropped white hair. "Milott and Strossberg came in right behind us. We searched the house." He paused and smiled faintly at the back of Susie's head. "When I got back here, she was peeping out the bathroom door."

I shook her gently. "I thought I told you to stay inside. What happened to the gun? Why didn't you squeeze off a round above his head?"

She pulled back reluctantly, mopped at her eyes with the wad of toilet paper. "It—it wasn't there . . . taken it back to the den."

Halleran cleared his throat. "If you're talking about a scoped rifle, it's hanging above the fireplace mantel. A bolt-action .270, looks like to me." He hesitated and rubbed a square dimpled chin. "I think the guy made a try for it. There's a small vase busted on the brick ledge in front of the fireplace. But your husband's got it locked in the rack." He paused again. "I know you haven't had a chance to check, but did you have anything else of value lying around—silver maybe, or jewelry—"

"It wasn't a robbery," I said, taking out my handkerchief and handing it to Susie as the tissue began to come apart in her tugging fingers. She gave me a small grateful look, making no effort to move away from my arm still draped around her shoulders. The trembling had subsided to an occasional tremor, the tears to intermittent seepage.

He gave me a puzzled frown. "What then? The call didn't specify, but I just assumed—"

I tightened my arm around her shoulders, then let it drop. "Go pack a small bag, Susan. Just enough for a day or two. We'll come back later."

She stared up at me for a moment, slowly wiping dark eyes that seemed more deep-sunken than I remembered, saffron-tinted circles stark against pale skin.

"I can't guard you here, Susie. I couldn't even if I wanted to. It's too damn big and about as easy to get into as a box of Cracker Jack. Besides, it's Jack's house, too, and it wouldn't work out."

"All right, Danny," she said meekly. "I'll leave him a note."

"Do that," I said tersely, lighting a cigarette, watching her slender form pad barefooted down the hallway, filled with ambivalence I would have been hard put to define.

"What then?" Sergeant Halleran asked when she had disappeared through the door.

"Attempted murder," I said tonelessly.

Halleran's eyes widened. "Murder? Hey, I'd better get somebody from Homicide out here. Christ, I thought we had a peeper, even a burglar maybe—"

"Captain Sellers knows about it. In fact he put in the call."

Halleran smiled crookedly and put away his pad. "All the same, I'm putting in a call." He started down the hall, short and stocky, wise in all the ways a cop needs to be to cover his backside.

"We're not waiting," I said. "Tell Sellers to send his detectives to my house for his report."

He stopped and looked back at me, his lined face noncommittal. "He won't like it, Lieutenant." When I didn't answer, he shrugged and continued down the hall.

It had been more than ten years since I had been a lieutenant in the Midway City police force, longer still since Sergeant Leo Halleran had worked for me as a patrolman, but in a cop's mind, once a cop always a cop, and old habits die hard.

"I'm sorry, Danny," Susie said. She gave me a quick sliding glance as she swept past me through the door into my house, the overnight bag bumping my knees, finding an old, almost forgotten bruise.

"No sweat," I said. "I wasn't doing anything tonight anyway."

She put the bag down by the entryway closet and flashed me another look. "I don't mean that. I mean this whole . . . this mess we've gotten ourselves into."

We? I thought, almost grinning. She hadn't changed as much as I thought. I shrugged and stepped down into the den, walking automatically to the bar. The scotch bottle was where

I had left it, but I pushed it resolutely aside, leaned instead and took a cold bottle of Pepsi from the refrigerator.

"How about a straight shot of Pepsi on the rocks? That sound good?"

She nodded and sat down on the couch, balling my handkerchief in one brown fist, her other hand wandering aimlessly through the black hair hanging loose to curl at her shoulders.

I dropped the ice cubes into two brandy goblets and divided the Pepsi evenly. I gave her one along with a pat on the head. "Don't look so glum. Things could be a hell of a lot worse." I sat down across from her, tasted the drink, and grimaced.

"I don't see how," she said. "I've really made a mess of things."

"I can't see that," I argued reasonably. "A woman has a right to work in her garden without being shot at."

She closed her eyes for a moment, her long natural lashes startling black crescents against pale skin that had not yet regained its natural olive tint. She sighed. "I'm not talking about that either. I'm talking about us, Danny. You and me. We seem to be ... what's the word? Star-crossed lovers? Whatever it is, we can't seem to pull in the same direction at the same time. When we came back from the cabin I thought we finally had it all together. I thought ... and then I came home and saw you beating poor Jack half to—"

"Poor Jack?" I lifted my eyebrows. "I'd be interested to know what Jack had to say about that."

She made a small fluttering movement and shook her head. "It doesn't matter. I understand about jealousy and I know you despise weak men, and Jack, I guess, is essentially a weak man—"

"No," I said. "I'd like to know what he told you."

She took a drink of Pepsi and blotted her lips with my handkerchief. "Well ... he just said that he came here to beg you to ... to not take me away from him and ..." She stopped and smiled apologetically. "I know how spineless

183

that would have seemed to you, Danny. And I can understand—"

"Exactly what did he say, Susan?"

"He—he said you pulled a gun on him, made him go around to the woodbin at the end of the garage. He said . . . well, he said you began beating him with a piece of firewood, and that you kicked him in his . . . privates again and again."

"Damn, I didn't know I was such a mean bastard. And I suppose you believed him."

She put down the drink and began torturing my handkerchief. "I—didn't want to. I tried not . . . but there were bruises on his back and neck and his . . . his privates were all black and blue and swollen terribly. And his face . . . God, Danny his face was—is a mess." Her eyes lifted from her hands, met mine, dark and anguished. "I—I know, Danny, that there's . . . that sometimes there's a dark rage in you . . . a dark terrible rage . . ."

"And that scares you, makes you afraid of me."

"No, no! Oh, God, no, honey, I'm not afraid of you. But I am afraid for you."

"But yet you chose to stay with him."

She shook her head, her full lips working into a thin pink line. "No, not at first. I thought he was hurt a lot worse than he really was. I stopped by here when we came back to get his car, but you weren't here—"

"His car? His car wasn't here."

"No, not right here. He left it up at the shopping center on Regent and Highway 183. He said the motor was heating up—"

"You seem to have a lot of trouble with your cars' heating systems. I suppose he drove it home, though."

"Why, yes, he did, as a matter of fact." Her eyebrows knitted. "Come to think of it, he never did call the garage."

I could feel her perplexed eyes on me, but I was busy doing some more pondering. There was only one reason I could think of that would cause him to leave his car a mile away, walk through the heat of that particular September day: the son of bitch had planned on killing me, beating me to death with my own firewood, leaving the police to place it at the door of the Wagermans if he was lucky, attribute it to person or persons unknown if he wasn't. I remembered the hat pulled low over his sunglasses, the empty battered briefcase. Props. Just another salesman working the neighborhood. In broad daylight who would give him a second glance?

"Was it right, Danny? What Jack told me?" She watched me anxiously, the handkerchief rolled into a rope and wound around and between her fingers, her other hand tugging.

"No, it wasn't, but I'm not going to explain it to you. You'll just have to take my word for it."

She sighed deeply. "I wondered . . . I really did. I came by here that day when I brought him to get his car and you were gone. I came back the next day and you were gone again. I came back one more time and came in." She paused and smiled crookedly. "I listened to your phone messages. There was one from a woman named Jill thanking you for that wonderful night at . . . at the lake." She looked past me, her lips firming up. "I didn't think . . . after the way you . . . we talked, I just didn't see how you could do that . . . so soon."

"But you were back sleeping with your husband," I said lightly, feeling something slick slithering in my chest.

"Oh, no, I wasn't. We weren't sleeping together. He was too sore anyway. He still is." Her eyes came back and met mine squarely. "I couldn't have, Danny. You don't have to believe that if you don't want to."

"I'd like to believe it, Susan. But all this time how much longer were you going to keep up this farce, if that's what it was?"

She shrugged helplessly, her face miserable. "I don't know. I'd talked to Jack, told him I'd have to leave him, that I knew now I didn't love him the way I should, the way I love you. And he seemed to take it all right. He just asked me to stay until he'd completed some deal he's been working on with the Dohenys, some big sum of money they're going to invest in his business. He asked me to stay until that was finalized since Clarice is my friend. He's afraid she'd blame him for us breaking up and back out."

"Do you think she would?"

"No, Clarice isn't like that. She's too practical when it comes to money matters. She's actually awfully tight to be so rich. I think she's been burning a little because Jack's been making so much money for Mr. Doheny. He's really good at that, Danny."

I felt a grin coming along with an overwhelming desire to touch her, a need to feel her warm vibrant beauty in my arms. I put the glass of Pepsi on the fireplace ledge and pushed to my feet.

She was standing also, watching me with slightly parted lips, her eyes quick and alive with emotion.

I tried to think of something to say, something witty and charming—if not that, meaningful, at least. But all I could think of was: "Come here."

Minutes later we broke apart from a hard searching kiss that left us both a little breathless.

She leaned back against my arm, her face solemn, her eyes dancing. "Do you think I could take time to shower first?"

/28/

Texas has never been what you would call a land of milk and honey for private detectives. Hiring a private detective implies a certain lack of confidence in one's own ability to cope, and whatever else we may be, we are in general a self-sufficient lot. Finding people, a surprising amount of divorce work despite the relaxation of divorce laws, and repossessions compromise the bulk of a Texas private detective's workload. We rarely solve murder cases, hardly ever have shootouts with desperadoes, and never, never, get involved in high-speed auto chases. If your subject makes you, you may as well pack it in. Unless, of course, it's a repossession, but we don't like to talk about that.

There are some odds and ends: the tired executive or businessman who has been wondering what the girls do at those Wednesday afternoon bridge parties that leave his young wife rumpled and mussed, dreamy-eyed and puffy-lipped. Then there's the nervous housewife who finds her husband's sudden interest in bowling two nights a week with the boys a trifle suspicious, particularly since the tiny brown thread she stuck in her husband's bowling bag zipper a month ago is still there. A smattering of detective work for an occasional lawyer trying to find an out for his client, cruising shoplifters, and putting the arm on pilfering employees about rounds it out.

Few, if any, private detectives do all of these things. Many, like myself, specialize in only one or two. But Mort Grossman, if you could believe the neat gold-leaf lettering on his office door, did them all, expeditiously, discreetly, and well.

He was a small man, compact and muscular with short, no-nonsense blond hair and a David Niven mustache. Swift sure movements of small dainty hands and a crisp business-like voice projected an air of competence I happened to know he didn't possess. Our paths had intersected a few times in the byways of private detective land and I had always come away feeling an inexplicable need for a quick hot shower. I was never sure why exactly, unless it was the slate-green hummingbird eyes that never landed, the feminine hands that were never still, or the pallid skin that always looked freshly laundered and powdered.

And this time was no different. I quickly dropped the warm sinewy hand that tried to make up in stout for what it lacked in bulk, and sat down across the desk from him.

"Well, well, Dan Roman. Long time no see. When was the last time? Superior Court number three, wasn't it?" He showed me two white rows of neat little teeth clenched tightly between smiling lips.

"Yeah," I said, "and that takes care of the reminiscing and the amenities. We don't like each other, so let's not pretend. I won't waste your time and you better not try to waste mine or I'll kick your little ass all over this cruddy office."

He pursed rosebud lips and gave me a long thoughtful look, the green eyes skittering from one point on my face to another. He cleared his throat and leaned forward. "It must be really important for you to come in my office here and talk like that," he said earnestly.

"It's important," I agreed. "But I'd talk to you that way even if it weren't."

"Well," he said, his hands coming together on the desk top with a tiny plop. "What can I do for you?"

"Jack Farley, Midway City. Lives up on Cooper's Mountain."

His head dipped forward in a stingy nod. "Yes, I remember him. What about it?" His mouth was pursed again, this time in a tight round ball of disapproval. "You understand, of course, that Jack Farley was my client and that we have a confidential client-detective relationship and that my admitting that he was in fact my client has already breached that—"

"I'm not interested in your client. I want to know about the subject of your investigation—Dalton Wagerman."

His face lit up. "Ah, I see. You're working for the insurance company. I read where Mr. Wagerman burned to death—"

"You made a series of reports to Jack Farley relative to the activities of the Wagermans. I want copies of those reports."

His short fingers danced on the desk top, his eyebrows lifting in a sardonic smirk. "Oh? Just like that? I spend three weeks busting my ass and you walk in here and demand the fruits of my labor." He laughed a throaty laugh without humor and wet his lips. "Five hundred dollars, friend, and not a cent less."

"All right."

"Wha—?" He stared at me, openmouthed, the flitting hands still for once, his eyes meeting mine for a fleeting second before sliding away across my cheek.

"What did I say? Five hundred? Well, perhaps I was hasty. After all, three weeks' work . . . and since we're dealing with an insurance company—"

"You're dealing with me." I took out my wallet and separated five one-hundred-dollar bills. I tossed them across the desk at him. "I'll want a receipt."

"Hey, now wait a minute. Let's negotiate—" He broke off as I stood up and walked around the desk.

"You remember what I said when I came in here, Grossman? Did you think I was being cute?" I leaned down and jabbed him in the chest with a stiffened forefinger.

He knocked my hand away and leaped to his feet. "Hey, look, this ain't fair. You're a lot bigger than I am—"

"That's not my fault. Your folks should have drowned you when they found out. Besides, I'd have to touch you and that more than makes it even."

He blinked slowly, backing away, his arms windmilling in front of his dapper body. He cursed once, viciously, then threw up his hands.

"All right! All right! It's not that big a deal. Ain't a damn thing in them reports, anyhow—" He broke off, suddenly afraid he had said too much. "Don't get me wrong. They're good solid reports, it's just that they didn't—"

"Just get them, Grossman. Do you have a Xerox machine?"

"I've got copies," he said sullenly. "Farley's copies. I gave him weekly reports. He never came by for the final report. It's got everything in it: times, dates, places."

"As long as it's complete."

"I said it was, didn't I?" He glared at me belligerently from behind the filing cabinet drawer, his small hands busy flicking through file folders. I smiled and he crimped his lips into a plump pouty ball. "This kind of thing is frowned on by the state licensing agency, you know. I could probably get your license."

I shrugged. "You can have it right now if you want it. It's a year out of date."

He yanked a folder out of the drawer. "Then how can you work for the insurance company? That's gross misrepresentation. You could be—"

"You said I was working for the insurance company. I didn't." I stepped across to the cabinet and took the folder out of his hand.

"Then why are you interested in the Wagermans?" Avid curiosity had overcome his belligerence and brought his voice back to cordiality.

"It's none of your business, but they've dropped out of sight since the old man was killed. I'm trying to find them." I found the final report and compared the first entry with the first daily report, then leafed through the stack to the last one and compared that. Satisfied, I dropped the folder on his desk and folded the three sheets of paper into a long rectangle. I slipped it into my inside jacket pocket.

"What for?" Grossman's tiny fingers rubbed each of the hundred-dollar bills in turn, then did a disappearing act with the folded money.

"Never mind what for. I'm hoping something in here may give me a clue to their whereabouts."

The sardonic smirk came back on his thin face. "Lots of luck, friend. My biggest problem on that job was staying awake."

I returned his smirk. "No, I imagine trying to keep from getting stepped on would be your biggest problem."

I walked out in utter silence, grinning, and if curses could kill I'd have been dead long before I reached my car.

Disappointed, I dropped the neatly typewritten pages on the kitchen table and gripped the bridge of my nose between thumb and forefinger. Nothing. At least nothing that would help me find them. They seemed devoted to the theater, which I found a bit surprising considering their obvious lack of refinement and culture. But that might indicate only that I was guilty of snobbery. Simply because they were merciless thugs addicted to sadistic beatings directed at anyone who displeased them wouldn't necessarily mean they didn't appreciate the finer things in life.

On the other end of the spectrum they rarely missed either a Saturday or Sunday visit to the flea market in Fort Worth where Susie and Jack had seen them. They were pack rats of a sort, buying all kinds of broken objects, primarily metal, welding or otherwise repairing them and bringing them back the next weekend for sale. That could account for their meeting with Jack and Susie.

Another interesting fact was that they invariably used the meat market on Highway 157, stopping in Friday after work for a week's supply of meat. That could also account for Susie's first sighting of the Wagermans.

I opened another beer and lit a cigarette and thought about it, feeling a faint tingling tenseness across the back of my shoulders as one thought slowly wormed its way into my consciousness and refused to go away.

If the Wagermans in their normal course of living frequented the theaters, the flea market, and the meat market on Highway 157, then wasn't it possible the meetings could have been accidental? That left only the ball game at Ranger Stadium.

That, too, could have been a coincidence. Couldn't it? Susie
and Jack both had said the Wagermans appeared to pay her no
attention. Maybe there was a reason for that. Maybe—Jesus
Christ!—maybe they didn't even remember her! I closed my
eyes and tried to recall what Tony Wagerman had said that
night on the dam when I mentioned Susie. He had called it
"bullshit talk," had ranted about "the girl" being there of her
own free will. His sister. He had been talking about his sister,
had thought I was talking about her also.

I rocked back in the chair, my mind reeling. Jesus, was it
possible? Could I have started the whole damn thing with my
trip to the Wagermans' machine shop? Had I offended or
scared the old man enough to precipitate their reprisal beating
in my entry hall?

Surely not, I thought wildly, choking back a thin bitter
taste of bile as my stomach lurched threateningly. Surely to
God not. Nobody was crazy enough or prideful enough to
start a small war because of a few minutes of indignity, a few
threatening words. But even as the thoughts raced through
my mind I saw Dalton Wagerman's cold empty face in my
mind's eye and I knew I was wrong. Somebody could . . . and
maybe had.

I stared numbly at Grossman's report, the sickness building
in my stomach, a slow wash of black misery creeping over
me, hearing Susie singing in the bathroom and suddenly feeling an incredible rush of guilty shameful relief as I remembered the rifle shot that had clipped a lock of hair from her
temple.

The gunshot! The *two* gunshots! The one at the cabin and
the one at her home. They had to be the same man and both
had been directed at Susie. It would be an impossible coincidence otherwise. And that would blow my theory. The
Wagermans would have no reason to fire on Susie if they
weren't out to pay her back after all. And since the old man
was dead, that meant his sons would have to be carrying on
with his mindless crusade. I didn't believe that.

I breathed deeply, the relief so intense it was almost painful. Maybe we were back at the starting gate, but at least I knew I wasn't the one who had turned loose the horses.

Only one small thing still bothered me: How had the Wagermans known about the cabin?

/29/

The Wagerman funeral was a brief, bleak affair. Other than the mortician and his helpers, only six people attended the dismal interment: a man and woman and three teenage children said to be distant cousins of Dalton Wagerman; I was the sixth. Tony and Karl didn't show. And there had been no sign of Wagerman's daughter, Greta.

I drove home through a cold drizzling rain wondering about that. I had expected them to be there, had hoped that in the solemn atmosphere of man's oldest ritual I could talk quietly and rationally to Tony Wagerman, somehow convince him that his father's death had erased the past, that what had been done could be forgotten, *must* be forgotten and done with or I would have to kill him.

I was not the only one looking for the Wagerman boys. Because of the arson, Dalton Wagerman's death was being carried as a possible homicide and two of Homer Sellers's detectives had been assigned to the case. They too had attended the funeral in their own fashion, parked across from the cemetery entrance, watching the proceedings through binoculars. They had still been there when I left, an old rumpled veteran named Troy Black and a young detective I didn't know.

I turned the corner into my street and slowed, feeling a heavy thud in my chest as I saw the twin to Susie's Maserati parked beside hers. I angled into the curb in front of the house and stopped. I looked across the street.

Allen Dempsey, the off-duty policeman I had hired to baby-sit my house while I was gone, rolled down his window and stuck out his head. "She said it was all right, Dan. Said he was her husband."

194

I climbed out into the rain. "Okay, Al. You can take off now. I'll give you a call." I ignored his questing grin, the almost lugubrious look on his square face as he nodded and lifted his hand. "Gotcha, pal; see you later."

I crossed the yard swiftly. The front door was unlocked and I paused in the entry hall long enough to slip out of my damp jacket and clip a .38 to my belt. There were no voices, but I had heard the telltale squeak of my new recliner and I knew they were in the den; I stepped through the door quickly, my right thumb hooked in my belt not far from the gun.

"Hi, honey," Susie said brightly, leaping up from the edge of the couch and smothering me in an overdone hug, kissing me a trifle too loudly and too long.

I broke away from her and looked at Farley seated rigidly in my chair, his hands pressed flat on the arms, his narrow handsome face crisscrossed with veinlike red tracings, a large bruise high on his cheekbone glowing an ugly yellow-green. A small black scab festered at the corner of his lower lip, and one eye gleamed ratlike out of puffy plum-colored tissue.

"What do you want, Farley?" I kept my voice flat and toneless.

He lifted his hands, palms upward, and made a placating gesture. "I'm just leaving, Dan. I only came by to tell Susie—" He broke off and wet his lips, wincing as his tongue touched the scab. "I only came by to tell Susie what really happened here that day. I—I guess I lied about it. I was . . . I was pretty well stoned and crazy jealous . . . and . . . well, I just lied about it, is all, and I'm sorry." His lips worked as if he wanted to smile but found it too painful.

"All right, you've told her," I said, and stood waiting.

He grimaced wryly and pushed to his feet. He brushed a hand through tousled auburn hair and found a way to make the smile work after all when he looked at Susie. He shrugged almost imperceptibly and walked toward the door. "I'm sorry, Susan," he said, his voice suddenly faltering, the hand coming up to worry his hair again. "I wanted it to work . . . to work for us, baby. I really did." He hesitated in front of her for a moment, then moved on as she made no effort to touch him, her arms folded firmly beneath her breasts, a frosty smile on the rosebud lips, the clear brown eyes as cool and remote as they had been the day I came home from finding Doheny.

I felt a twinge of something that could have been simple male empathy, a faint stirring of something else that felt like anger at this callous disregard for a man who had loved her, still loved her without a doubt, and who had been working his tail off to provide the kind of life he thought she wanted.

I watched her watching him, puzzled. Like her mother, she had always been kind and generous, forgiving to a sometimes ridiculous extreme. And now, seeing this glacial indifference to the obvious suffering of a man she had presumably once loved brought a stirring of uneasiness, a stunning reaffirmation of what learned scholars have been trying to teach pussy-whipped males for centuries: Papa may rule the barnyard, but Mama rules the roost and that's where all the little eggs come from.

We watched him leave, silently, and after the door clicked shut I crossed to the bar and poured an ounce of bourbon into a shot glass. I threw it down, catching sight of her coming around the bar toward me, shuddering at the raw bite of alcohol, not really wanting her to touch me right then.

"I feel sorry for him, Danny," she said softly, patiently waiting at my elbow, her breath exhaling in a long faltering sigh.

I wrinkled my lips in a tight disbelieving smile and turned it in her direction. "You could have fooled me."

Her head lifted sharply, her face startled. "What do you mean?"

I shrugged. "You looked like the original snow maiden. The poor bastard was bleeding all over my rug and you were firing icicles at him—"

She chuckled and tugged me away from the bar. She slipped into my reluctant arms and squeezed my waist. "Men! You never read anything right. What you saw in my face was pity, Danny, nothing else. Jack's hurting all right, but it's not because of me. He never once mentioned me coming home, or love, or need today. All he came for was one more try for the money. He was totaled out when I told him that I was putting the house up for sale and signing the money away to charity. He wouldn't accept it. He begged, Danny, begged, but I told him it was too late. And it was then that I realized he never had loved me, that it was a calculated pursuit of money all along. If it hadn't been for Clarice, I would have given him the whole lot in the beginning. She was horrified that I gave him half even, without any strings. But she was raised with money, she knows about it. That's why she's held off investing with Jack, I guess, waiting to make sure how he did with Mr. Doheny and her friends."

"Why this sudden push by Jack for your money? You think he's in trouble?"

She nodded and leaned her head into my chest. "A little, I guess. He said he had to have at least one million to hold things together until the first of the year. That's when Clarice is supposed to invest. The way he acted, it must be quite a bit. I remember them talking about ten million once at dinner." She raised her head and kissed my cheek. "But Clarice and Jack were always talking money talk. Me and Mr. Doheny didn't pay much attention to them." She leaned back and smiled. "We talked about other things like music and books and . . . and life. Well, mostly he talked and I listened. He's a very entertaining man."

"Yeah," I said, "more than you know. Did the sucker ever come on to you?"

She smiled demurely and cocked an eyebrow. "Sometimes, I suppose, with his eyes. He certainly never said a word I could take offense to, or anything. But his eyes sort of . . . sparkled sometimes, and I got the idea he wasn't thinking about whatever he happened to be talking about at the time. It made me feel funny—" She broke off and giggled, rolling her eyes up to me. "It made me feel like a little tiny mouse about to be . . . to be devoured by a big old friendly cat."

"That's Big Boy, all right," I said sourly. "He has that effect on women, little white women most of all, I think."

She chuckled and turned into me again, pressing our bodies together from our knees to the point of her breasts. "Were you depressed by the funeral?" she murmured, her breath jetting against my ear. "Do you need a little uplifting experience?" Her body began to move. "Something to distract you? A happening?"

"Are you talking about making love again?" I said, smiling a little, dropping my hands to her waist, the sericeous feel of the simple dress she was wearing inordinately exciting against smooth unresisting flesh.

"I have to warn you that funerals make me randy: a reaffirmation of life, as they say. At times like these, I become an insatiable devouring monster."

"Mmmmm," she said, sagging, hanging by her arms around my neck, as limber as a peeled willow limb. "Devour me, do."

The telephone yanked us out of the hazy afterglow, that sweet limbo between the incredible exertion and the inevitable exhausted sleep. Susie groaned and picked up the receiver before I could stop her.

"Hello." Her voice sounded as small and tired as she looked.

"Uh-huh," she said, and let her arm fall toward me with the receiver. "For you."

"Hello, cowboy." Tony Wagerman's voice seemed to thrum with repressed glee. "Did I catch you at a bad time? Your little black-haired baby sounds plumb tuckered out."

"I've been wanting to talk to you. I've been trying to find you—"

"Yeah, so I've heard. Don't worry, friend, just be patient."

"I went to your father's funeral—"

"Conscience, cowboy?"

"Conscience? No, why should—"

"Don't shit a shitter, man," he snarled, his voice suddenly venomous, grating. "Maybe you didn't do it personally. But you goddamned sure had it done."

"You're wrong. I told you that night on the dam. We were even, even enough to let it stop there. You agreed, man."

"Uh-huh," he said thickly, his breathing heavy and rasping. "Maybe even until you could get one of your black bastard friends to drop a couple of flash grenades into the lube oil drums at the shop. My old man never had a goddamned chance, man."

"I'm sorry, but I never had anything to do with—"

"Bullshit!" He was yelling into the phone, his voice ringing, wild with anger. "You motherfucker! You did it or had it done and now you're going to pay for it. Or I'm going to. One or the other. You're going to fight me, man. Just me and you. Maybe I'm partly to blame because I could have stopped it sooner and didn't. But one of us, or maybe both, are going to die for his death. One for one, man, that's what it says in the good book. It don't matter much to me which one."

"Why did you try to kill Susie?"

"Don't start it again," he yelled. "That bullshit talk's not going to put me off. You be there tomorrow morning at nine o'clock. The woods down behind the dam. It's five or six acres, and the overflow creek runs right through the middle. I'll be at the west end of the dam; you come in from the east. We head for the woods at nine sharp. We'll meet somewhere near the creek. You be there or that cute little black-haired woman of yours will pay for it. Sooner or later, man. You can't keep her hid forever."

"Listen—"

"You be there, man." He hung up.

I replaced the receiver and looked at Susie; she was sound asleep.

/30/

I was there: in the faint chill of predawn darkness, driving Hector Johnson's four-wheel black pickup down the winding ranch road toward a ramshackle barn and corral we had once used as headquarters in a search for a missing five-year-old child. We had found the child, raped and broken and dead, tossed into the creek like so much refuse. We had ripped the small valley apart searching for the man, his spoor, anything that would bring him into our hands. We had not found the killer, but the details of the woods and surrounding fields remained burned in my memory.

Day was still a hazy pink promise over Dallas when I left the pickup, walking rapidly along a deeply etched cattle trail that followed the meandering stream across a small over-grown field to the woods. There was no moon and twice I had to use a small flash to cross feeder ditches. Each time I squatted on the other side in the waist-high weeds and brush and scanned the dark menacing outline of the woods, an impenetrable wall of blackness that revealed no telltale flicker of light, no unexpected sounds. Once I startled a small herd of cattle drinking, ghostly gray shapes that trotted sedately away, grunting and blowing indignantly at being disturbed in their morning ritual.

A cleared area perhaps fifteen yards wide separated the brushy field from the small forest. I paused in the edge of the brush, my hackles rising, a flutter of fear in my stomach. During the long sleepless hours of the night, a dawn arrival had seemed more than adequate to forestall an ambush by the Wagermans. But now, here, facing fifty feet of open ground, walking blindly into the unknown darkness, I felt a slow creeping horror I had not felt since the tortuous jungle alleys of Vietnam.

Suddenly the camouflaged jumpsuit I was wearing seemed a jeering mockery, the heavy comforting weight of the .357 Magnum slung around my hips a useless impediment. I felt naked and vulnerable, old and inadequate and totally alone. Panic shrieked its siren call and I had an almost overpowering urge to turn and crawl back the way I had come.

I stood upright instead and took a step forward into the open, a shock reaction bringing a spurt of adrenaline, a thunderous booming in my chest and ears. Filled with incredulity at my stupidity, I strode firmly across the open area, brushed through the thin line of undergrowth at the edge of the trees and into the warm enveloping blackness, weak-kneed and shaking, bursting nevertheless with a wild fierce exultation at this indisputable proof that I was still a man among men, however reluctantly. I put down the .30-30 and linked my arms around a handy oak, leaning my face against the rough bark until I stopped trembling.

Jesus, I was getting too old for this kind of shit.

He came thirty minutes later, quietly, but not stealthily, wearing camouflage clothing much like my own, brown sneakers, and a hunting cap with a pull-down veil. He carried a double-barreled shotgun in the crook of one arm and a camouflaged thermos dangled from his left hand. As far as I could tell in the pearly dimness, he wore a gunbelt around narrow hips that could have been a twin to my own.

I watched him come toward me through the thin stand of trees, padding almost silently in the layer of silt deposited over the years by rampaging overflow from the now innocuous creek, short and sturdy and unheeding in the blind recklessness of youth, the blithe assumption that old dogs are by definition lazy and careless, that by all that's right the game belongs to the quick and the nimble . . . and those few smart enough to find an edge.

He drew up thirty feet away on the other side of the creek,

his eyes sweeping along my shore, over and across my burrow behind a fallen elm, returning to his immediate vicinity, searching for a likely spot for his ambush, selecting finally an uprooted oak wedged against two large pecan trees a foot above the ground. It offered concealment and relative comfort, a place where he could have a leisurely sip of coffee and await the old stumblebum. I wondered if he was supposed to kill me on sight or hold me for Tony. I wondered also if he thought I wouldn't be able to smell the aroma of the coffee already wafting gently past my twitching nose.

He sat more or less wedged between two pecan trees, feet outstretched before him, the shotgun propped within easy reach. I waited until he had the thermos tilted again, then rose quickly to my feet and stepped out into the open, the Magnum in my hand.

"Freeze, man," I said, louder than I meant to, snaking back the hammer for emphasis.

Karl froze, startled into immobility, his left hand holding the thermos to his mouth, the right lying on his thigh, only inches from the gun. His fingers twitched, then jerked.

"Don't do it, boy. This isn't playlike. There's no going back."

But he was just too goddamned young, a product of the sixties and seventies, of hundreds of episodes of "Gunsmoke" and "Bonanza" where blazing shootouts were the order of the day, where good overcame evil in the end and the righteous always inherited the earth.

His hand with the thermos came away from his face and I saw the wild reckless grin and understood with a sinking heart that I had misjudged him; he was going to try me.

The moment was just too charged, too ripe to bursting with clichés of undaunted youth overcoming, the bright and shining images of brave young men bracing tired, cynical old gunslingers. Or maybe all he was seeing was his brother's wrath if he failed.

He yelled and threw the thermos in an overhanded sweep; an intended diversion while his right snaked the shotgun from against the tree. He had it in his hands when I shot him, and the last thing I saw before I saw him die was that crazy grin beaming out of the taut white face in my sight picture.

I went back to my burrow. I tried to remember if Karl smoked, then said to hell with it and lit one anyway. Tony would not come blundering in like his brother. He would know the single shot meant only one thing: one of us was dead. He would not know which one until he came in to see, but he would suspect the worst and act accordingly. A whiff of cigarette smoke would matter little in the end.

I was on my third cigarette when I saw the first flicker of movement that had none of the flashing jerkiness of either a squirrel or a bird. A distant hole in the foliage filled for an instant, then emptied again, a smooth movement a creeping man might make. Or a slowly grazing cow.

It was five minutes before I saw another. Closer this time, fifty yards away, a blurred outline that was most certainly a man. I pushed my cigarette into the loose dry silt and waited.

A squirrel chattered somewhere behind me and a blue jay screamed shrilly, dive-bombing toward a shaking limb high in an oak tree. The blue jay hit the limb in a welter of flashing wings and thrashing leaves and a small gray shape catapulted down the limb, rocketed around the bole of a tree, then disappeared into thin air. The bird flew away cawing triumphantly: another encounter of the violent kind concluded successfully.

"Hey, Karl!" The voice was close, too close, and for a second I hugged the ground in blind panic. "Hey, man, I know you're dead, but if you ain't, move something."

There was a short silence that was broken by a low monotonous cursing voice. "Goddamn you, Roman. You've killed my brother, too!"

I turned my head away from his voice, cupping a hand around my mouth to confuse the sound. "You killed him, Tony. You should have known better."

"Come on, man, let's step out and get this over with. Do it like men and not some kind of crawling animals."

"Sure, Tony. You first, buddy. Just step out there where your brother is."

"You son of a bitch!"

I had him located: a tangle of logs and silt-covered brush left from the last floodwaters, twenty feet up the creek from his dead brother, almost directly across from my own position. I cautiously widened my viewing aperture until I could press my cheek against the ground and see his entire tangle of driftwood. I couldn't shoot beneath the log because of the uneven ground, but he wouldn't be able to move without me seeing him, either.

"You satisfied now, Tony? Your father dead, your brother dead? You next. Are you happy now?" I saw a flash of movement near the center of the drift and fixed my eyes on the spot, a small triangle formed by a forked limb and a bunch of dead leaves.

"Don't ask me that, man. You started this crazy shit."

"Come on, Tony. If you had just left the girl alone none of this would have happened—"

"Goddammit! What business is that of yours? She's my goddamned sister, man!"

"I'm not talking about her and you know it. I'm talking about Susan. My woman."

"You mean your wife? I saw you two come home the other night. I coulda killed both of you if I'da wanted to. But I didn't. What the hell has she got to do with it, man?"

He was back at the small triangle again, his head moving minutely as he scanned my fallen log.

I lit a cigarette, giving myself time to think. He would see the smoke, but he knew by now where I was, so it didn't matter.

"Come on, man, what does your wife have to do with this?"

"She's the girl who testified against you at the trial, one of the girls house-sitting next door who saw you and your dad through the Crawford boy's telescope. She was the one who called the police thinking it was a rape. She was also the one your dad swore at the trial he would kill some day."

"Oh, that bitch. Yeah, man, I'da gladly killed her then if I coulda got my hands on her. So would Pa. But that was then, man. I don't even remember what her name was, for christ sakes."

"What about the dinner theaters? Casa Mañana? The Ranger baseball game in Arlington?"

"What about them?" His head appeared momentarily in an opening bordered by two dead limbs.

"Why did you go there on those particular nights?"

"I don't know what nights you're talking about, man. But it don't make any difference. We got them tickets through the mail. Reservations like. Some guy who said he was a public relations man or some such shit sent them to us free."

"What guy?"

"Hell, I don't . . . yeah, guy named John something . . . John Forbes. Called me one day and said he had a public relations business and if we liked plays and things like that he'd send us some free tickets if we'd be sure and go then, tell him what we thought. Said he wanted to make sure they had a good crowd . . . and like that." He stopped and I heard a sound that had the solid thunk of a double-barrel seating. "We like plays, but we didn't always go, either."

"Look, Tony. If you're telling me the truth, then somebody has been jerking us around. You and me, your daddy, Susie, everybody, man. Somebody's been stroking us, putting us through our paces like a goddamned dog-and-pony show—"

"Yeah, man, I'm telling you the truth." He stopped and uttered a short barking laugh. "But it don't matter now. Not a goddamned bit!" His head popped around the end of the drift, the shotgun swinging to his shoulder. He bellowed an inarticulate cry and pulled both triggers.

The air was alive suddenly with earsplitting sound and flying debris, dry-rotted chunks and splinters as my log disintegrated, a two-foot section disappearing in a cloud of choking dust before my startled eyes. My face stung in a dozen different places and I cursed fervently my solid-looking bulwark that had proven to be nothing but a thin hard skin with a rotten heart.

"Tony! Goddammit, man, this is—" I broke off and scuttled frantically backward along the log as I heard the snapping thud of the gun locking in again. Seconds later I shoved my face into the silt as another section of log exploded into the air above my head. I raised my head and caught sight of him ducking behind the drift.

I snapped off a shot from the .38 I'd taken from Karl's body.

He yelled, a gurgling cry filled with shock and pain.

I came to my knees behind the log and aimed at the end of the drift. My log was down to eight feet or so and wouldn't withstand another double-barreled onslaught of buckshot. I waited tensely, wondering where I had hit him, wondering if maybe he was dying or dead.

But he was neither. He was suddenly coming around the wrong end of the drift, left arm dangling uselessly, right hand kicking upward with the recoil of a big black revolver that had the concussive roar of big caliber.

Another, smaller section of log disappeared beside my face and I shoved frantically away from its spurious safety and rolled, firing each time I plopped on my stomach, rolling again, firing, seeing him jerk and stagger with each thunderous report, but coming on, his stocky legs churning as he hit the ankle-deep water of the creek, slipping and sliding on the bank, still coming, and I knew I was down to empty or maybe only one . . .

I rolled into a tree; I yanked the trigger and heard a dull click, dropped the gun and reached for my own in the same movement, my eyes on Tony, stopped now a dozen feet away, weaving, the gun pointed at my head, his lips peeled back in a grinning rictus.

"Too bad, cowboy," he said, his voice low and forced. "One . . . one more woulda done it. I'm dead here on my feet now. All I gotta do is fall. I got one more . . . I think. If not, man, you're home free." He licked his lips and coughed and my hand tightened convulsively around my empty holster as I tried to shrink into the ground, to disappear, to never have been.

The grating metallic rasp of the hammer cocking reverberated inside my head, and somewhere deep in the murky recesses of my brain a tiny frantic voice urged me to grovel, to beg . . .

The falling hammer clicked dryly: a beautiful wondrous sound.

Tony Wagerman's head bobbed once, his face slack, his eyes already dulling as they stared ahead into darkness.

"Too bad," he said, and toppled forward, falling blindly and free, like a tree chain-sawed at its base.

/31/

I changed the scene as best I could to make it appear to be a fraternal disagreement of some sort. I wiped Karl's gun and curled his hand around the butt, dropped it beside his body after I carried it near my burrow behind the rotten log. I traded my gunbelt for Tony's, found my gun among the leaves and dropped it near his hand and carried his .44 away with me. The ballistics would come out even and the .357 was a gun I had picked up a long time ago after a shootout with a gang of fledgling terrorists who had made the mistake of assuming peaceful Midway City would be a good place to practice tactics. It would not be traceable to me.

A mile away from my house I stopped at a service station and called the fire department emergency number. Using Homer Sellers's name, I sent two teams of paramedics hot-footing it to the aid of two victims of snakebite. Two old men, I explained, who had been bathing in one of the creek's deeper holes and who had stirred up a nest of cottonmouths, been bitten severely and needed two resuscitators immediately. Even before I hung up I heard the whining wail of a siren over the phone.

I hung up and smoked a cigarette, then called the police and told them much the same story, omitting Homer Sellers's name, telling the girl on the board that I didn't want to get involved when she asked who I was.

Satisfied that the careless feet of paramedics and uniformed policemen would destroy whatever integrity was left of the crime scene, including my footprints, I drove home, weary and depressed, wishing I had a drink, a lot of drinks, wishing I could turn back the clock.

Killing another human being is never very much fun. Not even when you're forced into it and can't be blamed. I knew that, but it didn't help. Killing the wrong men is even worse. I knew that, too, but there again, it wasn't really my fault.

"You're home early," Susie said, helping me out of the jumpsuit. "And I don't see any squirrels, thank goodness."

"Lots of squirrel," I said lightly. "But I guess I'm getting old. They were so cute I didn't have the heart to shoot any."

She picked up the jumpsuit and sniffed, then held it at arm's length. "My God, what have you been rolling in? Smells like stump rot." She sniffed again. "You must have done some shooting, though, because I smell gunpowder."

"Target practice. Did some stalking too. Getting all ready for deer season."

She clicked her tongue against the roof of her mouth, then smiled. "You and Tom Jeffers, you're nothing but a couple of little boys playing Indian. I'll bet Tom killed some squirrels, didn't he?"

"Yeah," I said, wondering why it was that one little lie always seemed to lead to another and then another. I crossed the hallway and went into the bathroom. I turned on the shower and stepped out of my shorts, then turned to find her watching me critically from the doorway. "How'd you get those little cuts and scratches on your face, honey?"

"I was crawling, got into some briars." I adjusted the water and stepped into the shower stall.

"Aren't you going to take off your sneakers?"

"They're muddy. Best way I know to soak them clean." I shut the door. I took off the Adidas and washed myself, and when I came out a few minutes later she was still there, sitting quietly on the commode, holding a towel.

Wordlessly she handed it to me, then got up and stood leaning against the doorjamb, holding up her end of the silence until I had almost finished toweling.

"Tom Jeffers called while you were gone, Danny. He wanted to know if you'd like to go down to your land Saturday to check out the deer stands and put out some feed." Her voice was dry and flat, her eyes quietly punishing.

I knotted the towel around my waist. I crossed the short distance between us and cupped her face in my hands.

"I wondered," she said. "I wondered why you would go off hunting with things the way they are right now. But I didn't say anything. I thought you needed to get away, needed the relaxation . . ." Her voice trailed off.

"All right, I lied," I said harshly. "I didn't like doing it, but it was necessary and I can't tell you why. You'll have to trust me, Susan. I need your help. I learned something this morning that scares me silly. But I can't tell you about that, either. Not right now. Somebody's been winding our springs and watching us dance and laughing himself sick and I don't know who or why yet."

"I don't understand, Danny. What are you talking about?"

"I'm not sure myself. I have some ideas, but they're damn vague mainly because I haven't had time to think them through."

Her eyes probed mine for a moment, then she sighed and melted against me. "All right. For good or bad, Danny, I'm in your hands. But treat me gently, please. For some reason I feel awfully fragile right now."

"You're not fragile," I said, kissing her lightly. "You're tough as an old boot. It's just that you look so tender, so delectable on the outside. Inside you're whipcord and old rawhide. After what you've been through, most women would be making wallets at the funny farm."

She laughed. "My, you're getting almost maudlin in your dotage."

"I think there's an insult in there somewhere." I kissed her again. "Say, didn't you mention picking up the rest of your clothes today?"

"Well, that was before you went . . . went hunting. If you're too tired, we can wait."

"No, today will be fine."

"Do you think we should call first? What if he's there?"

"That would be fine. I have a few questions I'd like to ask him."

She brushed her hand across the wet ends of my hair and wiped her fingers on the towel. "What kind of questions, Danny?"

"Like if he ever heard of a man named John Forbes."

Her head lifted, eyes wide, then she burst out laughing. "How did you know about that? I don't remember telling—"

"Do you know a man named John Forbes, Susie?"

She shook her head, giggling. "No. There's no such person . . . well, there may be, but Jack just made up the name. He used it when we were calling real estate dealers about the prices of houses in our area. You know, checking on property values, actually just being nosy about our neighbors. They want a name before they'll talk to you and Jack always used John Forbes." She leaned back against my arm. "Why would you want to know about that?"

I shrugged. "Just a name I heard somewhere. Must be a coincidence."

She nodded sagely, pursing her lips. "I imagine there are a lot of John Forbeses around. It doesn't sound like an uncommon name, does it?" She wound her arm around my neck. "Do you want something to eat before we go?"

I shook my head. "We'll stop and have lunch somewhere after we pick up your clothes. But just remember you only get half the closet space."

"Ah, now," she said, and kissed me long and lingeringly.

"Well, maybe three-quarters," I said, "but only if you hurry."

I drove past the four-car garage and parked as close to the front door as I could get without pulling onto the sparse wet grass.

"His car's not here," Susie said, relief evident in her voice.

"Maybe it's in the garage."

"He never puts it in there. Something's wrong with the automatic door openers. They don't work half the time." She made an exasperated sound and opened her door. "You'd think you could get garage doors that worked on a million-dollar house."

"Life is hard."

I lit a cigarette and watched until she went in the door, flipping her head in feigned anger, popping her posterior out the door again and giving me a finger wave.

I laughed and opened the trunk on the Monaco. I rummaged though the greasy toolbox until I located a battered pair of Vise-Grip pliers.

Susie had left the door ajar and I stood for a few seconds listening to her whistling somewhere off to my right. I had a general idea of the layout from her description and I turned to my left, went through the door at the end of the narrow entry hall. Obviously a study, or den, or whatever the hell they're calling them nowadays, the walls were lined with almost empty bookcases, the spaces between covered with a rough-textured material that looked and felt something like shellacked tow sacking. A dun-colored brick wall, complete with walk-in fireplace, held up one end of the long narrow room, and low-slung massive leather furniture gathered dust along the walls and in front of the largest single-pane span of glass I had ever seen. The room was as bright as outdoors and I could see the shimmer of sunlight on the blue water of the swimming pool.

I didn't much like the room, I decided, heading for the gun rack above the fireplace, the single gun standing out like the thumb on a hand with four missing fingers. The room was too damn big and cold-looking with all that dark leather and the walls covered with something I used to pick cotton in when I was a kid. And who needed two pool tables? Hell, who needed one? And come right down to it, who wanted a damn swimming pool in his living room?

I was grinning a little as I broke the lock on the case holding the .270 Remington, feeling the grin tighten as I worked the bolt and saw the dimpled cartridge in the chamber of the barrel. I worked the bolt again, and again, but the casing refused to budge. I nodded happily and latched the bolt tight, tossed the gun on one of the leather couches and headed for the phone on the darkly gleaming desk.

I found the Midway City phone directory in the lower left-hand drawer. There were only two gun shops listed, but since one was circled heavily in black ink I didn't have to guess which one Jack had used.

"Midway City Gun Shop."

"Yes, this is Jack Farley. I brought my .270 Remington in a while back—"

"Yes, sir, Mr. Farley, I remember the gun, sir."

"I—uh, was wondering about the bill? Exactly what all did you do?"

There was a short silence, then a small clearing of a throat. "Just what you wanted, Mr. Farley. I don't think fifteen dollars was excessive—"

"No, no. I just couldn't remember off the top of my head what it was you did."

Another silence, then a cough. "The casing, sir. It was lodged in the barrel. Don't you remember, we had that discussion about the ammunition that guy sold you with the gun. I told you not to use it, that it had been either overloaded or the casings had been used too many times. The casing was split, sir. I had a devil of a time getting it out." He hesitated. "Then, of course, I dismantled the gun and cleaned it all up for you. I don't think the charge was—"

"Oh, yeah, now I remember. Sure, no problem. Fine job. Thanks a lot." I hung up and automatically reached for a cigarette, my spine tingling.

/32/

We made two trips, had lunch at a Mr. Beef on the way home with the second load. I sat where I could keep my eyes on the car stacked to the roofline with dresses, blouses, pants, designer jackets, and hanger after hanger of what looked like pants suits to me but was something she called coordinates. A full-length chinchilla and a mink stole lay carelessly across the back of the front seat and the trunk of the car was jammed with shoes and miscellany.

I helped her unload, a lengthy process since each article had to be shaken, brushed, and eyed critically before being hung in the closet. "I'll sort through them later and call the Goodwill," she said once, plaintively, when it became apparent that every square inch of the closet space in the house would fall far short.

"In the meantime," I said, "I'll string lines in the living room and one of the bedrooms and we can hang the overflow along the walls of the garage."

She smiled sheepishly. "It's not that bad. Honestly, I didn't realize I had so many things. But things do accumulate, you know."

"Right. Come on, let's take a breather. I could use a cold beer along about now."

I opened the beer while she cleared away a stack of her favorite books we had piled on the kitchen table. She ran a wet cloth across the table top and picked up Mort Grossman's report where I had left it. "What's this?"

"Mort Grossman's report on the Wagermans. I stopped by his office and picked up a copy."

"Mort Grossman? Who's Mort Grossman?" She sat down

and sighed. She ran her hands along the length of her ponytail and picked up her beer. She tasted it and made a face.

"Private detective. The one Jack hired when you became upset about the Wagermans. You didn't know about it?"

She shook her head wonderingly, her eyes wide. "No, I didn't." She picked up the report and opened it curiously. "I wonder why he didn't tell me?"

I lit a cigarette and sampled my beer. "Probably didn't want to add to your worry. He wasn't at all convinced that the Wagermans intended to do you harm."

She looked up with a puzzled frown. "Did he tell you that?"

"Yeah. The day I came by your house. You were at a wedding shower."

She shook her head slowly, the frown deepening. "I don't understand that. He seemed very concerned. He talked about it all the time, so much so around Clarice and Mr. Doheny that it got to be almost embarrassing." She nibbled at her lower lip and went back to reading.

"I'm sure he had his reasons," I said lightly, busying my hands with my cigarette and beer, feeling a sudden compulsion to tell her the thoughts that had been caroming around in my brain since Tony Wagerman's death. But the thoughts were still too fragmented, too amorphous, tenuous threads without cohesion or continuity. All I had was a gun with an empty casing lodged in its chamber: that and dark suspicions. And that was almost nothing at all.

The dark sleek head lifted again, smooth brow marred with puzzlement. "This doesn't make any sense."

"What doesn't make any sense?" I repeated inanely, lurching upward out of my reverie.

"This report. Look at the dates. The last one is dated June twenty-second, and I didn't see the Wagermans until the July fourth weekend. Do you think Mr. Grossman could have made a mistake?"

"Are you sure about that, Susie?" I took the report out of her hands and flattened it on the table.

"Of course I'm sure. We were having a cookout party on

July fourth. We went to the meat market to get some fillets on sale. They were six for—"

"And that was the first time you saw Dalton Wagerman? The first you knew about him being out of prison?"

"No, I didn't say that. We knew he was out. He got out sometime in March. Betty Asterman told us that. She thought she saw him driving a van in Dallas and got her brother-in-law who's a cop to check it out. He was released on parole sometime in March."

I refolded the report and pushed it to the center of the table. She was right. The reports had begun on the first day of June and ended on June 22. Three weeks more or less. Jack Farley had told the truth about that, whatever else he may have lied about. But why almost two weeks before Susie had seen Wagerman for the first time? And another two weeks before she became convinced that he was stalking her, that there was something to be feared?

"Did Jack know about the trial before you saw Wagerman that Friday? Had you told him the story?"

She nodded, her eyes searching my face. "Yes. Back in March when Betty told us he was out. I had almost forgotten about it until then." She hesitated. "Maybe he got to thinking about it and got worried—"

"That sounds reasonable," I said. "He has the look of a worrier."

She pursed her lips thoughtfully. "He did mention it a few times, come to think of it. I guess maybe it was on his mind." Her face softened. "Maybe I was wrong about him . . . a little bit. If he was worried about me, he must have cared . . . a little, at least." She looked at me, then glanced out the bay window. "Maybe I should have helped him. Given him some more money, I mean. He's worked awfully hard—"

I snorted. "Him and about ninety million other people in this country. Hard work is no guarantee of anything, Susan, least of all success. If hard work insured success, this country'd be rolling in millionaires, hell, the whole damn world—"

"Hey," she said mildly. "Don't get rabid on me." She picked

up one of my hands. "I know you're not really jealous of Jack, Danny—"

"Like hell I'm not!"

She smiled and fluttered her eyelashes. "I don't mean about me. I mean the money and the big house and the cars and things, the power that goes with the money. Jack loves it. He loves dining in fine restaurants, tipping big, going first-class on vacations, buying his suits in Rome or Paris, flying to exotic places for the weekend—"

"I like money," I said. "I'm not exactly a Neanderthal. I like a nice place to live—and I have that. I like steak once in a while—and I have that. I have a two-year-old Dodge that can't compare with your Maserati for power and looks, maybe, but it gets me there in comfort and I rarely have to worry about an overheating engine. I like power, too. But power that I generate. Not something that comes from a fat wallet on my hip. Anyhow, the only real power I'm interested in is power over you." I caught both of her hands in one of mine and squeezed, leaning forward across the table and giving her my steely-eyed Bogart look, complete with twitching lip. "And I got that, baby."

Her eyelids fluttered again and she simpered coyly. "Would you care to prove that, big boy?" It wasn't a bad Mae West imitation, but she could have done better than "big boy."

"Later, kid," I said, and kissed the pouting lips. "I've got some important stuff to do. Stuff you dames wouldn't understand, see?"

She giggled. "That sounded more like that little fat ugly man . . . what's his name?"

"Edward G.," I said, "and he wasn't just an ugly little fat man. He was a sweet kindly man who loved to grow flowers. He just happened to have a rasping voice and a talent for looking mean. He was just an actor. We're all actors in one way or another. Some more than others. That's an important thing to remember, Susie—we're never what we seem to each other. We all have things to hide, no matter how open and honest we appear to be. Dark mean things a lot of the time.

217

Things we think about at three o'clock on a sleepless night, things we'd maybe like to change and can't, things we've done and wish we hadn't, but we can't change that either."

"Lordy," she said. "You sure go from carefree to heavy awfully fast."

I stood up and drew her into my arms. "It's the times, babe. Transition. Change. Low emotional flash points. We watch soap opera drama one minute, the next we're listening to canned laughter and nonsense. With that kind of emotional seesaw going on inside us all the time, is it any wonder that casual horror and degradation become yardsticks by which we measure the quality of our world, our lives? The unthinkable becomes tolerable, the tolerable becomes acceptable, and finally the norm."

"Hey, lighten up." She gripped my chin and shook it. "Here I've been thinking sexy thoughts and wondering how to get you in bed and you've been brooding." Her voice was humorous but her eyes were troubled. "I keep getting the feeling, Danny, that you're trying to tell me something. What is it?"

I shook my head and cupped her face between my palms. "You're too fragile, too vulnerable. I need to toughen you up a little, is all. Besides, what I said earlier is true. I have something to do, something important to both of us."

"That's not fair."

I grinned. "Life is hard. Besides, when you were brought into this world kicking and squalling, nobody promised it was going to be fair."

She wet her lips and played her trump card. "You're not going off and leaving me here alone? What if—?"

"No what if's, Susie. It's all over. After you went into the house this morning, I heard it on the car radio. The Wagermans are dead. The police believe they had a falling out, shot it out, and killed each other."

"My God," she said softly, her eyes glowing liquidly, only inches away from my own. "I can't believe it. They were brothers!"

I shrugged and tried out a wry smile on her. "That low

emotional flash point I was talking about. They lived close to the surface. Their veneer was thinner than most, I think, or maybe they had a thicker pride. A bad night and the wrong word: sometimes that's all it takes. Brothers have been killing each other ever since Cain and Abel."

She leaned into my chest and shivered. "God, I can't believe it's all over."

"All over," I echoed, clamping my tongue between my teeth to keep from adding "almost."

I kissed her and eased her out of my arms. I picked up Grossman's report and slipped it into my inside jacket pocket. I buttoned the jacket and felt it pull tight across the bulk of the gun and remembered that I needed to lose some weight, realized at that same moment that I hadn't had a drink for about twenty-four hours and that something was eating me alive inside. But I envisioned the long walk to the bar, the dark sorrowful eyes carefully turned away, and sighed.

"One thing, babe, if Jack Farley should show up pecking on the door, don't answer it."

She nodded, then wrinkled her brow. "Why not? There are some things we need to talk about."

I put my hands on her shoulders and pressed until she winced. "We'll worry about that later," I said harshly. "I've admitted to being jealous, Susan. Let's leave it at that. If I come home and find him here, I'll whip his ass again. Understand?"

"I understand," she said coolly, "but you don't need to yell at me."

"I'm sorry," I said. "I just wanted you to know how I felt."

"I understand how you feel, but after all, he was—is—my husband."

" 'Was' is right," I said. "And now you is my woman."

Her lips lifted a little. "And when is I going to be your wife?"

"Just as soon as we can put asunder these unholy bonds of matrimony."

She stretched and put her arms around my neck again. "Is that a proposal?"

"I proposed every time I made love to you. This is more like a promise."

"Good," she said, tilting her head in preparation for a heavy kiss. "I happen to know you never break a promise."

I pulled free a couple of minutes later to breathe.

"Well, hardly ever," I said.

/33/

I wrestled with it all the way to his office: looked at it from all four sides, from upside down and all around, as the song goes. It still came out the same way, no matter how much it tried to squirm and wiggle and dance, it fell into place like the last run-through in a game of dead man's solitaire, each fact clicking into place like your last chip in a faro dealer's tray.

I chain-smoked and fretted at the traffic and alternated between inordinate pride, abrasive self-disgust, and dismay. Pride that I had finally swept the cobwebs from my eyes and seen the spider, disgust that it had taken me so long, that three men had died needlessly and I had almost lost the woman I loved because of my bumbling ineptitude, dismay that I had not been able to look beyond the spiny starfish to the cold-eyed barracuda lurking in ambush.

My one, my only consolation was that he had been even more physically inept than I, bungling two attempts on her life out of ignorance, or incompetence, or maybe both. But physical maladroitness aside, there was a flair of genius about his plan, a bold choreography that spoke of cold cunning, a deep instinctive understanding of the human psyche as it really is, and an old law that says: for every action there is a reaction.

Assembling the players for his little drama had been easy; they were already there waiting in the wings, scripts in hand. The wizardry lay in the manipulation, the careful movement of the players about the stage, the master's hand directing from the shadows, the actions and reactions inevitable and true.

All except me. I had not been given a role, had been a

walk-on written in at the last moment, designated to last barely past the first curtain. But ignorant, whiskey-soaked, love-whipped dolt that I was, I kept popping up in scenes I had no lines in, creating, as they are fond of saying, a tempest in a teapot.

And, as often happens in this cliché world of mice and men, I was still standing at the final curtain, one hand on the rope, the other on my gun.

"He isn't here," his secretary said, batting long false eyelashes at me. She was cute and plump and cuddly with long free-flowing blond hair that gleamed with golden highlights from the sunlight flooding through the room's single window. "He wasn't here yesterday, either." She pouted prettily and tapped one long-nailed finger against her chin. "I haven't been here very long and I don't know him very well, but he almost always lets me know where he's at."

"Where he is," I said.

She nodded vigorously. "Yes, that's what I said: 'Where he's at.' I don't know where he's at." She tilted her head like a cunning puppy. "Could I have your name?"

I couldn't resist. "You wouldn't want it, honey, it's a boy's name."

"Oh . . . oh, I see." She tittered and carefully parted her lips in that practiced smile.

"That was cute, but what I meant was, could I take a message, give him your name?"

"Sure. Tell him the grim reaper was here."

She obediently picked up a pen. "Is that spelled like 'graham cracker'?"

I leaned down and patted a precious little hand. "Never mind, honey, I'll come back sometime when you know where he's at."

"All right," she said brightly, straightening, tugging at her bodice coyly, managing to jiggle her fat little breasts in the process. "I'll still tell Mr. Farley you were here, Mr. Reaper."

She tilted her head in the other direction. "If that's all right?"

"That's fine. Have a nice day."

"Why, thank you!" she said, as if no one had ever thought to say that to her before.

The house was silent. Not a beam groaning. Not even a stud creaking. Not yet old enough to have a history, or ghosts, it was simply open space surrounded by walls covered over with a wooden rod. Egregious opulence for its own sake. With none of the stately elegance of mansions of the past, it was simply a loud and graceless statement of wealth without dignity, without gentility.

I wandered the halls almost soundessly, in and out of five bedrooms that showed no signs of previous occupancy, each one cheerful and bright, tastefully decorated in modern pastels, muted reds and greens and browns, ornate expensive-looking woods and frilly curtains, bathrooms of marble and tile and gleaming white porcelain.

The sixth bedroom. Larger than the others with its own wood-burning fireplace, it had a cozy nook for reading, or working, or maybe just watching the valley below, the erratic, inexplicable antics of the less fortunate ones. Decorated in subtle shades of green and gold, it had a warm yet slightly sterile tone. It had the look of being occupied, not lived in, and yet, seeing the immense circular water bed with its rich brocaded cover, I felt a sharp pang of jealousy.

"Shit," I said aloud, and turned toward the almost empty closets, saw the two suitcases at the end of a nearby love seat, the suit bag draped across a chair.

Going or coming? I wondered, walking over and lifting one of the bags, testing its weight, then carrying both to the bed.

I found nothing more incriminating in the first than shirts and shorts, an expensive bottle of men's cologne, a small case containing an ornate set of men's hairbrushes, neatly rolled up socks, and a dozen handkerchiefs.

I found the money in the second one: a solidly packed

brown paper bag crisscrossed with rubber bands. Two hundred thousand dollars in hundred-dollar bills. Beneath the package of money I found the ledger. A thin leather-bound book edged with gold, it was wrapped in a pair of purple pajamas.

Only the first ten pages had been used, with each page bearing a neatly inscribed name in a block provided for that purpose. A single figure followed each name, obviously a dollar amount, and farther down and to the right a column of smaller figures had been carefully inked in red followed by a date. Three of the pages were marked with a large black X crisscrossing the entire page.

Obviously a simple personal record of dollar receipts and subsequent dispersal, all but one of the ledger sheets balanced out, the sum of the red-ink figures equaling the initial figure.

The first and oldest, dated fifteen months earlier, bore the name of Henry Doheny followed by the sum of one million dollars. Unlike the others, there were no red-ink figures listed on the debit side of his ledger.

That would fit what Big Boy had told me, I thought. He had invested a million dollars with Jack Farley, receiving in return quarterly dividends of 25 percent or more. But something puzzled me: if the red-ink figures represented quarterly payments and dividends to clients as they seemed to do, why wasn't Big Boy's ledger sheet marked accordingly?

But staring at the almost blank page brought me no answers I didn't already have, and I finally closed the ledger and wrapped it carefully in the pajamas.

I lit a cigarette and sat down on the edge of the bed. Farley wasn't coming: that much was evident. But going where? A long weekend in Vegas? Atlantic City? The Riviera? Somewhere where a large amount of cash would be necessary. Two hundred thousand dollars wasn't exactly walking-around money even for people who thought in millions. And why cash? Credit cards and checkbooks were still the normal medium of exchange unless I had missed something by not watching the evening news lately.

I dropped ashes on the gold-toned rug and idly rubbed them in with the toe of my boot. Could he be running? Taking what he could grab handily and fleeing in search of greener pastures, a more hospitable terrain? But if so, why? There it was again. Why?

He had no way of knowing that I had found him out, and if he suspected, he would be smart enough to know there was no evidence, no way of proving what I knew in my heart to be true. Most of my evidence lay on cold slabs in the Midway City morgue.

The .270? I had the gun, but it proved nothing beyond the fact of corroboration in my own mind. There were no ballistics to match up, no corpus delicti, thank God. He had only his own ineptitude and fear to blame for that. The first time at the cabin the trajectory had been right on, only the aim had been bad. And no second try because of a faulty casing splitting in the barrel. So all he had to do was run.

The second time in his own backyard he had fared no better. His aim had still been bad, closer maybe, but still no Panda bear. Whatever the reason, a faulty bullet, bad aim, or scope misalignment, he had missed and had been forced to come down out of the hills, come out into the open to finish the job once and for all. The groundwork with the Wagermans had been laid, the scene set, and without a doubt the gun would have somehow found its way into one of the Wagermans' possession.

But imagine his surprise when he found her locked behind an almost impregnable door instead of cowering in some dark corner as he had expected. Imagine the shock of hearing wailing sirens so soon after the police had left the first time. But giving credit where credit was due, it had been a stroke of genius to lock the gun in its accustomed place above the fireplace before fading back into the night. Doing so had solved two problems instantly: denied the possibility of that particular gun being the one used in the attack and prevented some very pointed and awkward questions had he been stopped before he managed to get down off the mountain. He had had only one small, almost insignificant, piece of bad luck: smashing the small vase in his haste to rack the gun. It had been almost insignificant because it meant nothing to me at the time beyond focusing my attention on the gun, emphasizing the incongruity of Jack Farley owning the gun in the first place.

By his own admission, and in the course of amiable arguments during his stay at my house, he had made his antigun, antihunter position eminently clear. Why then purchase a gun that was designed primarily for that one purpose, the hunting of game? And why from an individual instead of a gun store? Certainly not because of the small savings involved.

Why, then?

There was only one reason I could think of: he wanted a gun that could kill from a distance, and he wanted one that couldn't be traced to him. And that was probably his reason for not purchasing new ammunition: to avoid having to identify himself and sign a log. He obviously didn't know what a farce that law had become.

I got up and walked over to the fireplace. I threw the cigarette butt into a welter of half-burned logs. I picked up the lone wedding picture that Susie had left for him on the mantel. They made a good-looking couple.

I felt another pang, milder this time. I avoided Susie's face, looked at his smiling one, and saw the ashen face of his father, cold and grave in death as it had never been in life.

"Too bad, boy," I said aloud, my voice curiously muted by the heavily textured walls, absorbed and attenuated by the acoustical ceiling. "You should have stuck to what you know. To margins and stocks and bonds or whatever the hell it is you make money with. You should have stayed up here in your fine home and left the real people out of your schemes. We're malleable and you can manipulate us up to a point. But then we sometimes go rogue, become unpredictable. Maybe you don't remember about that. Guns and killing. That's not your bag. You broke the rules. You stepped into my world and now I'm going to have to take you down. I couldn't sleep nights knowing the man who tried to kill the woman I love is walking the streets somewhere alive and kicking."

I sighed and put down the picture. I lit another cigarette and, restless, wandered out of the bedroom.

Unaccountably despondent, I walked the halls until they eventually led me to the den. I sat behind the desk, twirling in the swivel chair, smoking moodily, the sliver of pool I could see beyond the glass doors cool-looking and inviting.

A huge rubber ball hung suspended on the lip of the water, immobile, held in place by an invisible anchor. A multicolored, polystyrene water-chair hugged the far corner, and a pair of clear goggles lay abandoned on the coping.

I got up again, stretched, bored with waiting. I crossed over and pushed through the glass doors, walked around to the end of the pool—and found Jack Farley floating facedown in the water. Dead.

Except for his suit coat, he was fully dressed. Impeccably so in gray pants and vest that had the soft sheen of silk. Glossy black shoes, pale gray silk socks, and a subdued maroon tie completed the ensemble. I saw that much when I maneuvered him to the shallow end and gingerly inspected his pockets. Nothing. Not even a wallet.

Where do rich people carry their money, I wondered? Maybe in brown paper bags in their luggage.

I let him slip back into the water. There was a large discolored spot on the edge of his chin, but no blood that I could see. I looked at him for a moment more, wondering exactly how he had died. Then I walked back along the hallways again to the bedroom.

His coat was where I remembered seeing it, draped across the arms of the clothes caddy in the corner near the circular bed.

His wallet was in the inside pocket, along with a large white envelope addressed to Clarice Doheny. I fingered the envelope, turned it over a time or two in my hands. I almost ripped it open, had one corner gripped tightly between my fingers. But I didn't. Maybe I would have if the damned thing hadn't already had a stamp on it. I shoved it into my own inside coat pocket instead.

/34/

"Off the top of my head, it looks like an accident." Dr. Alonzo Heart picked at a small blue scab on the back of his hand. He winced as the scab came loose and fluttered to the floor, then held out his hand and flexed his fingers to see if they still worked.

"You don't think that bump could have been made by some sort of instrument, say like the human fist?" Homer Sellers shuffled his feet and snuffled, automatically reaching for his coat pocket.

"Sure, hell yes." The tall distinguished doctor ran a hand through his silvery hair. "A goddamned meteorite coulda done it, for christ sakes. All I'm saying right now is he probably drowned as a result of a fall into the water, striking his chin on the pool coping as he fell. That's what it looks like to me right now. After I have a chance to get into him, maybe I can tell you different. But right now, that's it."

"Any idea how long ago?"

"Not real close. Lying in that warm water didn't help any. I'll say between twelve and twenty-four hours, somewhere in there—probably."

Homer grunted. "That's what I like, decisiveness."

The tall doctor picked up his bag from the edge of the desk and grinned amiably. "That's as decisive as it gets until I get my knife on him."

"Jesus Christ, you make him sound like a side of beef."

Heart shrugged. "At that point that's all he is; not as good, in fact. You can't eat him."

Homer turned toward me, the lower half of his face hidden

behind the handkerchief. "Well, let me know as soon as you can, huh?"

"Gotcha, Homer." Dr. Heart grinned at me and winked, then turned and walked jauntily out of the room.

"Son of a bitching ghoul," Homer growled. "I sure hope he never gets his goddamned hands on me. Did you ever notice? They look like chunks of raw pork crawling with worms."

"Maybe it's the heartbreak of psoriasis," I said.

He whirled abruptly and sat down in Jack Farley's swivel chair. "All right, talk to me, tell me what the hell you were doing here."

"I told you, Homer, I came back to get this pair of shoes that Susie forgot." I picked up one of the pair of red shoes I had scrounged up before the police arrived. "I bought these for her a long time ago. You know how sentimental she is."

"I know how she is," he said, his tone softening. "But I don't always know about you. And you and her didn't notice anything when you was here earlier?"

"Not a thing. I did notice, however, that the suit coat to the pants he's wearing is in the master bedroom."

"Yeah, we already got that." He shoved out of the chair, paced over to the glass doors, and stood watching the two detectives down on their hands and knees inspecting the coping.

"What do you think, Dan?"

I struggled out of the soft clinging leather couch. "I think the doctor may be right. His shoe soles looked to me like they're leather. All that tile out there. It'd be easy to slip." I moved to the swivel chair and sat back down.

"How's she going to take this, do you think?"

"Hard. You know Susie. She'll try to blame herself and she'll cry some. But she's got a logical mind and deep down she'll know no part of it was her fault."

He cleared his throat and blew his nose again. He came back to the desk and sat down on one corner. "I haven't told you, I guess, but I'm glad you two are back together. You just see if you can keep it that way this time. No reason you can't marry her now. Right away, if you want to."

I nodded and lit a cigarette and we sat silently listening to the voices out in the pool room, an occasional laugh. He stood up and paced around the room, stopped at one of the electronic games. "You ever play these things?"

"He was the one, Homer. Jack Farley was the one trying to kill Susie."

"What?" He turned slowly, his bright blue eyes widening. "Did I hear you right?"

"You heard me right. He tried twice. Here, the other evening, and once at the cabin."

"At the cabin? You didn't say anything about that."

"We haven't been doing much talking lately, Homer. Besides, I didn't want you worrying any more than you already were. There wasn't a damn thing you could do about it."

"How do you know?"

"His gun, for one thing. A .270 Remington deer rifle I have outside in my car. He fired only once at the cabin. He had time to fire at least once more and possibly twice, but there was a good reason why he didn't. The casing split and lodged in the chamber. The same thing happened here the second time. He was using bad ammo and he was a lousy shot. Otherwise she'd be dead."

I told him about the gun shop, what the gunsmith had told me.

"That doesn't prove anything except that he was hardheaded and maybe dumb. He could have gone out and tried out the gun again—"

"No. Susie said they had just delivered it from the shop."

I lit another cigarette and told him about Mort Grossman, the Wagerman investigation that started a month before it should have, about the tickets from a man named John Forbes, that John Forbes was Jack Farley's favorite alias.

"Who told you that? About the tickets, I mean?"

"Tony Wagerman," I said. I took a drag on the cigarette and looked him in the eye. "That night out on the dam. I didn't believe him then, but I didn't know then who John Forbes was, either."

"I guess you heard about the Wagerman boys?"

I nodded, returning his stare placidly. "Seems incredible that two brothers would turn on each other that way."

"Yeah," he drawled, "don't it?" His eyes searched my face.

"Speaking of the Wagermans," I said, watching one of the detectives pause in his slow crawl around the pool, lower his face until his eyes were only inches from the coping. "They weren't the ones who bushwhacked me in my entry hall that night."

Homer's head swiveled toward me, bushy eyebrows lifting. "How do you know?"

"They were professionals. The Wagermans would have broken something. They tended to get carried away. And at least one of them was black. Farley hired him. Hell, he could have been there for all I know. Or at least close by. He knew about Doheny, knew how he was when he passed out. They weren't worried about him waking up. The Wagermans would have been. Besides, the language was wrong. 'Jiveass' and 'honky' aren't words the Wagermans would have used." I stopped and stood up, paced around the desk, then walked over to the glass doors and stood watching the activity around the pool. "I should have realized that a lot sooner than I did, but I guess I was wallowing in too much self-pity over losing Susie to think about anything too clearly."

Behind me Homer made a grunting sound of agreement. He blew into his handkerchief and coughed harshly. "I'll buy that."

"The thing that bugged me for a while was how did Jack know where the cabin was? Susie said she had never told him, and you said the same thing. It turns out that I told him, or as same as."

"I don't follow you."

"I called him from Butler Wells. I ran out of time and money. He had the call put on his phone. All he had to do was call the operator back after we hung up. Once he knew the town, it was a cinch. I was born and raised in that area, sooner or later he would have found someone who knew where my cabin was located."

"None of this really proves anything, Dan."

"I know that. I couldn't prove it even if he were alive." I hesitated. "What I can prove with what I know now is that he's been running an investment scam on some pretty rich people in the area."

"Scam? What kind of scam?"

"One that don't make much sense on the face of it. Not until you know that it was simply bait for a bigger fish, a cagey old matriarch bloated with eggs, watching the small fry feeding, waiting until the game was worth—"

"What the hell are you talking about?"

"Okay. Jack Farley accepted investment money from wealthy clients, primarily Henry Doheny and some of his friends. He guaranteed a return of twenty percent. He also guaranteed the principal with a ninety-day notice in writing. I don't know a hell of a lot about the financial world, but I would imagine he had a lot of takers once they were convinced he wasn't nuts or a crook. But he was selective. He accepted only close friends of Clarice Doheny. And he paid off like clockwork, making sure Clarice Doheny heard about each payoff. She was the one he was angling for, the big fish. They were talking in terms of ten million dollars or more. The rich, by definition, are greedy, my friend. That's the heart of any scam—greedy people. Once Jack Farley had his hands on Clarice's money— poof, no more Jack Farley."

Homer nodded thoughtfully, his lips pursed, eyes glistening. "I can understand the scam, the buildup, but what I don't get is how he could continue paying them people twenty percent on their money if he wasn't making anything."

"He couldn't, and that was the rub. He was using the pool of investment money to make his quarterly payments and he was running dry. That's why he needed Susie's million, to last until the first of the year, until the deal was closed with Clarice."

"How do you know all this?"

I shrugged. "A lot of it's guesswork, but there's a ledger in Farley's suitcase that makes it pretty plain what was happening."

"Why didn't he just ask Susie for the money?"

"He couldn't take the chance. Susie and Clarice are tight, and Susie can't keep anything from anybody, you know that. She also uses Clarice's stockbroker. Too many ways Clarice could find out. One whiff of the wrong scent and that old broad would run like a turpentined cat." I crushed the cigarette with a savage jab of my fingers. "So the son of a bitch decided to kill her instead."

Homer sat down on the arm of the couch, a half-smile on his lips, his eyes shrewd. "And that's what you were doing here? You were going to brace him. Were you going to kill him, Dan?"

"I might have," I said evenly. "It could have turned out that way. I don't think so. His plan demanded absolute secrecy. My knowing should have been enough."

"Unless he managed to kill you?"

I shrugged. "That's true. But he tried that once before."

His eyebrows lifted, creating the row of inverted V's. "When?"

I waved a hand. "That doesn't matter. He didn't succeed, obviously. None of this really matters now, Homer. He's dead and that's that, as they say." I stood up and dropped my cigarette into the coffee cup I had been using as an ashtray. I started across the floor toward the door. "I have to go."

"Hey, wait a minute, dammit. Why wouldn't he have just hired someone to kill her, make it look like an accident, maybe? Why go to all the trouble with the Wagermans?"

I stopped and made a gun with my hand, cocked it, and pointed it at him. "Time. It's not an easy thing to find someone to do a killing, to do it right. An unknown murderer would have brought an investigation, automatically put him under suspicion. Time and delay. He needed the money fast. The Wagermans were ready-made fall guys. With Susie dead and no cloud over the estate, he could borrow money against it if he had to, if the probate proceedings took too long. And he knew he couldn't stand a long investigation. Expediency, buddy." I fired my hand at him and left.

I mailed the letter on my way home, turned it over in my hands one more time, then shoved it into the chute before I changed my mind. I'd done some things in my life I wasn't proud of, but reading other people's mail wasn't one of them. And in the end it turned out best that way.

There were an astonishing number of people at Farley's funeral. Clarice Doheny and a large group of people with her I didn't know. Big Boy was nowhere to be seen. I wasn't too surprised. He had always said he hated funerals. After the service I finally met Clarice Doheny face-to-face and found out why Big Boy wasn't there: he and HONKY 1 had taken off again.

/35/

When I found him, he was where I had left him the last time, beneath a giant pecan tree on Jesse Coldwater's place near Houston. Parked in almost exactly the same spot as before, the big blue-and-white rig streaked with mud and bug-spattered from six days of running before the winds of autumn and the last gasp of a dying September.

It had been harder than the times before; he wasn't leaving any clues, and the motor home, as big as it was, was just another rich man's toy among many. But I was trying harder, and maybe that made the difference. I had some advantages; over the years I had amassed a considerable list of his favorite haunts, and a seven-foot black man traveling with three small white women tended to stick in people's memories. I found out he had three women with him at a honky-tonk near Houston.

I had no trouble identifying Clara and Jill, but the third one had me puzzled. Maybe a hitchhiker he had picked up along the way, or some bored barmaid with road fever and a yen for black power.

We crisscrossed the state twice. He had a two-day head start and for four days I went at a dead run, sleeping only when my body said to hell with it and brought down my eyelids like the final curtain on a bad play. I spent the third night in a motel room soaking away accumulated grime, but the rest of the time I slept in the backseat of the Dodge, eating bologna-and-cheese sandwiches washed down with cold beer. I was in and out of bars all over the state, but I left even more sober than when I went in. Being around a bunch of damn drunks is a sobering experience.

Most of the time I spent behind the wheel, wearing out rubber and burning gas, smoking innumerable cigarettes and grinning wolfishly every once in a while, thinking about his big black eyes in the rearview mirror with a dry mouth and a pounding heart whenever a green car with a white vinyl roof hove into his view. I could tell by the way he was running that he knew I was back there somewhere. The pattern was different and he was doubling back, circling, coming in on his own backtrail. He was running scared and that made me feel good.

I almost caught him on the third day in Austin. Barreling down the freeway on my way to Buzzy's Place in San Antonio, I met him coming up the other side of the highway. It could have ended right there, maybe should have, but there was a concrete-and-wire barrier up the median and by the time I found an exit and doubled back he was gone, off the freeway and headed west to San Angelo. A fact that cost me almost a full day's circling and searching to discover. Evidently he had seen me also.

But I found him. As I always had before. And for the first time I found some pleasure in it. Always before the chase had been the thing, the finding a sorry anticlimax. Something finished, something done, a long dull trip home before me and nothing there that mattered a damn after Susie left.

But it was different this time, and a curious mixture of satisfaction and anticipation shivered in my stomach and dried the saliva in my mouth as I rolled the Dodge along the tracks HONKY 1 had left in the soft earth.

I parked and got out, stretched the miles and an almost sleepless night out of my tired muscles, studiously ignoring the faces peering out at me through tinted glass. I could see three white blurs and one black one in my peripheral vision and I heard excited feminine voices, a rumbling baritone, and the sound of pounding feet.

He was waiting at the door, a grin as wide and toothy as a hayrake, and gleaming eyes.

"Hey! Hey, man, this shines! This really shines, man!" He

grabbed me and hugged me, his big hands patting the small of my back, raking my sides as he pushed me back, beaming.

"Man, it's great to see you, but I thought you was through with all this shit." His right hand scraped through the furry mat on his chest, then dropped down to hitch up his chartreuse shorts, came back up to plow through curly black hair.

I grinned at him. "You know me, I'm an unpredictable lout." I swiveled my grin toward the three women grouped loosely in a semicircle behind him. Clara and Jill and a third face that sent a tiny ripple of shock thudding in my chest. Meg Wainwright. She caught my eyes and grimaced wryly before she looked away.

"Well," I said, the grin still holding, reaching for my cigarettes. "I see you have your usual complement of ladies. Hello, Clara, Jill, Meg."

"Hidy, Dan," Clara bubbled. "My, you're looking good. Better than a ripe watermelon."

Jill nodded coolly. "It's nice to see you again. You're looking well. A little tired, but well."

Meg nodded silently.

"Hey, man, get on in here and sit down. Clara, honey, why don't you fix us a little something—what'll it be, Dan'l? You name it, man, you got it." Big Boy bustled around, making shooing motions at the women clustered behind him.

"Maybe a beer, Big Boy, and a few minutes of your time."

"Whatta you mean, a few minutes? Man, we got all the time in the world. You're a dadgummed week early, you know. I figure we can have us a high old time and still get back in time to make old Clarice happy." He guffawed half-heartedly and slapped the dinette table as he sat down. He looked up, his glance ricocheting off my cheek. "Uh, how pissed off is old Clarice, anyway?"

I shrugged and sat down across from him. "You broke the rules. It hasn't even been a month yet."

"Aw, hell, I know that." He scraped a hand across a two-day growth of beard. "But, man, there's too much shit going on. You just don't know. And old Jack Farley getting killed

thataway. Man, I can't stand funerals." His face sagged sadly.
" 'Specially a fine young feller cut off in his prime like that.
Why, I never knowed a finer feller than Jack—"

"He was a sick son of a bitch," I said. "A greedy sick son of
a bitch who tried to kill his wife for her money."

"Aw, man—" He broke off and lurched to his feet. "You
ladies come on. Why don't I dig you some lounges out of that
storage bin. You all can sit out yonder under the trees and
chitchat while Dan and me talk. That okay with you?" He
made herding motions with widespread arms and the three
women silently moved toward the door. He lumbered down
the steps with Jill and Clara close behind. Meg hung back, one
hand fiddling with a drawstring at the bottom of the short,
sleeveless blouse she was wearing.

"I was right about Loren. He didn't want me. He wanted
the money. He already had my replacement picked out." She
gestured vaguely. "Hank gave him his money. Hank, he's a
good man, Dan."

"He's a prince," I said. "And I'm sorry about your husband.
He fooled me. That doesn't happen too often."

She smiled uncertainly and edged toward the door. "I just
wanted you to know."

I nodded and watched her trip lightly down the steps, trim
and lovely still, but strangely asexual, and I went back to the
night in the motel room and wondered what combination of
chaotic emotions had brought about such intense desire, the
obsessive need to protect and preserve the sanctity of a woman
who had just slept with three men for money. Perversity, I
decided finally, nothing but plain damned perversity.

Big Boy came pounding up the steps and through the door.
"Hey, buddy, you ready for another brew?"

"No, thanks, I'm holding fine."

"Damn," he said, flopping into his seat, "it's getting hot
again. Damned air conditioner ain't working worth a fart." He
raked a heavy hand across his forehead and wiped it on his
shorts, giving me a rueful grimace. "You really mean that
about Farley?"

I finished my beer and dropped my cigarette through the hole in the can. "The whole thing with the Wagermans was a scam, Big Boy. He planned on saddling them with her murder."

"Aw, man, I can't believe—"

"From the beginning. He had a private detective following them for three weeks. He needed to know their habits, their likes and dislikes. He used what he learned to set them up. He engineered all the meetings between Susie and the Wagermans. He egged her on while pretending to scoff at her fears to me. He made sure she went to the police, both County and Midway City. All their friends knew about it. You know that, you must have heard the talk at dinners and parties."

He nodded slowly, his brow furrowed. "Yeah, we all talked about it a lot, I guess. But I didn't think anybody took it too seriously. I know I didn't."

"Right. But Susie took it seriously, and everyone knew that. They put it down to an overactive imagination, paranoia, or whatever. But if she had turned up shot by a mysterious stranger, who would you think the police would go to first? All they'd have to do is find the gun on the Wagermans and their ass would have been mud. And planting the gun would have been duck soup. They lived in an apartment and left their trucks out on the street like everyone else who lived there."

"But, why, man? Why'd he want to do a thing like that?"

I shrugged and collapsed the beer can between my fingers. "Money. He wanted the rest of her money."

He shook his head vehemently. "I can't believe that. The kind of woman Susie is, she would have given him the money if he'd asked her for it, if she thought he needed it."

I nodded, smiling a little, poking another cigarette into the corner of my mouth. "That's the truth. She would have. But he couldn't ask her, you see." I lit the cigarette and puffed a stream of smoke across the table at him, watching it break across the handsome features that had a curious tinge of gray beneath brown.

"Ask me why," I said softly.

"Why?" he echoed obediently, the tip of his Adam's apple barely visible through the thick neck muscle as it leaped upward convulsively. "Why not, for christ sakes?"

"The scam," I said. "The big scam. The ten-million-dollar scam. One hint that he was almost broke, that he needed operating money even, and the whole thing would have come apart like a dandelion in a thunderstorm. He was the boy wonder, you see. He was making people bucketsful of money every day of the week, presumably lining his own pockets in the process. After all, nobody works for nothing. Everything he did, or said, his entire life-style, was dedicated to projecting that image. The charming young genius with the Midas touch."

Big Boy threw up his hands. "Man, you done lost me. I don't know what the hell you're talking about." He tilted the beer can and emptied it, mangling it with one squeeze of his hand.

"All right, I'll make it clearer. Clarice Doheny. Ten million dollars. You must have heard the talk around the dinner table. Even Susie heard that much and she couldn't care less about money talk. She'd rather talk about movies and plays and books and life. The things you and her talked about, she said."

"Yeah, man, she's one smart little lady." He lumbered to his feet. "I need another brew. How about you?"

"No thanks."

He opened a drawer, took out a dish towel, and wiped his face and neck.

I reached down and took the .32 out of my boot and stuck it between my thighs.

He popped the tab on the beer and sat down. "Yeah, I knew about the ten million. Couldn't miss it. They talked about it enough. She was getting ready to lay it on him."

"Not quite yet," I said. "The first of the year was the target date. He had her sold, but your wife is a cautious woman. The responsibility of all that money seems to weigh heavily on her shoulders."

"Yeah," he said sourly, carefully linking circles on the table top with the sweating beer can, then erasing them with a savage swipe of the towel. "She's careful."

I nodded amiably. "And her caution created a problem for our young hero. He was broke, or very nearly so, and he had three more months to go. Three months of heavy payments to his investors, and to top it off, Clyde Zimmerman had served notice that he was withdrawing his half million. That was a half million that Jack didn't have and the money would be due and payable on October thirtieth in accordance with the investment agreement that investors could withdraw without penalty with ninety-day prior notice."

"How do you know that?" He was watching me steadily, the whites of his eyes clear for once, the black centers as shiny as black marbles.

I shrugged. "I'm a detective. I find out things." I ducked my head and smiled ruefully. "Actually, Clarice told me about Zimmerman and we found out the rest from Jack's two sets of books."

"Two sets?"

"One for Clarice and one that showed things the way they were. I guess that one was for the IRS."

He made a fist and banged the table. "Aw, man, are you telling me he was going to take Clarice's money and head for the hills?"

"Yes and no. He was going to take *part* of Clarice's money . . . the rest of it would have gone to his silent partner." I returned his gaze steadily. "The actual split was sixty-forty, I believe."

His hands closed convulsively on the beer can. I watched the foaming liquid spill through the triangular hole and over his fingers to the table. I dropped my right hand into my lap.

"Two things I have to tell you right now, Big Boy. One, nothing can be proven with Jack dead." I took a deep breath. "The other one is that if you come at me I'll blow your goddamned balls off."

He laughed harshly, the musculature of his bare chest appearing to swell and tighten, a heavy purple vein popping out in the center of his forehead. "You ain't armed, man. I checked you out when you come in."

"You didn't check far enough, asshole," I said, lifting the gun barrel to the table top, then dropping it again. "I don't want to shoot you, man, but if you want to piss out of a tube and talk in a high voice the rest of your life, just try me."

He hung suspended, the conflict clear in his bulging eyes and swollen muscles, his lips pulled back and fixed in a fearsome rictus.

I tightened my grip on the gun and thumbed back the hammer, but my heart wasn't in it. "Listen, man, nobody's after your ass. I think you probably killed Jack and that's fine with me. It saved me the aggravation. He was running out with your last two hundred thousand and I guess that was reason enough. I don't know if you knew anything about his plan to kill Susie or not, and I don't want to know. I'd rather believe you didn't. Anyhow, the greatest crime, the real crime, was against the Wagermans. As for you, all we know for sure is that you were masterminding the scam to bilk Clarice out of ten million dollars, that you and Jack set it up. But that's between you and Clarice. That's the reason I'm here. She sent you a message."

I eased the envelope out of my jacket pocket with my left hand and tossed it on the table in front of him. "You have a choice to make. There's a cashier's check for two hundred thousand in that envelope, the two hundred thousand I found in Jack's bag. Along with a copy of the letter Jack sent to Clarice. It was in his coat pocket ready for mailing when he was killed. I know because I mailed it. He not only was running out on you, he was sticking you with the blame." I stopped and watched him slowly shrinking, the shiny eyes receding, settling back into their dark sockets as he stared at the envelope. He made no move to touch it.

"You can cash the cashier's check and keep moving on. But that's the end of it; there won't be any more from Clarice. Or you can go home. Get rid of HONKY 1. No more binges. No more two-week jaunts into the high lonesome with your pretty little friends. Nine to five and home for dinner with Mama at seven. Vacations in Acapulco and Rome and scenic Mediterranean cruises. All the normal things you common garden-variety rich folks do for pleasure. That's her deal, Big Boy, and I'm pretty damn sure she means it." I lifted my pants leg and put the gun away, grinning a little at his sagging face.

"Aw, man," he said, his voice almost a whisper. "Why you helping her lay all this bad shit on me? I thought you and me were friends, man. It's because I'm black, ain't it? You wouldn't do this to me if I was white."

I slipped out of the booth. "First of all, I'm not doing anything to you. Clarice is your wife, remember? And you're wrong, man, we weren't friends. Not yet we weren't. But we were damned close. Close enough that you being black didn't matter a damn to me. Close enough that this hurts like hell."

"Hey man, I didn't know he was trying to kill Susie. If I had, I'da done it a lot sooner—" He broke off, finally looking up, then shrugging and going on. "I'da done it sooner. I thought it was them krauts, the Wagermans."

I nodded, then turned and walked out the door, detouring on my way to the car to say good-bye to Hank's harem. I got a hug and a kiss from each and a bit of unexpected wisdom from Clara. "It's over, isn't it, Danny?" she said sadly, her eyes brimming with unshed tears.

"Maybe," I said. "He has a choice to make."

"It's over," she repeated, shaking her curly head. "It's been different this time. He's been running away from something— himself, I think."

There was nothing more to say that would matter to them. I walked back past the mobile home to my car.

I was grinning a little when I settled in my seat. Grinning because it was finally over and I had my woman back and a crazy September was almost gone. Grinning, remembering Big Boy's ludicrous face, the haunted eyes leaking crocodile tears down coffee-colored cheeks, a tragic portrait of a man who has seen his destiny and understands that life is nothing more than a complicated mosaic of small achievement and personal tragedy, and that whimsical fate's final decree is oftentimes awesome and eternal.

A modest retribution for four dead men, two beatings, and a busted friendship.

Not a heck of a lot, maybe, but I'm not hard to please, and it sure beat the hell out of killing him.

I was whistling to the tune of Willie Nelson's "On the Road Again" when I reached the highway. Home was a far piece away but I was glad of that. I needed the time to crank myself up out of my melancholy malaise, time to ponder the future with Susie home again.

I settled back in my seat, lit a cigarette, and decided that life might be a keeper after all.